RACHANEE LUMAYNO

I0639011

HEIR OF
ILLUSIONS
AND
OTHERS

KINGDOM LEGACY BOOK SIX

Editing and proofreading by Tom Loveman

Cover art by Fiona Jayde Media

Thank you for reading, I hope you enjoy Heir of Illusions and Others!
If you have the time, please leave an honest review on Goodreads or wherever you
purchased this book! Thanks!

ALSO BY RACHANEE LUMAYNO

CONTENTS

JOIN THE NEWSLETTER

HELLO DEAR READER!

Here's a fun fact for you—the first book in the Kingdom Legacy series, Heir of Amber and Fire, was inspired by a character in a Dungeons and Dragons campaign that I never got to play. Even though the game never happened, the character's backstory stayed with me, and became the basis of Jennica's story.

Since the first book had such strong ties to tabletop gaming, a friend suggested I create a campaign set in the world of the Kingdom Legacy series. And so *The Mysterious Magical Emporium* was born, and I'd love to send you a FREE copy! Just sign up for my newsletter at www.rachanee.net/newsletter, and your new campaign will be sent to you right away.

So grab your friends, grab some dice, and grab a copy of *The Mysterious Magical Emporium*, and get ready to spend some time in the kingdom of Calia with your new friends, Jennica, Beyan, and Taryn!

PROLOGUE

Two years ago

THE PEDDLER WATCHED, ONE eyebrow raised, as the young man approached him on the road. Despite the young man's fine clothing and clean-cut appearance, he had a look of desperation about him. Ah, well. The young were always passionate about something, and it was following those passions that got them into trouble. The peddler pulled his mule to the side of the road to allow the young man's horse to pass him by.

But instead, the young man halted his horse. Dismounted. Practically grabbed the peddler by the collar, he was so frantic. "You're a traveling peddler, are you not?"

No, I'm the King of Calia, the peddler wanted to say sarcastically. But sarcasm never won him patronage.

"Indeed I am, sir," the peddler said instead, touching the brim of his threadbare cap respectfully. "Are you looking to sell something?"

The young man perked up. "I am. Is there anything you're looking to buy?"

The peddler eyed the young man's horse. "You've a fine mount, sir. Would you be willing to part with him?"

The young man frowned. "I—I would prefer not to. I've a long way to go, and it will only be longer if I have to travel on foot."

"Hmm. What about your clothes, then? I'd be happy to sell you something if you don't have a second outfit on you, and you'd still have money to spare."

The young man looked down at his clothing, as if just remembering what he was wearing. "I don't have a change of clothing. I ... kind of left in a hurry. And I—no, I don't want to sell this, either."

"You don't want to sell your horse, you don't want to sell your clothes," the peddler mocked. "What do you want to sell, then? Or be on your way, if all you want to do is waste my time."

"No, I—" The young man stopped and waved his hand in the air. "What about this?"

A shiny gold ring glinted in the sunlight.

"Perhaps," the peddler said. "Let me take a look at it."

The young man tugged the ring off his finger. He held it a minute, reluctant to let it go. Sweat started to bead on his forehead.

"Well?" The peddler held his hand out. "Do you want me to look at it, or not?"

"I—" The young man seemed to be having trouble forming words.

The peddler reached out, his dirty, gnarled fingers closing over the gold band the young man held between his fingers. A jolt passed through the young man, and he startled, but the peddler didn't seem to notice. He took the ring from the young man and held it up to the light, turning it this way and that.

The young man panted slightly, getting his breath back.

The peddler bit the ring, then inspected it again. Satisfied, he said, "It's genuine, all right. I'll take it."

The young man blew out a breath, and then the two men engaged in a round of haggling. They settled the price and the peddler paid the young man, commenting, "This little ring will be worth something once I melt it down, I'm sure."

"Melt it down? But—can't you see ..." The young man trailed off.

"See what?" the peddler asked.

"Ah, it's not important. It's not mine anymore, anyway. Do whatever you want with it."

"I will." The peddler touched the brim of his cap again. "Thank you, sir."

"Thank you. Good day."

The young man mounted his horse and rode off. The peddler watched him go, then turned back to look at his new acquisition.

When he had touched the ring, he had felt the spark signaling the presence of magic. But now, as he studied the ring closer, he realized its magic was for something extremely specific, and something he had no use for.

"Worthless piece of junk," he muttered, shoving the ring in his pocket.

He withdrew his hand. Instead of the gnarled, dirty fingers the young man had seen, the hand that emerged was pale and perfect, with long black fingernails. The peddler's form changed as well, growing taller, younger, leaner. Long golden hair flowed down his back, with two black strands highlighting his pale face.

King Balor, King of the Unseelie Court, sneered at the waning sunlight overhead. Fortunately it was nearly sunset, although being out in the daylight at any point was taxing on the Unseelie Fae. As the King, he had a higher tolerance than his subjects, but not by much.

The useless magic ring felt like a boulder in his pocket. He sighed. Collecting magical items was proving to be a worthless endeavor. He was searching for something ancient and specific, an item that had most likely been lost or buried by now.

There had to be another way to unseal the gods' prison. Gathering random magical pieces wasn't working, but perhaps tapping into a very specific kind of magic would do the trick? It was worth trying. Perhaps it would also allow him to wander the Gifted Lands at any hour, not just during the evening to right after sunrise.

He smiled to himself. Think of all the havoc he could create, if he could stay aboveground for longer.

And if his idea failed ... well, as a Fae King, he had all the time in the world to come up with another plan.

All the time, in all the worlds.

1

CHAPTER ONE

THE PALE BLUE-GREEN JEWEL winked in the sunlight that streamed through our large front windows.

"I think this will be a better fit for you, Endri," my father, Pazho, said.

He shook his long, white-blond hair out of his eyes. "Tourmaline is a stone of stabilization, of protection. And," he winked, "it matches your eyes."

"Ha, very funny, Father," I said, widening my dark brown eyes at him.

"You never know. Perhaps your other self will have blue eyes."

I smiled sadly as I reached for the teal-colored, slightly translucent pendant. It was a lovely jewel, and would probably make a good soulstone for me. But ...

"We've tried two others, and neither of them worked," I sighed. "Perhaps we should just accept that I'll never be able to transform."

Pazho closed my fingers around the gem. The thin leather cord attached to it trailed from my closed fist. "Oh, Endri. Don't say never. You'll get it soon, I'm sure."

I gazed out the window. Our next door neighbor was outside, beating her rugs on the stone path. Dust clouded up, and she stopped to sneeze.

I sighed again and met my father's concerned eyes. "I'll try, Father. But it's hard not to be discouraged."

"I understand." He patted my hand. "I'll go and get all the things we need for the soulstone creation."

Pazho stood up and disappeared into the kitchen. I opened my hand and studied the tourmaline, and the faint scar on my palm next to it. Yet another cut was coming. Great.

Here in the kingdom of Annlyn, the people were able to shift forms, learning at a young age which animal would be their second self. By adolescence, the shapeshifters had mastered their ability, usually with the help of a soulstone. The more you used your soulstone, the more your magic became tied to it. So, picking a gem to become your soulstone was quite important. Fully connecting yourself to your soulstone required a small ceremony that involved a bit of bloodletting.

I had merged with two other soulstones before this, and both times the gems had ultimately failed.

With the first soulstone, I had been unable to transform, even after years of trying. Pazho, after much observation, had decided that perhaps I hadn't merged with the soulstone like we had thought, and we got rid of the jewel.

The second soulstone cracked right after I joined with it.

The failed soulstone issue wouldn't have been so worrying, except for one other fact: I was past the age of my majority. Everyone else had mastered shifting by the age of thirteen or fourteen. When my birth parents had brought me to Pazho, a well-respected scholar, for help, I had already been fifteen, much older than other first-time shifters.

They never came back for me. I never saw them around the capital city, where Pazho lived. Perhaps they had left the kingdom of Annlyn altogether.

I suppose they knew, deep down, that I'd never master shifting, and they had decided it was a convenient way to be rid of me.

But Pazho and his mate, Denaan, never made me feel inferior, even though the cloud of my failure always hung over my head. Instead, they had taken me in, quietly adopting me—and proving to be truer parents than the ones who had left me behind ever were.

Pazho, his arms full, dropped several items on the table in front of me. I began organizing them, used to the routine by now. The candle went to my left. Bandages and towels, to my right. The small black pot I moved in front of me. I picked up the pitcher and poured water into the pot, while Pazho heated a knife in the fireplace.

Hmm. Something was missing. Oh, yes—I jumped up and walked into the kitchen, scooping up some jars of dried herbs on the open pantry shelf.

"Thank you, Endri," Pazho said. "There was too much for me to carry."

"You're welcome," I said, as I added a scoop from each jar to the pot.

Pazho finished heating the knife and placed it on the table to cool. I hung the pot on a hook over the fire.

While I waited for the water to boil, I said to Pazho, "Do you think this time it will work?"

Pazho nodded. "Of course it will. This time we have the perfect jewel for you. And, remember, you're not the only one who is a late shifter. Queen Jennica of Calia was a late shapeshifter, and now she's quite adept at transforming."

I smiled indulgently. Whenever I felt down about my lack of shapeshifting ability, Pazho often invoked Queen Jennica of Calia. I had never met her, but apparently a few years ago she had met my father, and he had given her the gem that would become her soulstone. She had been around my age—nineteen—when she first learned to shift into her dragon form. I refrained from commenting that the queen already had a background in magic, so she at least understood the theory even if she couldn't do it. And she hadn't even *known* she could become a dragon until she met my father, so she hadn't known what she was missing.

I acutely knew what I was unable to do.

Also, from the stories my father told me, Queen Jennica had shown signs of shapeshifting power when she was young. I had never manifested any powers—hence my abandonment on Pazho and Denaan's doorstep.

My silence must have spoken volumes to Pazho, for he stood up and embraced me. "We'll get it this time, Endri. We will."

Tears pricked my eyes. His encouragement gave me hope—as did the knowledge that he didn't view it as a "me" issue, but a "we" issue.

The water in the pot started bubbling. I grabbed a towel and took the pot from the flame, placing it carefully on the table.

"Shall we?" Pazho held up the now-cooled knife.

I nodded and held out my hand, palm up. Pazho made a quick cut near my old scar, and tipped my hand sideways so my blood dripped into the pot. I scrunched my nose, disgusted by the odd metallic herbal smell in the air.

When the water turned muddy, he put the necklace into the pot, pendant first. *"Junctus.* May the two become one. *Fiat."*

There was a flash, and I gagged as the sickly smell grew stronger. Then it disappeared. The pot was empty, except for my necklace.

I grabbed a strip of cloth and bandaged my hand, then reached into the pot and grabbed my new soulstone. It shimmered in my hand, bright with new magic and full of promise.

Just like the other ones had.

"How does it feel?" Pazho searched my face, wide-eyed and curious.

I touched the stone with my good hand. It felt warm, and hummed with a pleasant energy. "Not bad. Time will tell, I guess."

"I guess," Pazho echoed. He sounded disappointed, as if he expected a stronger reaction. I felt a bit guilty for not being more enthusiastic, but I also didn't want to get my hopes up again.

My father sighed. "Well, let's clean up. And then we can try—"

There was a knock at the front door.

Pazho frowned. We had been so busy with the soulstone, we hadn't noticed anyone approaching the house.

He stood up and opened the front door. A middle-aged woman fell into the room, frantic. "Oh, Pazho! I'm so glad you're home! I need your help, right away!"

2

CHAPTER TWO

PAZHO RAISED AN EYEBROW. "Mistress Laina. Please, come in."

He waved the woman into the room, pulling out a chair at the table for her. I hastily moved the items sprawled across the table to one side, but Mistress Laina didn't seem to notice—or care—about the mess.

While I cleaned up the remnants of our spell casting, I eyed our guest. She was breathing heavily and her face was red, as if she had been running. Her dark brown hair, streaked with white, had been pinned up earlier, but was now partially coming undone. She shivered, despite the fire in the hearth.

"Madam, what seems to be the matter?" Pazho asked.

Mistress Laina visibly fought to compose herself. Taking in a shaky breath, she said, "I was walking in the hills, the ones just north of town. By Lake Vitrum. You know, where Fan normally brings the sheep. Although I think she takes longer out there than she needs to, so she can meet up with that young Roger."

I brought a few items into the kitchen so Mistress Laina wouldn't see me roll my eyes. You had to feel a bit sorry for her—not only was she a widow, but she had lost her two sons about a year ago as well. But she was also a notorious busybody, probably because she had little else to fill her days with. If you told her something, most of Annlyn would know within the hour. At least in the kingdom's capital city. It would take a few more days for the outlying farms and villages to find out.

As I returned, Mistress Laina was finishing her story. "And they were all just standing there, wandering about. No fights between any of them. And no soulstones, either."

"Perhaps they're not shapeshifters, but merely mundane animals," Pazho said.

"I know what I saw," the woman insisted. "And I know how it *felt*, too. My skin was prickling and I kept thinking someone was watching me. Please. It needs to be looked into."

Pazho nodded. "Don't fret, madam. I'll go to the hills with you."

"Oh, thank the gods," Mistress Laina said, her relief evident. "If you don't mind, I'd like to stop at my home first before going back out there."

"That's fine. I have a few things to finish up here, and then I'll come get you."

Mistress Laina stood. "Thank you, thank you so much. I know people don't always believe me ... so, thank you."

She left, closing the door behind her. Pazho sat, lost in thought. I tidied up a bit more, eyeing him, but he didn't say anything. Finally, I coughed a bit to get his attention.

My father looked up, frowning. "Oh, Endri. Is the smell still bothering you? You should have said."

I shook my head. "No, no, I'm fine. What's going on?"

Thoughtfully, Pazho looked out the window, although Mistress Laina was long gone. "It seems we have a random menagerie of animals outside of Annlyn."

I frowned. "I hardly think a bunch of sheep is cause for concern."

Although Annlyn was full of magical animals that were also people, there were also regular, non-magical animals that lived in the area outside the capital. Birds and rodents in the forests, livestock on the farms.

And as far as the magical animals went, the normal predator-prey relationships didn't apply. For example, Pazho's second form was a grey wolf, while his mate Denaan could transform into a majestic elk. Although the two often teased each other, they had never wanted to outright kill each other, from what I could tell. Even though their natural instinct would demand it.

Pazho shook his head, his hair falling in his face again. I made a mental note to buy him a hair ribbon, even though he lost them constantly. "Not from the way Mistress Laina described it. She said there were a few animals just wandering around—a lion and a zebra, two rabbits and a fox. No fighting, which you'd expect. But not a soulstone among them, either. So are they Annlyn animals, or mundane ones?"

"Ah. I see. They're too exotic to be native to this area, but then, if they're mundane, how did they get here?"

"Exactly my thoughts." He surveyed the table. "Did you need any help cleaning?"

"No, I can get the rest. It's pretty much done, anyway."

"Very well." Pazho stood up and grabbed a cloak hanging on a peg near the door. "I'm not sure how long I'll be. Please tell Denaan I may not be in tonight."

"All right." I paused, feeling unusually uneasy. "Father?"

Pazho stopped with his hand on the door handle, a question in his eyes.

"Be careful," I said.

He kissed the top of my forehead. "I will, my dear boy."

Pazho slipped out the door and headed down the street, while I stood there watching him leave, the tourmaline soulstone dangling uselessly between my fingers.

3

CHAPTER THREE

"ENDRI! ENDRI, WHERE'S THAT water?"

"Coming!" I scooped up the bucket, taking care not to spill any water even as I rushed to the Red Antler Inn's back door. I nudged the door open with my foot. "Here it is, De—"

A tin cup whizzed through the air, hitting the wall just to the right of the door.

I sighed. "Denaan, could you aim a little further away next time? You could have hit me!"

The stocky innkeeper looked at me sheepishly, wiping his wet hands on his perpetually stained apron. "Sorry, Endri. That one just slipped out of my hands."

I laughed. "At least you're throwing unbreakables now." I set the heavy bucket down and picked up the tin cup. It sported a huge dent near its handle—although that could have been there before, since most of the dinnerware in this place was chipped, dented, or cracked.

Fortunately, the patrons of the Red Antler didn't notice, or didn't care. They came for the food and stayed for the company, and could have cared less about the quality of the plates and cups.

Speaking of which ...

I snatched up my own apron—slightly cleaner than Denaan's, although not by much—and grabbed a knife. The dinner crowd would be here soon, and there was no time for dallying.

"Oh, by the way," I said. "Pazho wanted me to tell you he might not be in tonight."

Denaan raised an eyebrow. "Really? And why not?"

"He wanted to look at something outside of the city." Briefly, I told him about Mistress Laina's visit.

Denaan snorted. "That's it, then. He won't be in tonight. You know how he gets. He'll lose track of time and stay out there for days, until he finally realizes he's tired and hungry."

I laughed. That would definitely be like Pazho. He had a brilliant mind, but tended to forget the basic necessities if he was studying something. Denaan had forced Pazho into the habit of stopping by the Red Antler Inn each night, just to ensure Pazho ate at least one meal a day.

I finished slicing the cheese I had been working on, and started in on some potatoes. Denaan gave me a sideways glance as he continued his work. "My goodness, Endri, you're fast. My old fingers aren't as nimble as they used to be. What would I do without you?"

I smiled at him. "You'll never have to find out, Father. I'm happy to help."

We settled into a rhythm of peeling, chopping, and cooking.

Since I had come to live with Denaan and Pazho, this was how I spent most of my nights. Days were for studying, or helping Pazho with his research. Although, according to Denaan, it was more making sure that Pazho didn't do anything foolish in the name of research.

We heard the front door of the inn open and close.

"Piedra? Piedran? Is that you?" Denaan called out.

Two teenagers, a boy and a girl of about sixteen, flitted into the room. Fraternal twins, they were Denaan's niece and nephew, and often helped out around the inn.

"Hello, Uncle," Peidra, the girl, said.

"Hello, Endri," her brother Piedran said. "How have you—"

"—been?" Piedra finished. "Mother says hello. She wanted us to tell you, Uncle—"

"—that she'll be in later tonight, with some pies." Piedran spoke just as fast as his sister. "Can we help you—"

"—with anything?"

Denaan flicked a towel at the two of them. "Go set up the dining area, will you?"

"Of course, Uncle. We'll have it done—"

"—in no time." The two of them exited the kitchen.

Denaan shook his head, but a smile teased the corners of his lips. "Hummingbirds. I love them, but they're exhausting."

I chuckled. "That makes sense, for someone like you."

He snorted. "Elks aren't known for rushing into things. Unless it's absolutely necessary, of course."

"In which case, may the gods help whoever gets in your way."

He laughed, and we settled into our cooking rhythm once more.

Soon the Red Antler's front door opened and closed again. And kept opening and closing. The inn, always a popular spot for locals and the rare tourists we got in Annlyn, was busy tonight. The earlier quiet was replaced by a steady hum of chattering voices and happy eaters. I lost track of how many times Piedra and Piedran flew in and out of the kitchen, their arms full of food or drink or dirty dishes. My world narrowed down to chop, cook, clean, repeat.

Eventually the chaos slowed—less food to prepare, and more things to clean. Which meant, as always, that the night was winding down.

I swiped a sweaty hand across my forehead, trying to brush my dark brown hair back from my eyes.

Denaan wiped his hands on his already damp apron and stretched, rolling his shoulders. "What a night. Was it just me, or was it busier than normal? For a moment there, I thought we were going to run out of potatoes."

I checked the basket on the table. "We definitely ran out of leeks."

Denaan sighed. "Well, I suppose there are worse problems than selling out of our food supply." He looked around. "And I don't think Pazho ever made it in tonight. I'll have to bring something home for him, if there's anything left."

"We might have some pie still." I checked the pie dishes on the counter that the twins' mother had left at some point in the evening. "Nope, never mind. It's just crumbs."

I gave Denaan a sheepish look. "I should have remembered to set something aside. It got so busy, I just stopped paying attention to anything other than my work."

Denaan smiled. "You really are Pazho's son, even if you do get your cooking skills from me."

I smiled back. In the three or so years since I had come to live with Pazho and Denaan, they had never made me feel like I was anything less than family. Even though we weren't blood related, in any way. And even though I could never fully repay them for their unending kindnesses towards me—taking me in, feeding and clothing and teaching me—they never made feel like I *had* to repay them. They had never had children, but now that they had me—admittedly much older than the age most children would be adopted—they were happy to have me around.

The twins fluttered into the kitchen, arms laden with stacks of dirty dishes.

"Piedra, Piedran." Denaan addressed his niece and nephew. "Do either of you know if Pazho came in tonight?"

"Hmm." Piedra's brow furrowed in thought. "No, I—"

"—don't think so." Her brother wore the same expression. "Mother was the—"

"—only family that came by. Odd, really. Uncle—"

"—Pazho usually stops by to at least say hello."

Denaan nodded, frowning. "Well, he probably stayed out too late researching whatever it was and went straight back home. At least, he better have gone straight back home. I swear, if he's not there when I get back—"

A scratching sound at the inn's back door made us all pause. The scratching came again, more insistent and accompanied by a low whine.

Curious, I opened the door. The creature on the other side had been leaning his full weight against the door, and when I opened it, the grey wolf tumbled into the room. The wolf picked himself up and shivered, panting slightly.

I gasped.

Blood completely covered the grey wolf's normally pristine muzzle, dripping down to stain his chest and legs as well.

4

CHAPTER FOUR

I REACHED FOR THE wolf, half-picking him up to bring him inside. Although I wouldn't be able to fully carry the beast's weight, I could at least help him a little.

Denaan grabbed some linen towels and rushed forward to help me. Together, we carried the wolf in front of the kitchen hearth. Denaan wiped at the wolf's mouth, while I looked up at the twins, who hovered nearby, worried. "Bring some water, please. And extra towels. Hurry!"

The twins flitted away. The wolf began to cough, emitting a sort of bark-and-wheezing sound. Denaan stroked the wolf's head, trying to calm him down, but the wolf began to change form under his hand. In the place of the grey wolf, the tall, lean form of Pazho appeared.

Pazho's coughing subsided. His face scrunched up and he was smacking his tongue and lips. Blood coated his mouth and part of his cheeks, and stained his long, light white-blond hair. He spat into the fire.

Denaan looked worried. "Pazho, my goodness. There's so much blood."

Piedra and Piedran returned, one holding a glass of water and the other holding more clean towels. Pazho took the glass, rinsing his mouth with a little water before spitting into the hearth again. The fire sizzled and crackled upon impact.

Pazho rinsed and spat once more, then wiped his mouth with one of the towels. "Fortunately, it's not mine. But it does leave an awful taste in one's mouth."

"Pazho, what happened? If this isn't your blood, whose blood is—"

Pazho held up a hand to fend off Denaan's questions. He finished off the last of the water, this time actually drinking it instead of using it to rinse his mouth.

"Ah, that hits the spot. Now, then. What was it you wanted to ask me?"

Denaan rolled his eyes, despite his worry. "Pazho. An explanation, please."

The wolf-turned-man leaned against Denaan, taking comfort in his mate's solid presence. Although his earlier question had been flippant, Pazho seemed disturbed about something.

"So, I went to investigate Mistress Laina's story," he began. "It seemed terribly far-fetched, but she seemed so sincere, I thought it worth looking into."

"You know what a gossip she is," Denaan said. "You really thought she wasn't exaggerating?"

"I wish she was." Pazho sighed. "Just like she had told me, there were several animals just standing around, ones that aren't necessarily native to this area. And they did have that feeling of otherness about them, so I think her hunch that they were from Annlyn was correct."

"Did you recognize them?" I asked. "Did Mistress Laina?"

Pazho shook his head. "No, she didn't know who they might be, and neither did I. But I don't leave the city that much, so if they're from the outskirts, it's possible that I've never met them."

"And I'm here most of the time," Denaan said, waving one hand to indicate his inn. "So unless they come to eat here often, I wouldn't know them either."

"Oh," I said, disappointed. "Okay. But that doesn't explain the blood."

"I was getting to that," Pazho said, a little testy. Denaan raised his eyebrows, but neither of us said anything. Pazho was one of the wisest, most patient people I knew. If he was short-tempered, it was a sure sign that something had set him on edge.

Pazho stared into the fire. "The animals were just standing around, not interacting with each other, and not all that interested in Mistress Laina or me.

"But then, this odd feeling came over the area. Everything got eerily quiet, and then the animals exploded in a frenzy. They started fighting each other, and then, as one, they turned on us.

"Mistress Laina was able to shift into her other self, a parakeet, and get away. But I was surrounded. I shifted into my wolf form, but there were still too many. I fought my way through the group and ran like mad for the city."

Pazho wiped his mouth again, even though it was now completely free of blood. "I hope none of the injuries I may have inflicted were fatal."

Denaan patted his mate's shoulder soothingly. "You did what you had to do to survive. That's how it is in the animal kingdom."

"But that's not how it is in the kingdom of Annlyn," Pazho said sharply. "Our ability to reason is what sets us apart. Otherwise, we're no better than the animals we transform into."

We all fell silent, keenly aware of the truth Pazho had just uttered.

Finally, I ventured, "These animals. If they are from Annlyn, they should have transformed back into their human selves. Not attack you. Right?"

Pazho looked away from the fire then, his haunted eyes meeting mine. "I don't think they could have. None of them had their soul-stones anymore."

5

CHAPTER FIVE

"ARE YOU SURE I look all right?" I asked Pazho for probably the hundredth time.

"Don't fret," my father assured me, patient as ever. "You cut a fine figure. I'll be doing most of the talking anyway."

"But did we have to do this today?"

"We're way overdue to present you to His Majesty as it is. And since I have to meet with His Majesty anyway, we might as well get it over with at the same time."

I understood Pazho's logic, but it didn't stop me from feeling panicked and apprehensive.

We were hurrying down the gray, white, and black cobblestone streets towards the palace, our sandals slapping against the ground as we threaded our way through the Market Day crowds. Stalls lined both sides of the street, overflowing with produce, leather goods, jewelry, and other crafts. Children giggled and ran around while their parents shopped—or yelled at them to slow down. One child had a close call, nearly falling into one of the many fountains that dotted the city center.

After his discovery last night, Pazho had sent a message to the king first thing this morning, requesting an audience to discuss "urgent matters." He hadn't expected a response right away, and so we were all taken by surprise when just an hour later, a messenger had come by, saying that King Tahrin would see Pazho at midday.

Pazho had decided I should accompany him. For one thing, I had yet to be presented to the king, and at nineteen, I was six years past when most people were brought to the Annlyn court for the first time. For another—and probably the more crucial thing, although Pazho didn't want to admit it—my father wanted support when he went before the king with his tale.

I wasn't sure why. Pazho was well-known as a respected scholar. I was a nobody, and unknown to the king. And hadn't the king responded to Pazho's request almost immediately? He obviously held Pazho in high regard. My father would be fine. Me, on the other hand?

I guess we'll find out.

A few women crossed the street in front of me, separating me from Pazho, who was now several steps ahead.

"Excuse me. Pardon me." I tried to weave around them, but the little group planted themselves firmly in front of me, dawdling over a stall's wares.

Someone next to me giggled. "A herd of elephants could be running down the street, and you'd still never be able to come between the matrons and a good deal."

I turned to look at the speaker, and was instantly smitten.

A young woman about my age met my gaze, her big brown eyes twinkling. She pushed a strand of her wavy black hair away from her heart-shaped face, and I swear my heart skipped a beat. She wore a simple cream dress, similar to those I'd seen household servants wearing.

"We can test your theory," I said. "Are you able to transform into an elephant?"

She shook her head. "Sadly, no. But that would be lovely. They're such majestic creatures."

"Alas, I can't either." The shoppers had yet to move. And, if I was being honest, I didn't want to move either. I stuck out my hand in greeting. "I'm Endri."

She put a slim brown hand in mine. "Laersa. Are you shopping today?"

"Oh, no. I'm actually headed to the palace with my father."

"Oh? Perhaps I'll see you there. I've a bit of shopping to do, but I'll be there later."

"Really? Do you work there?"

A smirk played at the corners of her lips. "You could say that."

A vendor at a nearby stall called out to us. Well, to my new friend. "Lae-lae! Good to see you! Are you here to buy my vegetables?"

Laersa giggled. "Of course, Benton. You always have such lovely produce. Give me a moment, I'll be right over."

Another merchant waved at Laersa. "Come by my stall when you're finished with Benton!"

"I will, Teela."

"You're quite popular," I observed. "Everyone here knows you."

Laersa shrugged. "I'm a frequent customer."

Teela laughed as she addressed me. "Lae-lae's being modest. Not only is she a good—and generous—customer, but she helped me build this stall."

Teela waved proudly at her beautifully built booth. I nodded in appreciation. It was well-constructed and painted in a bright, eye-catching yellow. "And Benton's produce is only so good because Laersa has quite the green thumb."

"Hey!" Benton yelped. "I'm not that bad a grower!"

"You're not," Laersa reassured him.

"It's just that Laersa's better," Teela teased.

As the two merchants bantered back and forth, a shout from further away made both Laersa and me look up. The matrons had moved on, and the crowd had thinned. Down the street, Pazho stood waiting for me, his arms crossed.

"I need to go," I said, my face coloring. "I hope to see you again, Laersa."

"Likewise, Endri." Her face lit up in a radiant smile.

I floated the rest of the way to the palace.

6

- · -

CHAPTER SIX

PAZHO GENUFLECTED BEFORE KING Tahrin, pressing the back of the king's hand to his forehead in a gesture of respect. "Your Majesty."

King Tahrin smiled. "Ah, Pazho. Welcome, my old friend."

Pazho rose and motioned for me to come forward. I knelt down before the king, hoping my long, straight robes wouldn't get tangled up in my feet.

"And who's this?" The king scrutinized me with shrewd brown eyes set in a grizzled face. He waved his sceptre at me, a long, golden rod with a multi-colored cluster of jewels at the top.

"My son, Endri. Adopted by Denaan and me a few years ago."

"Ah. Well met, Endri."

I gulped, hoping my nervousness didn't show as I rose to my feet. "Thank you, Your Majesty."

"Adopted, huh? My condolences on the loss of your family."

"Well, they ..." My voice trailed off when I felt Pazho nudge me. "Thank you, King Tahrin."

The king leaned back in his throne. The twin throne next to him, with its red velvet seat and gold trim, was empty. King Tahrin had become widowed a few years ago, and had yet to remarry. "You're much older than most of the others who come to court for the first time. I'm sure that means you're already settled into a second self. Tell me, what is your animal form? Perhaps I've seen you around the kingdom."

"Oh. Uh." My mouth went dry. "I, uh—"

My father stepped in smoothly. "Endri has yet to find his second self, but we expect it to manifest soon."

King Tahrin raised a brow. "Already a man, and yet no sign of your animal form? That is unfortunate."

A flash of anger surged through me, but I kept my eyes downcast so he wouldn't see my emotions.

A rustling to the king's left caught my attention. A young woman had just entered the room and stood to the side, just behind the throne. She gave me a sympathetic smile, and I recognized her as Laersa, the servant from the marketplace.

She winked at me as if we shared a secret.

I grinned back. Her smile grew wider. I was so taken with the enchanting creature that I nearly missed what King Tahrin was saying.

"... I understand your concern, Pazho, but I don't think it's necessary to study them any further." The king frowned at my father. "From what you say, there's not that many of them. Any curiosity on our part could attract attention from outsiders."

Pazho dipped his head in deference, but I could see his hands moving slightly behind his back. My father wore his soulstone on his right hand, a flawless ruby set in a simple silver band. When he was agitated, he tended to twist the ring around his index finger or rub the gemstone.

"Your Majesty, I wouldn't have brought this matter to you if I didn't think it was important. I know that Annlyn's policy of isolation has kept us safe thus far, but—"

The king sighed noisily. "For generations, in fact. Our jewelry trade gives us all we need from the other countries. Keeping them at arm's length ensures they do not learn our secrets. Secrets which could be used against us."

"Respectfully, I would argue that the rest of the Gifted Lands is already aware of our secret. Despite the fact that non-shifters cannot see the animals within Annlyn's borders."

King Tahrin's lips thinned. "And who is responsible for that? You, and Joichan. And the blasted dragon had the nerve to leave and escape my wrath."

"Your Majesty—"

"No." King Tahrin stood, slamming his golden sceptre against the floor. "We are done here, Pazho. Frankly, I was hoping you wanted this meeting to apologize. Instead, you fill my head with crazy stories about wild animals."

A knock at the doors of the throne room caught our attention.

"Yes? What is it?" King Tahrin called out.

One of the doors opened a crack. A guard stepped in, clearing his throat. "Forgive the intrusion, Your Majesty. The ambassador from Graenir has arrived."

"I am nearly done here. Send them in once these two leave."

"Yes, Your Majesty."

The guard backed out of the room, closing the door behind him.

Pazho turned back to King Tahrin, one eyebrow raised.

King Tahrin flushed. "Pazho, it's because of you and Joichan that I am even forced to entertain the idea of alliances with the other kingdoms. Not that any alliance means I willingly disclose Annlyn's shapeshifting abilities."

He sighed, and his eyes turned sad. "We used to be such good friends, you and I. But your ideas are dangerous. Now, please leave.

Our audience is ended." His eyes narrowed. "And don't you even think about going back into the hills to study those strange animals."

Pazho bowed stiffly, then turned to leave. My normally composed father trembled all over. He started walking towards the wooden doors at the other end of the throne room.

I turned to go as well, but not before exchanging one last glance with the beautiful servant girl. I wondered what she thought of the whole exchange. As a servant, she probably witnessed a lot of political discussions.

Pazho was several steps ahead of me. I rushed forward and put my hand on his arm to steady him. Father stopped and looked at me, then patted my hand and allowed me to guide him. We passed several other servants, who studiously avoided looking at either Pazho or me.

As we reached the exit, we nearly bumped into a tall, stately woman who was waiting just outside the room to enter. Two long, pale blond braids framed her face. She was adjusting the high collar of her long-sleeved silk blouse—a surprising choice to wear in the warm southern kingdom of Annlyn. We tended to favor lightweight linen or cotton clothing. Perhaps she had yet to discover our local dress. In this heat, I was sure she would search it out soon enough.

Standing behind her, two guards held a large, fabric-covered object between them. With the wrappings over the item, I couldn't tell what it was they were holding, but I guessed it was probably a painting, from the shape of it.

"Oh!" Startled, the blond woman put a gloved hand to her mouth. Her green eyes widened. Gaining her composure, she moved to the side to allow us to pass. "Forgive me."

Pazho said, "It is we who should be begging your pardon, Miss—?"

"Allisandra, of Graenir."

"Ah. Welcome to our fair country." Pazho bowed over her hand, then leaned forward conspiratorially. He whispered, "His Majesty's in a bit of a bad mood today. Sorry about that."

Allisandra chuckled. "That's how it usually is, in my line of work. Thank you for the warning."

"Of course." Pazho nodded to Allisandra, then indicated to me that we should keep walking.

As Allisandra entered the throne room, with the guards trailing after her, I heard King Tahrin say behind us, "My dear, you're a princess. Why can't you dress like one? No one will take you seriously if you insist on dressing like a servant. One day you'll rule in my place, and you should start acting like it."

I glanced back. Laersa now sat on the formerly empty throne next to the king. She laughed, a lovely, lilting sound. "Oh, Father. These clothes are so much more comfortable, and—"

Pazho and I walked into the hallway beyond. The doors closed behind us, their echo reinforcing that we were no longer welcome.

We continued on, but my mind was reeling. She was the Crown Princess?

7

CHAPTER SEVEN

"THAT FOOL! THAT OLD, stubborn fool! His refusal to listen, to look to the future, is going to be the downfall of us all!"

I nodded, only half-listening. My mind was still back at the palace, focused on the servant girl. I mean, the princess. Pazho had held his tongue during the walk home, but the moment our door closed on the outside world, he let loose his frustration.

Denaan walked in, drying a dish with a linen towel.

"I hope you're not talking about me," he said mildly. "I've been home all day."

"No, I'm talking about King Tahrin," Pazho fumed. "He's so slow to act—if he does at all! And now, when there is a problem right at our doorstep, he'd rather ignore the issue!"

Denaan didn't respond, just silently held out the now-dried dish to his mate.

Pazho waved it away. "No, thank you. Just because being destructive helps you feel better, does not mean I share the same proclivities."

Denaan shrugged. "I prefer to think of it as testing for quality. Besides, I don't throw things around as much anymore."

Both Pazho and I turned to Denaan, eyebrows raised. He smiled sheepishly. "For the most part."

I laughed, and even Pazho chuckled. My smile, as I watched my two fathers joke around, was one of genuine relief. I had never seen Pazho so upset before. Denaan's temper often ran hot, but Pazho had always been mild-mannered, and rarely got angry.

Pazho sank into one of the plush chairs by the hearth, looking weary.

Denaan said, "I'll make us some tea." He walked back into the kitchen.

I stood around awkwardly. Wanting to feel useful, I said, "Father, how about I take your cloak? Your boots? So you can get comfortable."

Pazho gave a little sigh, but allowed me to take his cloak and boots. Once they had been neatly stored, Denaan came back in, holding a tea tray with three green cups and a little green teapot. I took it from him and began serving while Denaan sat down next to Pazho.

I handed a steaming cup of chamomile to Pazho, then Denaan. Sitting back with my own cup, I asked, "Father?"

Both men looked at me.

"I guess I didn't realize until today's conversation with the king, but—why *do* we hide our shapeshifting abilities from the rest of the Gifted Lands? Is it really that bad?"

Pazho smiled at me, but his eyes were sad. "Oh, no, Endri. Once, we may have worried about a stigma attached to becoming animals, but Queen Jennica's successful rule in Calia proves that our gifts would be embraced in other lands."

Denaan grinned. "They don't even keep a standing army in Calia, since she took the throne."

"Yes, the sight of a large, golden, fire-breathing dragon is probably enough to make most armies reconsider invasion." Pazho paused. "When I helped Jennica find Joichan, who also could transform into a dragon, I had no way of knowing the repercussions of their meeting until months, even years, later. By then, rumors of the two Calian dragons had spread over much of the Gifted Lands. Not that I would have counseled either of them to keep their abilities a secret. But King Tahrin was furious when he found out my part in the whole thing, and our friendship has never been the same since."

Denaan took his mate's hand, rubbing his thumb over the back of Pazho's hand in an attempt to soothe him. "King Tahrin is just trying his best to keep Annlyn safe."

Pazho snorted. "If 'keeping Annlyn safe' means denying progress, then I disagree. He used to be much more forward-thinking, before the death of his queen. Now, he just hides away in his fancy palace, and he expects his people to hide themselves as well."

Denaan hugged Pazho to him. "It's that fire of yours that I love so much. You worry about the people; I'll worry about tonight's dinner."

Denaan gave Pazho another squeeze before standing. "And speaking of which, I should get to the Red Antler and start preparing. Endri, will you be along later?"

"Of course, Father." I nodded at Denaan, then eyed Pazho. "But I might be a little late, if that's okay with you."

Denaan nodded. "Of course. You're a good son. I'll see you at the inn."

After Denaan left, Pazho sighed and leaned back. "My apologies for silencing you earlier, Endri."

"Ah, yes, I noticed that. I meant to ask you about it."

"If King Tahrin wanted to believe that your family died and that's why we adopted you, I saw no reason to correct him. He may be the king, but the true reasons aren't his business."

I raised an eyebrow. "You mean, the fact that my birth family thought I was worthless and hopeless and saw you and Denaan as easy targets to saddle an unwanted son with?"

Pazho blinked, sitting up. "Endri...."

He reached out to hold my hand, but I pulled back. "Don't get me wrong, I'm grateful you and Denaan took me in. It's just ..."

When I didn't finish, Pazho prompted, "Just what?"

I shrugged, not even trying to hide the hurt lacing my voice. "Days like today remind me of why my family left me. Even the king thought something was wrong with me, when he found out how old I was. I've lived off your generosity for so long, but I'm not able to reciprocate in kind. I can't even shapeshift, no matter what I try."

Pazho took my hand. This time I let him.

"Your family barely deserves that title. They may have given birth to you, raised you for a few years, but when it mattered, they failed you horribly. I wish I could take back the damage they did to you through that failure."

I nodded, turning my head slightly so he wouldn't see the sheen of tears in my eyes.

"Look at me, son."

I did, rather reluctantly.

Pazho smiled. "You are one of the best things to ever happen to Denaan and me. Every day with you is a joy and an honor. I know you're going to learn to shift, one of these days. When you do—you'll be unstoppable. And I, for one, cannot wait to see that day."

8

CHAPTER EIGHT

I SMILED BACK AT Pazho. He held my gaze a moment longer, then his smile faded as he looked out the window and heaved a big sigh.

"Father?" I asked hesitantly. "What are you going to do? About the animals in the hills, I mean."

He didn't look at me, but I could hear the sadness and frustration lacing his voice. "What can I do? My king has ordered me not to go back. So, I guess I must obey."

"It will be all right," I said, although I was aware of how hollow my words sounded.

Pazho nodded, but still wouldn't meet my eyes.

I cleared my throat and stood up. "I'll clean up around here, and then I'll head over to the Red Antler to help Father."

I collected up the tea set and carried the tray to the kitchen. Cleaning dishes normally wouldn't take me too long, but I didn't want to leave Pazho while he was in such a melancholy state. After drying the teacups for the third time, I had to admit I couldn't draw out the chore for much longer. I put the dishes back in the cupboard and called out, "Father? I'm going now."

From the other room, Pazho called back, "Endri—before you go. Can you come in here for a moment, please?"

I put the towel I had been holding down on the table, then walked back into the front room, curious. Pazho now stood by the window. He held something in his hands, and looked down at it as he rolled it over and over between his fingers.

"What is it, Father?" I asked.

Pazho stopped twirling the object in his hands. He held it out to me. "Take it."

I reached for the item and studied it. It was a small figurine of a blue dragon, about the same shade as my teal tourmaline soulstone. Its white-streaked wings were half-raised, but not in fear or flight. Instead, the magnificent creature looked like it was ready to defend something—perhaps its territory, or maybe its kin?

"It's beautiful," I breathed, turning it over in my hand. "The craftsmanship is exquisite."

"It was a gift from Queen Jennica," Pazho said. "Her father-in-law, Kye, makes wonderful carvings of dragons, memories of his time as a dragon Seeker."

"Fascinating." Although dragons—both the regular and the shapeshifting kind—were a common sight around Annlyn, I had never seen an ice dragon in person before, just in books. They didn't exactly favor the hot, desert climes of the southern Gifted Lands, preferring the snowy, colder areas up in the north.

"Thank you for showing it to me, it really is wonderful." There was something about the little sculpture that drew me in. I found I didn't want to part with it, although I knew I would have to. Reluctantly, I held out the figurine to Pazho. "Here you go."

He waved my hand away. "Keep it. I want you to have it."

"Are you sure?" Even as I spoke the words, my fingers curled around the little dragon.

"Yes. It's not just a carving, you see. It also contains a bit of magic, a calling spell. It will link you with Queen Jennica, or perhaps her advisor, Taryn, up in Calia. Other mages, as well, if you know who you are calling."

"Really?" I frowned down at the little figurine. "How?"

"Just concentrate on who it is you're trying to contact. They will hear your call, and answer. If they need to get in touch with you, they can reach you through that carving. So it might be wise to keep it on or near you, in a safe place."

"But how can I contact the queen—or anyone, really—if I don't know what they look like? Or sound like? Don't I need to have some familiarity with them for the spell to work?"

"It helps, yes. But just focusing on the person should be good enough. I would demonstrate, but there's not a lot of magic left in that figurine to experiment with. It was one of the queen's early experiments with that kind of magical infusion, and is considerably weaker than her more recent attempts. But it's a rare item—you won't find any new calling items that look like that anymore." He smiled. "I understand Kye didn't want to give away too many of his dragon sculptures. Even though he has quite the collection."

"Why are you giving this to me?"

Pazho's smile faded. "Just a precaution. I hope you won't have to use it, but if something should happen to either Denaan or me, then leave the capital city and go to Joichan's former residence. Then contact the queen. You should be safe from prying eyes, both magical and mundane, in Joichan's cave."

I blinked. "What? Where? How do I find it?"

"It's a cave set in the side of the mountain just west of the capital city. The casual observer won't be able to see it—it's hidden by magic, and I believe all the spells Joichan used on it are still active. But now that you're aware of it, you might be able to spot it, if you're deliberate and careful. Once you actually reach the cave, you'll always be able to see it. Climb straight up, you'll come across it. If that cave could keep him safe from the best dragon Seekers for years, it will definitely keep you safe as well."

"It's warded?" At Pazho's nod, I frowned. "How am I supposed to get in, then?"

"The ward has a way of knowing who is hostile to the cave or its inhabitants, and who is not. As long as you don't go there with any ill intent—like wanting to destroy the place or steal from it—then you should be able to enter."

He paused, then chuckled. "Oh, and you might want to bring some rope."

I eyed my father with some skepticism. But he looked completely sincere.

My blood ran cold.

"Nothing's going to happen to you. Either of you."

Pazho sighed. "I hope not, Endri. I hope not."

9

---·---

CHAPTER NINE

I HURRIED TOWARDS THE Red Antler Inn, keenly aware of how late I was to help Denaan. He usually began prepping for the evening meal around mid-afternoon, and from the look of the sun low in the sky, the Red Antler would soon be open.

But he would want me to take care of Pazho, I reasoned. Even though my tardiness would put extra work on Denaan, I also knew my father wouldn't be upset with me. If anything, he'd tell me to go right back home and make absolutely sure Pazho was all right.

When I reached the Red Antler, I saw a small crowd milling around out front. I recognized one of our regulars and called out to him.

"Arnon! What's going on? Why is everyone just standing around?"

The heavyset man turned to me, his face breaking into a smile when he saw me. "Endri! Good to see you, my boy!"

He gestured at the door. "The door's locked, although the Red Antler should have been open at least an hour ago. Do you know why Denaan hasn't opened up the place yet?"

I frowned, looking at the inn. The windows were dark, when normally the inside would be lit up from the glow of candles on tables and the room's hearth. "I don't know, Arnon, but I'll go find out. Excuse me."

I walked around to the back of the Red Antler and pounded on the kitchen door. The door opened a crack, and Piedra's scared face stared back at me. Then, once she realized it was me, she opened the door fully and grabbed my hand, pulling me inside.

"Endri! I'm so glad you—" Piedra stopped, waiting for something. Her face grew confused when whatever she was waiting for didn't happen.

"Are here," she finished lamely.

For a moment, I shared Piedra's confusion. Something felt odd, but I didn't know what. Then I realized—"Where's your brother?"

Piedra sniffled and wiped at her face. The scant firelight from the two candles on the table showed tracks of dried tears on the girl's cheeks. "I—I don't know. He went out to look for Denaan, but he hasn't come back yet. Endri, do you think—"

"Wait, what?" I put my hands on Piedra's shoulders and steered her to a chair. "Sit. Start at the beginning."

Piedra sank down slowly, wringing her hands. "Piedran and I got here around mid-afternoon, like we usually do. Uncle Denaan wasn't here, but we didn't think anything of it. We got the extra key and let ourselves in."

She held up a small, slightly dirty brass key. I recognized it as the spare key Denaan kept hidden in a dirt-filled pot just outside the kitchen door. Not under the pot, mind you, but buried in the pot's dirt. There were also three other similar-looking pots next to the one that held the spare key, all filled to the brim with dirt as well. Denaan figured no one would be so dedicated to finding a spare key that they would dig around in four full pots of dirt.

Denaan. I hope he's all right. Somehow, I had a feeling I would not like what Piedra had to say.

My hummingbird cousin continued to fidget. "We waited around for a while, but Denaan didn't show. You weren't here, either, so we thought maybe you would both arrive at the same time. So we went outside for a bit, just to work off some nervous energy—"

I smiled to myself. Boundless energy came naturally to the twins.

"And Piedran found this in the back." She pulled a leather cord from her pocket and handed it to me.

My breath caught as I examined the cord. I recognized the braided pattern, made of brown, black, and white—a gift from Pazho and me to Denaan a few years ago. But—

"It's missing its soulstone," I said. The cord's middle had a small loop to hold the soulstone, but the loop had been cut. I examined the cord more closely. Not cut, exactly. Slight fraying on the edges told me that perhaps the gemstone had been yanked or torn away.

Piedra nodded. "Yes. And since we remembered Pazho's story from last night—"

My eyes widened. "Oh, gods. You don't think that Denaan—?"

"Maybe? I hope not, but then the dinner crowd came, and Denaan still wasn't here, so Piedran went out to find him." Her voice hitched on a sob. "And my brother hasn't come back yet, either."

I paced around the kitchen, trying to gather my wild thoughts. "Okay. All right. First, uh ..."

I looked around the room. Even if we did want to open the Red Antler Inn to patrons, we'd be hours behind actually getting food on the tables. "I think the first thing we should do is tell the crowd that the Red Antler is not going to open tonight."

"Okay," Piedra said. Her dark eyes clung to me like a lifeline, although I doubted my ability to keep either of us afloat during this crisis.

"Okay," I echoed. "Next, I'll walk you home, make sure you get there safely. I—When—" I just stopped myself from saying *if* "—your brother gets back, he'll probably go straight home, especially once he sees the Red Antler is dark. I'll get Pazho, and then ... and then ..."

I had no idea what we would do next. Run to the hills? Go to the king again? I may have had no idea, but I was confident Pazho would.

"And then everything will be all right." I hoped.

Piedra nodded, sniffling. She stood. "I'll go tell the crowd."

She disappeared out the back, leaving me alone with my thoughts. I slipped my hand in my pocket, touching the ice dragon figurine there for reassurance. Should I use it to contact Pazho? No—he had made it clear it was to be used in an extreme emergency. And while this whole thing was cause for alarm, it wasn't an emergency.

Yet.

Piedra returned. "All right, I've told them. They're not happy, and they wanted to know why. I—I told them we didn't have enough food for tonight."

"It's not a complete lie," I remarked. I looked around the room one last time, even though there was nothing to clean, and blew out the candles on the table. "Let's go."

I followed Piedra out the kitchen door, taking the brass key from her to lock it. Looking at the four pots of dirt, I hesitated, wondering if I should hide the key again. *I'll just hold on to this for now. Denaan won't mind.*

As Piedra and I walked around to the front of the Red Antler, most the crowd was gone, save for a few lingering regulars grumbling to each other as to where they would find their dinner. We avoided their pointed stares and angry questions, keeping silent as we headed to the twins' home.

Fortunately, my cousins lived close to the Red Antler, and it wasn't too far out of my way to escort Piedra. We soon reached her home.

"Be well, Piedra," I said, giving her a quick hug goodbye. "If you need anything—"

"What's that?" my cousin interrupted me, pointing at the sky.

It was hard to tell, since twilight had already fallen as we walked home, and moonrise would happen soon. I looked where Piedra pointed. Darkness approached, like a sudden thunderstorm, but it didn't look normal. Flashes of red lightning punctuated this complete blackness, and the air fairly sizzled with the feel of magic.

"Piedra, get inside!" I said, as she fumbled for her house key and jammed it into the lock. She opened the door and we both fell inside as the blackness covered the sky of Annlyn like a heavy, opaque blanket. I slammed the door against the night.

The blackness rolled over the city. Crimson flashes lit up the sky, before the odd storm cloud completely passed by Annlyn.

The sky lightened a fraction, and true night shone down. I looked out the window, sighing in relief when I saw the full moon in the sky.

"Piedra, I don't know what that was, but it's gone now," I said.

A light buzzing sound answered me.

My heart sank as I turned around. Moonlight streamed through the window behind me, illuminating a little green, white and gray hummingbird. Her wings, a blur from continuous movement, continued to buzz as she flitted up to my face.

I looked down. When people shifted, their first layer of clothes transformed with them—a good thing, or Annlyn's trade would have to be in textiles and not jewelry, just out of necessity from the constant form changing. But outer layers didn't shift, and so my cousin's thin cloak was now lying on the floor. Amidst the pile of clothes, I found her soulstone—still attached to its cord, but the formerly lustrous white pearl was now cracked and dull.

"Piedra, what happened? Can you change back?"

A plaintive chirp was her only reply.

10

Chapter Ten

As much as I hated leaving Piedra, it was now more urgent than ever that I find Pazho. After a few more—admittedly inane—words of comfort, I left my cousin's house and headed out into the night.

As I rushed along, weird sounds filled the air. The tinkling of Annlyn's many fountains could still be heard, but above it, discordant noises arose.

The braying of a donkey. The lowing of a cow. The wheezing cry of a llama. Something dark flew by my head. Spooked, I batted at it, and heard the owl hoot in my ear before I saw it fly away.

My steps slowed as I paused in the middle of the street to listen.

Some animals roamed the area, as the night was still young, but the majority of the sounds were coming from—indoors.

"Oh, gods."

I ran.

I didn't stop until I reached the front door, frantically fumbling through my pockets for my house key. If I could have run through the door to save time, I would have.

My hands trembled as I inserted the key into the lock.

The door swung open. Inside, all was dark and quiet.

"Pazho? Father? Are you here?" I called out.

Only silence.

I felt around on the side table by the door for the unlit candle we always left there. My hands were shaking so much, it took me three tries to light the darn thing. But finally I had a little light to see by.

I held up the candle, surveying the room. Everything looked the same as it did when I had left earlier in the day.

"Father? Pazho, hello?" I walked through our front room, and into the kitchen.

And stopped at the sight before me.

The kitchen also looked like it had when I had been home earlier. Still tidy and clean, with the exception of the towel I had been using to dry dishes—that was still on the table where I had left it.

But I hadn't left the back door open.

The moonlight shone in through the door. Beyond, I could see part of the long alleyway that ran behind our house. But no sign of Pazho.

Something glinted on the floor. Feeling numb, I picked it up.

The silver ring with its single ruby winked dully up at me. A deep crack marred the formerly flawless finish of the bright red gem. Father hated being without his soulstone, and even when he transformed into his grey wolf form, the ring would stay looped around his paw.

If Pazho's soulstone was here—then where was Pazho?

I called Pazho's name several more times, but he didn't show. Deep down, I knew it was futile, but I didn't want to give up hope. Finally, though, I had to admit that he was gone. I shut the back door, my mind racing.

Denaan was gone. I had been counting on Pazho's help to find him. Now that Pazho was gone too, who could help me?

I thought about our earlier meeting with King Tahrin. Something was definitely amiss in Annlyn. He'd have to believe the tale now, and go investigate.

I slipped Pazho's ring on my right hand, absentmindedly rubbing the cracked stone. Wearing Father's ring—and doing the same action he would when feeling worried or upset—made me feel better. I would find Pazho and Denaan. Somehow.

I left the house through the front, walking down the cobblestone road towards the palace. The cheerful market stalls from the daytime, now empty, looked like twisted skeletons and grotesque ghosts in the moonlight.

A dark shape peeled itself from an alleyway and meandered into the street. I halted, my heart pounding.

The shape solidified into a large tiger. It yawned, showing its sharp white teeth, but didn't attack. A pig squealed and streaked down the street, with a deer bounding after it. The tiger showed no interest in either animal.

Those must also be transformed citizens, I realized. There were very few natural animals in Annlyn's capital city, other than the occasional horse or cat or dog. So, most of the animals wandering the streets were probably Annlynians who had shifted against their will, like my cousin Piedra had.

I gave the tiger a wide berth as I continued on. I didn't think it would harm me, but I also didn't want to take any chances. Perhaps I should have checked to see if it still had its soulstone, but I preferred not to get that close.

As I walked, I saw more animals wandering the streets. Broken windows or half-open doors hinted at how all these animals got out. One building had a particularly large hole in a side wall. Probably a rhinoceros or elephant had lived in that house.

Elephant. I wondered how Laersa—*Princess* Laersa—had fared. I seemed to be the only human in all of Annlyn.

Finally, I reached the palace. On the walk over, I hadn't thought about how I would get in. When I reached the building, I realized, perhaps I should have.

The portcullis was down, and beyond that, the heavy wooden doors were firmly shut. Nearby, a goat pawed at the ground—and at his guard uniform, now lying in a shredded heap near the castle wall. It looked like he had ripped his clothing from his body while he transformed. I didn't even know someone could do that. A second goat had parts of a torn uniform hanging from his mouth.

Oh, dear. I was beginning to think there would be no help from the king, or his men.

11

Chapter Eleven

"Psst! Hello, down there!"

I looked around, then up. Princess Laersa was looking down at me from an upstairs window, her wavy black hair fluttering in the wind.

"Laersa!" I blurted out without thinking. "I mean, Princess! Uh, that is, Your Highness—"

"Who's there? State your name and business."

"It's Endri. From the market. I met you in the market. And I was here earlier, with my father, Pazho. He wanted to talk to the king about—"

"Endri!" The princess leaned out further to get a better look at me. "I remember you, and your father! Yes, this is good. I'm glad you're here. I'll come down and get you. Go around the palace, and stop when you see the vegetable garden."

"Uh. Okay."

Princess Laersa's head disappeared. One of the goats—the one who had been pawing at his uniform—bleated at me.

I sighed. "Yeah, I know. Real smooth, right?"

I reached out and plucked the clothing from the second goat's mouth. "That can't be good for your digestion."

The goat gave me an impassive look, then bit into the uniform again.

"Suit yourself." I let go of the clothing and headed around the side of the castle.

Under the light of the full moon, I discovered the vegetable garden easily. I didn't have to wait long. A creak from the castle wall caught my attention. Princess Laersa poked her head around the plain door—most likely the servants' entrance—and beckoned.

"Come in!"

I hurried over and slipped through the door. Lit sconces lined the stone walls, giving off plenty of illumination. A family of rabbits hopped along, while a snake slithered in the opposite direction.

Princess Laersa pinched my arm.

"Ow!"

"Oh my gods, you *are* human," she breathed. "I thought I was the only one in all of Annlyn who hadn't transformed unwillingly."

"No, you're not alone," I said, rubbing at the spot she had pinched to make the pain fade quicker. Then what she had said registered. "Wait a minute. Don't you have a second self?"

"No." She regarded me, wide-eyed. "You mean—you can't shapeshift either?"

"No."

We stared at each other for a moment, silent. Then we both burst out laughing.

"Here I thought I was the only one!" I said.

"And I thought *I* was the only one in the whole kingdom who couldn't shift," Princess Laersa said. Her voice turned sad. "It's not something Father wants anyone in Annlyn—or beyond—to know. Although it's getting harder to keep it a secret as I get older."

"I'm sorry," I said.

"Don't be. I'm sure one of these days I'll figure it out. When Mother died, I should have already come into my transformation powers by then. But I was too distraught to really concentrate—and Father kind of ignored me for a while. I think I reminded him too much of her. A few tutors tried to help me shift, but I seem to be blocked somehow, and I don't know what to do about it."

She looked at me curiously. "How about you? Why can't you shift?"

I shrugged. "I seem to be blocked as well, like you. My birth parents tried for years to help me transform, but I just couldn't. They finally brought me to Pazho the scholar for help. And they never came back for me. Pazho and his mate, Denaan, were kind enough to take me in. Eventually, they sought out my birth parents, who then officially disowned me. So Pazho and Denaan adopted me, and have been a better family to me than my birth parents ever were."

I sighed. "But even though I've been studying with Pazho for years, I still can't shift, either."

Impulsively, Princess Laersa hugged me. "Well, we'll figure it out. Together."

I smiled. "Thanks."

When she released me, I noticed a cloth wrapped around her left hand. "Your Highness, are you all right? What happened?"

I clapped a hand over my mouth, embarrassed. "I mean—uh, please forgive my impertinence."

She laughed. "There's nothing to forgive. I thank you for your concern."

She raised her bandaged hand. "This was just a result of me being clumsy. A little nick, nothing more. I'm just lucky no slivers of glass got stuck in my hand."

"Oh, I'm sorry to hear that."

She waved away my concern. "We probably can't stay here. But I'm not sure where we could go."

I blinked. "We?"

"Well, of course. I'm not staying here by myself. And I'm sure you don't want to be wandering around alone, either."

She had a point. And I couldn't exactly leave her while Annlyn was in this state. What with her being the Crown Princess, and all, of course.

Pazho's advice came back to me. "I have an idea. There's a cave just outside the city that my father Pazho said I should go to, if something happened to him or Denaan. He said someone named Joichan used to live there. Also, Pazho gave me something to contact a friend of his."

I took out the ice dragon figurine from my pocket and showed it to Princess Laersa.

"Ooh, that's beautiful," she said. "But how is that going to help us contact anyone? And who are we contacting?"

"There's a calling spell on it," I explained. "As for who we're supposed to call—Queen Jennica of Calia."

Eyebrows raised, Princess Laersa said, "I thought you were just a commoner. I didn't realize you had such high connections."

Stung, I commented, "And I thought you were just a servant. I didn't realize you were the Crown Princess."

We both fell silent again.

Then, from Princess Laersa: "Let's start over."

She curtsied before me, laughing. "Greetings, good sir. My name is Princess Laersa, the future ruler of Annlyn."

I smiled and bowed. "Well met, Your Highness. I am Endri, of Annlyn."

"Well, Endri, now that we are acquainted with each other, what should we do about this problem that seems to have taken over all of Annlyn?"

"I'm not sure, Your Highness, but I'm sure as we discuss it further, we will come up with a good solution."

Princess Laersa grew somber. "I wish I knew what happened. I was at dinner when suddenly the air felt funny, like it does before a big storm. Everything went dark, even though all the sconces were lit. But they hadn't gone out—I nearly burned myself testing that theory. It was like someone had thrown a curtain over them so their flames couldn't be seen. When the light came back, everyone in the palace began transforming into their second, animal selves."

She shuddered. "A soldier even ran in to give a report on what was happening in the capital city—that everyone out there had suddenly shifted, too. He transformed into a dragonfly right before my eyes, and then a bird flew in and snatched him away."

"Oh gods. That's horrible." I quickly filled her in on what had happened earlier at the Red Antler Inn, with my cousin Piedra, and then back at my home. I also told her what I saw in the marketplace on the way to the palace.

She nodded. "I think—if we're going to go to this cave your father mentioned, we'll need supplies. Food, weapons, clothes."

"And rope," I added, remembering Pazho's half-jest.

"Good idea." My spirits soared at the small praise. "Let's start with weapons, then."

12

CHAPTER TWELVE

PRINCESS LAERSA LED THE way through the palace halls. Piles of clothes—coats, vests, aprons, hats—littered the floor, from where people had transformed. A panther crossed our path, while a monkey hanging from the rafters hooted at us. A sparrow flew across the room, while a red-tailed fox jumped up on a table and yipped at it.

The walls twinkled, even though there was minimal light in the area. Looking closer, I realized a mosaic of colored tiles and little mirrors decorated the walls.

I thought back to when I had been here earlier, with Pazho. Now that I really considered it, the hallways leading to the throne room had looked like this as well. In my nervousness, I hadn't paid attention. My steps slowed as I took it all in.

"These are beautiful," I said, running a hand over a blue-and-yellow patterned tile. "Are all the walls in the palace like this?"

Princess Laersa stopped, beaming at my obvious admiration. "Yes. Each tile is hand-painted, and every hallway is in a different color. My mother had it specially commissioned by her favorite artist here in Annlyn."

"They're exquisite." I leaned in to look closer. "And all the mirrors?"

The princess shrugged. "Mother said they helped make the halls look bigger. Personally, I don't see the point. We live in a palace. How much bigger does the building need to be?"

She had a point, although it would probably be considered rude to actually agree with her out loud. Or would it be rude to not agree with royalty? I had no idea about the etiquette of that. Instead, I said, "I wonder how the artist got all the little mirror pieces? He or she must not be very superstitious."

She looked at me curiously. "Superstitious? What do you mean?"

I chuckled. "You know. The old saying about a broken mirror being unlucky."

Princess Laersa's face suddenly shuttered. "Then perhaps that's the reason why my mother died. All that unluckiness, all around the palace."

She turned on her heel and started walking again. Feeling chagrined, I followed after her.

We continued on in silence. The tiled walls really were beautiful. Even if I now knew better than to comment on them.

Too bad I couldn't say the same for the smell, however. I wrinkled my nose at the strong scents that assailed it, then sneezed.

Princess Laersa laughed at my expression, breaking the tension between us. "There's going to be quite a bit of cleaning to do when this is all over. You can't have this many animals in a confined space without them needing to eventually defecate."

I chuckled. "It might be easier to just build a whole new palace."

To my surprise, the princess stopped mid-hallway. An oversized patterned vase with the ugliest, gaudiest flowers I had ever seen stood in front of an otherwise blank wall. The vase was nearly as tall as the princess.

"I didn't even know flowers came in those colors," I remarked, eyeing the bright red, orange, and yellow blooms. Their striped patterns clashed horribly with the vase.

"Everyone turns a blind eye, because it's such an eyesore," Princess Laersa remarked absently as she ran one hand over the wall just behind the vase. "Which is perfect for—ah!"

A small, hidden door, mostly concealed by the large vase and its even taller flowers, opened in the wall. The princess turned to me, beaming. "We could take the long way through the palace, and have to watch out for all the animals. Or we can go through the hidden corridors."

I nodded, grabbing a torch from the wall before we entered the darkened passageway.

The princess moved through the hidden passage with confidence. Following after, I asked, "I take it you use these passages often?"

I saw the back of her dark head bob up and down in a nod. "When I was a little girl, I would hide in them if I got in trouble with Father." She giggled. "It helps that one of the entrances is in my bedroom. Later on, after Mother died, I found them a convenient way to listen in on Father's council meetings, since he wouldn't tell me anything going on in the kingdom."

She turned a corner, and I hurried to keep up, even though she didn't seem to need the torchlight.

"These passages are also a convenient way to escape the palace," she said. "I'd often use them to sneak out at night. Not to do anything illegal, mind you. But just to go find an open field, lie back, and look at the stars." She sighed. "I miss those days."

She stopped at a plain door and opened it, revealing a room full of weapons. A rack of spears stood against one wall, next to another rack of swords. Metal and wooden shields of various sizes leaned against another wall, and I spied a table with several bows piled on top. Another table in the corner held a few items currently under repair.

"Ah, here we are," Princess Laersa said. "What kind of weapon do you prefer?"

I shrugged. I was a scholar and a cook, not a soldier. If I actually used one of these things correctly and took down my opponent—and not myself—it would be a miracle.

"This should suit you." Princess Laersa handed me a sword, and a belt to carry it. She also took one for herself, and then grabbed a bow and a quiver of arrows. "Would you like a bow and arrows as well?"

I shook my head as I gestured to the sword, now belted at my waist. "I'll have my hands full enough with this."

"I prefer archery over close combat, but it can't hurt to be prepared," Princess Laersa said. She eyed me. "How well can you use a sword?"

"Not that well," I admitted. "I spend more of my time studying or cooking than fighting."

"I'll teach you," she said, flipping her long black hair over one shoulder. "Now, for food."

I followed the princess through the palace's twisty hallways. I thought she would go back through the secret passageways, but now that we were in this wing of the palace—the storage and preparation areas for the servants, it seemed—we apparently didn't need to use the tunnels again.

In addition to our weapons, we gathered food for the journey, a set of traveling clothes for both of us, and bags to store everything in. Some tin bowls, cups, and utensils. A few water skins. Oh, and some rope.

In the last storage room, Princess Laersa surveyed our items. "I think we have everything. Ready to go?"

"Now? It's still night."

"I don't see any reason to stay around here," she pointed out practically. "And the sooner we reach this cave of yours, the sooner we can contact Queen Jennica."

"It's not *my* cave," I grumbled, but started packing the bags. Handing one to the princess, I hefted the other onto my back. It was a touch heavy, but nothing I couldn't handle for a few hours' walk. Climbing to the mountain cave, on the other hand, would be another story.

"All right, then. Shall we?" She headed out the chamber door without waiting for my answer. Sighing, I followed her.

Instead of going straight to the servants' side entrance, Princess Laersa turned a corner, heading towards the front of the palace.

I thought she was in a hurry to leave this place. But I didn't say the words out loud.

The princess stopped in front of the broken doors of the throne room. One of the wooden doors hung off one hinge, threatening to fall at any moment. The other door now sported splintered wood surrounding a gaping hole. I wondered what shapeshifters had been here when the forced transformation occurred.

Princess Laersa pushed the splintered door open.

There was a new addition to the throne room since I had last been here. A large, gilt-framed mirror hung on a wall to the side of the twin red velvet and gold-edged thrones. Unlike the doors, the mirror was perfect and intact, its glass polished and gleaming.

Princess Laersa followed my gaze. "Oh, that. It was a gift from the royals of Graenir. Ambassador Allisandra brought it with her. I think it's a bit much, don't you?"

"I'm not sure what your father would do with a mirror," I answered honestly. "Except maybe make sure his hair looks good before he holds court?"

She giggled. "I'm not entirely sure either. He said something about wanting to learn how mirror magic works from the mages of Graenir."

"Well, at least it matches the rest of the decor."

The princess giggled again, but her laughter died when we got a good look at the rest of the room.

Atop the red velvet of the King's throne sat a black-and-gray raccoon. A bejeweled gold crown encircled his body. The King's sceptre lay askew on the floor.

I stayed in the doorway, watching as the princess approached the twin thrones at the far end of the room.

She knelt before the throne, getting eye-level with the little beast. The raccoon turned his black-rimmed eyes on the princess.

"Oh, Father. I'm so sorry this happened to you—to everyone. I need to leave now, to find out who did this to you. But I swear, I will make this right."

The animal chittered. Princess Laersa held out a finger, and the raccoon touched his paw to it.

"I'll be back soon, Father. I promise."

The raccoon-king chirruped again, and the princess stood up. She walked towards me as she wiped her eyes. "Let's go." She swept by me.

I bowed to the animal on the throne. "We'll fix this, Your Majesty. And I'll watch over your daughter."

The raccoon growled, then snorted. Was he making those noises from instinct? Or because he thought I was a poor bodyguard for the Crown Princess?

I wasn't sure which.

13

CHAPTER THIRTEEN

PRINCESS LAERSA AND I left the palace through the servants' entrance, making our way to the front under the light of the full moon. The goat guards were still milling around near the closed portcullis, although the torn uniform had disappeared. I side-eyed the goats as we walked by. That would definitely be hard on the stomach later.

The princess stopped to pat them on the head. "Hello, Francis and Madra."

One of the goats bleated in return.

I chuckled. "How can you tell them apart?"

"I can't. But I know it's them, they've been the front gate guards for as long as I can remember."

We exited the palace courtyard and approached the empty marketplace. It didn't look as creepy as it had when I came through earlier. Perhaps it was because many of the stalls were now occupied by various animals. A squirrel slept on a stall countertop, while a few birds roosted on the wooden frame above. A Great Dane curled up by another stall.

My sandals squished under my feet. Pulling one up, I realized I had stepped in a small puddle of muddy water. The trickle that fed into it came from a cracked fountain nearby. Apparently the animals hadn't been careful when wandering around Annlyn.

Princess Laersa marveled at the animals as we went by. "The messenger wasn't kidding," she said. "Whatever hit Annlyn transformed everyone at the same time."

She eyed a pride of lions that took up a sizable space in a large gap between stalls. One of the lion cubs tumbled into the street. A lioness detached herself from the group and delicately picked up the cub between her teeth, bringing it back to the group. The rest of the pride stared back at us, unblinking.

"Should we be worried?" Princess Laersa whispered to me. "Do you think any of them are ... hungry?"

"We'll be all right," I said. "When Pazho investigated something like this the other day, he said none of the animals showed an inclination to give in to instinct. And since everyone's just turned, I doubt their animal sides have completely taken over."

"All right," the Princess echoed, but she didn't sound very confident.

We continued on in silence.

An odd prickling sensation began to crawl over my skin.

Princess Laersa stopped walking and grabbed my arm. "Something's wrong. The air feels heavy. Do you feel it?"

I nodded. Remembering what had happened before, I looked up.

The black storm cloud had returned, the red lightning providing occasional bursts of eerie light. It moved slowly over the nighttime sky, blanketing Annlyn and blotting out the stars and moon.

"Oh, gods. It's back," I said.

"What's back? What are you talking about?" The princess followed my gaze, turning a worried glance towards the sky. "What is that?"

"That cloud ... I think it's responsible for all of Annlyn shifting."

Princess Laersa gasped. "What should we do?"

"Just keep going," I said, with a confidence I did not feel. "The last time this happened, it made everyone transform. Well, we can't shapeshift. So we should be safe."

"Okay," she said doubtfully. Her hand slid down my arm, and she slipped her hand into mine.

Despite the danger, I couldn't help but thrill at her touch.

We took a few tentative steps, although once the cloud completely covered Annlyn, we stopped, afraid of tripping over something. But we didn't have to wait long for the cloud to disappear. Just like before, it passed over in a matter of minutes, and soon the moon and stars reappeared to light our way.

We started moving forward again.

"Thank the gods," Princess Laersa breathed, looking up at the normal nighttime sky. "It was bad enough in the palace to feel it and see its effects on the people. To actually *see* the magic happening—what?"

I had stopped moving, and since we were still holding hands, she felt a slight tug. She looked over at me curiously.

"What is it?" the princess repeated.

I had been right about one thing—since neither Princess Laersa nor I could shapeshift, we were safe from the cloud's turning magic. But I had forgotten about the rest of Pazho's tale. We were safe from the storm cloud—but not its effects on the others.

The tiger I had seen on my walk to the palace padded out from the shadows, growling low as it bared its sharp teeth.

Princess Laersa's head turned, slowly, to take in the creature. "I thought you said we were safe."

The tiger now stood squarely in our path. He crouched, his ears flattened against his head.

The princess and I both started to back away. I hissed, "I said should. Should be safe. It wasn't definitive."

The tiger began stalking towards us.

"And I'm not afraid to admit when I'm wrong."

Princess Laersa snorted. "Let's hope we live long enough for you to be wrong about other things."

"Gee, thanks."

The tiger froze. We froze.

The animal snarled, then sprung.

I yelled and threw myself in front of the princess, covering her with my body as much as I could while we both crouched low. I cringed, expecting to feel sharp teeth ripping into my flesh at any moment.

A deafening roar sounded behind us. A large blur sailed over our heads, knocking the tiger to the side.

The tiger crashed into a stall, sending a flurry of annoyed, squawking birds flying into the air. A gecko scurried away from the ruined stall.

The lion that had slammed into the tiger roared once more as the tiger got to its feet. Answering roars sounded as the lion's pride padded forward to flank the tiger.

Princess Laersa whispered, "What should we do?"

"Get out of here," I whispered back. "But don't run."

We began to slowly move away, trying to keep an eye on the animals without drawing their attention. But we needn't have worried. The tiger, now surrounded by the lion's pride, was solely focused on the lion as they snarled and circled each other. A sudden escalation of sound told us the two big cats were now engaged in a fight.

By unspoken agreement, Princess Laersa and I picked up our pace. The growls, roars, and snarls soon faded behind us as we reached the city gates.

Princess Laersa gasped. "What happened here?"

Whatever the gate guards had turned into, they were no longer there. Annlyn's gates stood wide open, for any and all comers. In the moonlight, we could see several sets of animal tracks, suggesting some of the transformed had left the capital city.

"Perhaps the guards were admitting someone through the gates when the storm cloud first came through," I said.

The princess looked around in dismay. "We can't just leave the city open like this. Annlyn's already so vulnerable."

I eyed the system of levers and chains attached to the city gates. "That looks pretty heavy to move. And if we close the gates, how do we get out? Or back in?"

"We have to try. We can figure out the other parts later."

But even with both of us trying with all our strength, we couldn't get the gate mechanism to move. We debated cutting the chain, but aside from finding a tool sharp enough to do so—of which neither of us had that knowledge, nor did we want to take the time to hunt one out—we didn't want to do lasting damage to the gate. Finally, we settled for moving a few carts and wagons in front of the gate. It wouldn't deter anyone truly determined to get in, but it would slow them down a bit.

"And," I reasoned as we left Annlyn, "if anyone does get in, those lions and that tiger will make them think twice about their decision."

Princess Laersa's silvery laugh accompanied us down the road.

14

CHAPTER FOURTEEN

WE STOPPED TO REST just outside the city, when we were sure no animals—or at least, large, predatory animals—were around. The princess slept against a tree while I, too jumpy to sleep, kept a watchful eye out. Sunrise would come soon, and I wanted to start towards Joichan's former home once it was light out.

I had a vague idea of where to go—the mountain was easy to see in the distance, about a half day's walk due west. As far as how we'd actually reach the cave ... well, if we pushed ourselves in the morning, we could take a rest around midday and still have enough light to climb up. My gods, this would be easier if Princess Laersa and I could transform. Well, maybe. As long as we could both transform into animals that were able to scale the side of a mountain....

"Endri? Endri, wake up."

I startled awake to Princess Laersa gently shaking my shoulder.

I had dozed off, when I was supposed to stay vigilant and protect her. And I had already failed, less than a day later.

The princess looked sheepish. "I'm sorry to wake you—you seemed like you really needed your rest. But it's already past sunrise."

I eyed the position of the sun in the sky. I had missed sunrise, but fortunately it wasn't too much past that. I stretched, then rummaged in my bag. Finding an apple, I handed it to Princess Laersa. "Your breakfast, Your Highness."

She giggled and took the apple from me, while I fished around for another one. We ate our fruit quickly, throwing the cores into the scrub at the side of the road. I stood and held my hand out to Princess Laersa. "Shall we?"

She put her hand in mine—again sending that little thrill through me—and let me help her up. She brushed off her dress and then gave me a small curtsey. "Yes, let's go."

"If you could shapeshift, what would you want to turn into?"

I pondered Princess Laersa's question as we trekked through the forest that would eventually open up to Joichan's former mountain. "I ... I'm not sure. My one father, Pazho, can turn into a grey wolf. Denaan, my other father, transforms into an elk."

I paused. "But I'm adopted, so it's unlikely I would shift into either one of my fathers' forms. Then again, I understand that blood relations don't necessarily dictate what you'll become. At least, that's what Pazho used to say. He said it had more to do with personality and one's essence more than anything else."

"Oh, that's interesting. I never knew that, but it does make sense. I'd always wondered why not everyone in a family changes into the same kind of animal. What did the members of your birth family turn into?"

"Lemurs, all of them. Including my brother."

Princess Laersa looked at me curiously. "You had a brother?"

I nodded. "Yes. Older than me by two years. We—we used to be close."

"What happened?"

I sighed. "When it became apparent that I couldn't shift, but my brother could, my parents made their favoritism quite clear. And my brother, who used to stand up for me, started bullying me because I was different. 'Broken', in my family's eyes."

"I'm sorry," the princess said.

I shrugged. "Don't be. It is what it is. Although, sometimes ..."

The silence stretched out. Finally, Princess Laersa prompted, "Sometimes?"

"On the days when I'm really feeling low, because I still can't shift, I think they were right to abandon me," I burst out. "Maybe I really am broken, forever. And no one has any use for things that are broken."

"Hey." The princess stopped walking and put her hand on my arm, forcing me to stop as well. "Beautiful things can be made from brokenness. Nothing is irreparable."

I didn't say anything for a long moment. Then, "Wise words from one so young, Your Highness."

"Thank you, Endri." She bobbed a curtsey, then started forward again. "I can't take all the credit, though. My mother, may the gods bless and keep her forever, used to say that often."

"She must have been a very wise woman, then."

"She was."

"If you could shift, what would you want to be?" I asked the princess.

"Something that can fly, just like my mother. She used to transform into the most beautiful butterfly I've ever seen. Blue and green and gold wings—you could never feel sad or angry when she was in her second form." Princess Laersa looked up, where we could see glimpses of blue sky and sun through the trees. "I would love to soar up in the air, feel the wind on my face."

I looked up as well. A hawk circled lazily overhead. Remembering the majestic ice dragon figurine in my pocket, I murmured, "Something that can fly. I think I'd like that as well."

Princess Laersa giggled, drawing my attention. "Tell you what. If I'm able to transform into an animal that can fly, and I can carry you—either your animal or human form—then I'll take you up into the sky."

I chuckled. "Agreed. And likewise. I'd be honored to do the same for you."

"It's a pact, then."

We fell into a companionable silence as we continued on.

After a while, the rush of water from a river reached our ears. I was dusty, thirsty, and still exhausted despite my short sleep. I looked over at Princess Laersa, wondering if she felt the same way. She nodded enthusiastically.

We veered to the right, headed towards the water. It wouldn't be too far off our path—after all, we could still see the mountain in the distance.

We found the river soon enough. The sight of water perked both of us up.

"Race you!" Princess Laersa hitched the skirt of her dress up slightly, running towards the water.

I laughed and started to run after her, when the light caught on something in the grass.

"Princess Laersa! Stop!"

She giggled but kept running. I put on a burst of speed and slammed into her, knocking her to the side.

"Hey!" she protested, even as we both heard a whoosh of air and the clang of metal against metal.

"What was that?" Princess Laersa asked.

We both looked down. A corner of my robe was caught in an old, somewhat rusted snare.

"Oh my gods," the princess breathed. "Oh, no. Endri. Thank you. It ... It could have been my foot, caught in that."

"You're welcome," I said. "Now, how to get out of this thing?"

We spent some time trying to figure out how to open the darn contraption, but the snare was so old and rusty that the releasing mechanism refused to budge. Eventually, we just had to tear part of my robe, leaving the caught cloth behind.

"And this was my good robe, too," I said ruefully.

Princess Laersa laughed. "I'll have the Royal Tailor make you a dozen fine robes. When this is all over, of course."

"Of course."

She surveyed the area. "How did you know that snare was there?"

"I saw the light bounce off it. It looks fairly old, so whoever set this may have done it a long time ago, and forgot about them. Still, if there's one, there may be others."

Princess Laersa shuddered. "I'll be careful. Thank you again, Endri."

I nodded, glad I had been able to avert a crisis. Not only were we ill-quipped to handle an injury like a maimed leg, but if it had happened, Princess Laersa would be unable to climb to Joichan's cave. And I wouldn't be willing to leave her.

We moved slower after that. By the time we reached the river-bank, we had found two more snares, both as old and rusted as the first one.

"After all that, I think we've earned a rest," I said, earning a grateful smile from Princess Laersa.

We sat down on some boulders that jutted into the river. I picked up a few pebbles, skipping them across the water.

Princess Laersa pointed. "Hey, is that a cave over there? Is that Joichan's cave?"

I looked where she was pointing, shading my eyes to get a better look. A large black entrance yawned in front of us, just off the river.

"It's *a* cave," I said slowly. "But I don't think it's Joichan's cave. Pazho was very clear, Joichan lived in a mountain cave. Not one on the ground."

"Perhaps he got it wrong," Princess Laersa said. "How many caves can there be around Annlyn?"

She stood up. "Let's go look."

"We really should get going," I said. "It's already past midday, and we don't want to be climbing at night."

"We won't go too far in. And if it is Joichan's cave, then we don't have to go on to the mountain. And we can call Queen Jennica sooner."

She strode towards the cave. Hastily, I stood up and followed her, doubting her judgment, but also my memory. Maybe this *was* the cave Pazho had meant?

Princess Laersa disappeared into the gaping blackness. With trepidation, I followed her in.

15

CHAPTER FIFTEEN

PRINCESS LAERSA WRINKLED HER nose. "Ew. It smells disgusting in here."

I breathed deep and instantly regretted it. A stench of rotting meat hit my nose, making me gag. "Oh, you're right. Ugh."

The light from outside the cave angled just enough for us to see most of the cave's interior. Ahead of us, on a ledge just above our heads, I could see a mass of leaves, twigs, and grass, with an occasional shiny glint showing as we drew closer.

Princess Laersa put her sleeve up to her nose, breathing through the fabric. "What is that?" she wondered, looking up at the ledge.

As I studied it, I realized the leaves, twigs, and grass were woven in a haphazard pattern, to form something circular and solid that disappeared into the darkness of the cave that the light didn't touch. "It looks like ... a nest. A very large one." The shiny part glinted again. "With—with *gold* woven in it."

The rotting meat smell was stronger in this area. I put my own sleeve up, breathing shallowly. The gold woven into the nest fascinated me, and I moved forward to get a better look.

My foot ran into an obstacle of some sort, and I heard the sound of metal hitting the wall. "Huh?"

I looked down. The "something" was a half-decayed corpse—an adventurer, from the looks of their rotted clothes. My accidental kick had caused the former adventurer's helmet to fly off their head, and I unfortunately got a good look at what was left of his face.

I screamed. Princess Laersa, upon seeing the body, also screamed.

A golden head popped up from the nest. It looked like a baby eagle, but when it opened its mouth, a weird sort of roar-screech emerged. It hopped up and down, fluttering its wings, and then put two small lion-like forelegs on the edge of the nest.

A gryphon.

Another baby golden eagle head popped up. And then another.

"Oh gods." This was not good.

"Endri?" Princess Laersa whispered. "I don't think this is Joichan's cave."

The gryphon babies started chattering at us, bobbing up and down in their nest. The first one climbed out of the nest, a little unsteady in its lion body, but still moving steadily.

"Nice gryphon. Good gryphon."

The other two baby gryphons decided to investigate us as well. They climbed out of their nest to join their sibling, quickly encircling us.

The princess and I stood back to back, bracing ourselves for the inevitable attack. But the gryphons didn't pounce. Instead, they kept chirp-meowing at us. The first gryphon walked up to me—I winced, turning my head—and nosed my bag.

"I think they're hungry," I said in realization.

"Of course they're hungry." Princess Laersa's tone implied I was an idiot. "And we're on the menu."

"No, I mean, I think they can smell the food in our bags." Slowly, carefully, I slid my bag from my shoulders and opened the flap. The gryphon nosed my arm, nearly making me drop my knapsack.

I reached into the bag and pulled out an apple. The gryphon chuffed impatiently. I tossed the apple away from me, nearly hitting the poor dead adventurer with it.

All three baby gryphons rushed towards the apple, but only one of them got it, gulping it down in one swallow. The food now gone, six golden eyes turned and fixated on me.

"Princess Laersa," I hissed as I rummaged through my pack again. "I'm going to count to three. On three, get ready to run."

"O-Okay," she said, her voice laced with fear.

The baby gryphons tired of waiting and started advancing on us.

"One." I emptied my pack of apples, slinging the much lighter bag over one shoulder.

"Two." Shifting the weight in my hands, I made ready to throw.

"Three!" I hurled three apples in quick succession towards the back of the cave, as far as I could throw. The gryphons followed the movement, scurrying to the back of the cave. Princess Laersa had already started running, and I hurried after her.

Behind me, I could hear the baby gryphons fighting and snorting and pawing and munching. The last of which, unfortunately, was over all too soon. I sneaked a look behind me. The gryphons had finished eating and were coming after us.

I turned and lobbed more apples at them.

They jumped in the air, knocking each other over in their attempt to get the fruit. Princess Laersa and I were nearly at the cave's entrance. I must have been tired, because I hadn't thrown the apples very far. And the babies polished them off much faster this time.

"Princess! Give me your bag!"

She half-turned as she slipped the bag from her shoulders, throwing it to me as we ran. I—surprisingly—caught it, fumbling with the catch. I was beginning to lose energy, from the extra weight, the effort of throwing, and the lack of sleep.

The baby gryphons were moving towards us again.

I reached into the bag, throwing apple after apple after apple. One of them bounced off a baby gryphon's nose before rolling away, making the fledgling roar-mew in indignation. But there was enough food there to keep them occupied—long enough for Princess Laersa and I to slip out of the cave and back into the sunlight.

We didn't stop running until we were hidden among the trees again, well away from the river.

When we felt the gryphon cave was far behind us, we stopped to catch our breath. I plopped down on the hard, grassy ground, leaning against the fallen log the princess had found to sit on.

"I'm sorry for not believing you," Princess Laersa said. "You even warned me that wasn't the right cave, and I didn't listen. I could have gotten us killed."

"It's okay," I said. "I mean, it's not *okay*, but—hey, I was wrong about how safe we'd be, back in the marketplace. Which nearly got us killed there. So—I guess that makes it even?"

She laughed. "I guess. But let's not continue this trend."

I grinned. "Agreed. Look on the bright side—at least we got out of there before the mother came back."

A shadow flew overhead, catching our attention. In between the trees, we caught flashes of a large winged creature with an eagle's head and a lion's body, heading towards the direction of the baby gryphons' cave.

I looked at Princess Laersa. She looked at me. As one, we both stood.

"Break's over."

"Let's go."

16

CHAPTER SIXTEEN

OUR DETOUR IN THE gryphons' cave had cost us some valuable time. By the time we reached the mountain base, the sun hung low in the sky.

We craned our necks to estimate how high we'd have to climb. I thought I saw a slight indent in the mountain face, but I wasn't entirely sure. Remembering Pazho's words, I knew the only way we would truly find Joichan's cave was to just climb up and hope to come across it. Since we couldn't see the cave entrance, we had no way of knowing if we'd only have a little way to go—or if we'd have to go to the summit.

"It doesn't seem that bad," Princess Laersa said. "There's a path, to start, at least."

I raised an eyebrow at her. "And after that? Then what? How many mountains have you climbed?"

She blushed. "None. I was just trying to stay positive."

I sighed. "So now, the question is, should we try to find the cave now? Or wait until the morning?"

"I guess we just wait until morning. We'll be fresher then, and we'll have more light for climbing."

I nodded. "Okay, then. I'll gather some firewood."

The princess looked around. "What should I do?"

That was a good question. I didn't think princesses were knowledgeable in camping—I barely was, myself, and I certainly wasn't royalty—but I wasn't going to voice either of those thoughts. Instead, I said, "You don't mind helping?"

She crossed her arms, annoyed. "Just because I'm the Crown Princess doesn't mean I'm helpless. And we're in this mess together."

I smiled, surprised. "Okay. Great. Uh ... I guess ... clean up our camp area? And then—since you're much better with a bow and arrow than I am—hunt for tonight's meal?"

She smirked. "I can do that, especially since someone quite literally threw away pretty much all of our provisions."

"It was for a good cause," I protested. "Not getting eaten is high on my list of priorities."

She chuckled and turned away to prepare our campsite. Smiling to myself, I headed into the woods.

When I returned, with an armful of twigs and pine cones, as well as some wild onions I had found, Princess Laersa had finished getting the area ready. She grabbed her bow and a handful of arrows. "My turn to go exploring."

"Happy hunting."

She gave me a brilliant smile before disappearing into the trees.

I turned my attention to setting up a spit for cooking later. Although I wouldn't consider myself an adventurer, I did know how to cook, thanks to years of working alongside Denaan at the Red Antler Inn. By the time Princess Laersa came back, I had our fire all set up.

"Wow," Princess Laersa said. "I'm impressed."

"Thanks." I nodded at the rabbit in her hands. "I am too."

"Thank you." She sat down and took out her eating knife. "Now, to skin this thing."

I eyed her curiously. "I'm surprised. Not about your skill with weapons, although I suppose for a royal that could be unexpected. But just—"

"How a princess is trained in woodcraft?" She grimaced down at her messy hands. "When I was little, my family used to spend time in the wilderness. Never for very long, and always with guards nearby. But it was a way to bond as a family, and get away from the pressures of palace life." She shrugged, still not looking up. "When Mother died, that was it. No more trips away. Just nonstop work for Father."

Princess Laersa handed me the skinned rabbit. I skewered the meat on the long stick, then busied myself with other meal preparations. "If you don't mind my asking, how did the queen die?"

The princess stared into the fire as I cooked. "Desert sickness. She had shifted into her butterfly form and gone outside the city. I believe, when she landed, she kicked up something, on a leaf or on the ground, that was toxic to her animal self. By the time she flew home and shifted back, she was already close to dying."

"Oh, gods, I'm sorry. That's horrible."

Princess Laersa kept her eyes on the flames, as if the fire would reveal some long-held secret. "Perhaps that's why Father didn't care much if I could learn to shapeshift, after that. If I couldn't shift, then I couldn't die like Mother had."

I didn't know what to say to that. So I just focused on cooking, instead.

The princess cleared her throat. "Is there anything I can do to help?"

I indicated the wild onions I had found. "You could cut those up."

She instantly reached for them, peeling and slicing. Soon the smell of roasting meat and fried onions filled our camp. I prepared a bowl for Princess Laersa and handed it to her, then made one for myself.

"Mmm," she said after her first bite. "This is delicious. Where did you learn to cook so well?"

"Thank you." I tucked into my own bowl. For what I had to work with, not bad. "My father, Denaan, runs the Red Antler Inn. I help him there most nights, ever since they took me in." I smirked. "And I may have taken some spices from the castle's kitchen when we were gathering supplies."

"As Crown Princess, I officially pardon you." She giggled, then took another enthusiastic bite. "I've never been to the Red Antler, but once we get back, I will make sure Father and I are frequent patrons. This really is wonderful. Your father would be very proud."

I smiled, then sobered at the thought of Denaan. Where was he? Where was Pazho? Were they still near Annlyn? Had something bad happened to either of them? And what about their soulstones? At least I had Pazho's, even if it looked unusable. But—

A hand clamped over mine—the one holding my inert spoon.

"Stop," Princess Laersa said gently.

"Huh?" There I was, showing off my smooth verbal skills again.

"You're letting your mind run away with your worries. Don't. We'll find your fathers. And we'll make this right."

"How?" I wondered.

"I don't know. But hopefully this Queen Jennica will have answers." She sighed, looking up at the blank mountainside. The sun had disappeared over the horizon, and the purple of twilight was around us. "I'll feel better once we find this cave. I feel very ... visible ... out here."

"I know what you mean." We were camped in a small clearing, with the mountain on one side and trees on the other. But being out in the open wasn't what made me feel on edge. I just felt like something was out there, watching.

And waiting.

We banked the fire and settled in to sleep. Perhaps we should have set a watch, but we were so tired from the day's events that sleep claimed us both quickly.

17

CHAPTER SEVENTEEN

THE MOON HAD RISEN by the time I woke up, a prickling sensation crawling over my skin.

Looking up, I saw a dark cloud moving over Annlyn's capital city in the distance. It was disturbing, to see part of the night sky blotted out by darkness while around that abnormality, the stars and moon still shone.

I shook Princess Laersa awake.

"Mmmmm?"

"Princess! Princess, wake up! We need to get going!"

"Hmm? Why?" she asked groggily, sitting up.

I pointed to the city. "That thing, that black cloud is back. But there's nothing left there for it to look for, except—"

"Us." The princess was on her feet now. I hastily packed our things, while she threw dirt and leaves on the fire to smother it.

The darkness over Annlyn swirled around, as if looking for something.

"Come on." I started up the mountainside, Princess Laersa behind me.

While the full moon lit the path upwards, the foliage and rocks along the way cast shadows that forced us to go slower, picking our path carefully.

And speaking of shadows ...

The swirling darkness over Annlyn had stopped. It moved a little north of the city's gates, then grew smaller as it moved east.

I breathed a sigh of relief. Although my relief was short lived.

The path ended in a wall of stone. From here on up, we'd have to climb.

"I wish I knew how much further the cave is," I said. "I suppose we could just stay here and wait for daylight."

Princess Laersa was staring off into the distance. "No, we can't."

The black storm cloud was back over Annlyn. And beginning to move our way.

"Oh, gods."

I ran my hands over the rock wall, frantically searching for handholds. I scrambled up the mountainside, Princess Laersa on my heels.

A quick look over my shoulder told me that while the blackness was indeed heading in our direction, it seemed to be taking a meandering route. It was definitely looking for something—or someone—but it hadn't figured out where that thing was.

Princess Laersa's voice floated up to me. "Endri ..."

"I see it."

My arms ached. It was painfully slow-going, since I couldn't see the handholds and had to spend precious minutes feeling my way up the mountain. At one point, my foot slipped, making me yelp and causing a small sprinkle of rocks to fall.

"Ouch!" Princess Laersa called up. Her voice sounded further away than I expected. I looked down carefully—regretting my decision right away—and saw that she was far behind me.

"Sorry. Are you all right?"

"I'm fine. Just—keep going. It's—it's still headed this way."

I took a quick moment to catch my breath. Then the moon shone directly on the rock wall, and I nearly fell off in my surprise.

The rock around my hand glowed. And, as far up as I could see, other glowing circles lit up in random intervals, each less than an arm span's width across.

"Princess! Can you see the handholds?"

I could hear the wonder in her voice. "Yes. Oh, thank the gods. That will help immensely."

"I'll wait for you." I estimated we were about halfway up the mountain at this point.

"No, no, keep going. I'll be fine. Besides—" her voice suddenly sounded worried "—I think it spotted us."

Oh, gods. I started climbing again, forcing myself to go faster. I focused on one glowing circle, thrusting my hand into the rock, then concentrated on the next one. *Don't look at that black cloud. Just keep climbing.*

The luminous rocks brought me to a ledge. I scrambled over the edge, grateful for the moment to rest. I looked down. Princess Laersa was still fairly far down. Despite the magical assistance, she wasn't moving any faster than before.

I looked up. The cloud floated halfway between us and Annlyn, and in that moment I felt like, if a big black fog had eyes, it had seen me and pinpointed my exact location. Flashes of scarlet light crackled through the sky, as if to say, *Found you!*

"Princess, hurry!" I hissed down at her.

She looked over, then gasped. Although she tried to go faster, I could see she was having trouble.

Frantically, I looked around. A rock jutted up from the ledge, making a perfect anchor. I quickly fished the rope out of my bag and tied one end of it around the rock, then tossed the rest of it over the side. Looking over the side again, I called down to Princess Laersa.

"Grab the rope! I'll pull you up!"

She flailed for the rope once, twice, then grabbed it. She began scrambling up the rope, while I began pulling her towards the ledge.

Meanwhile, the darkness was making a beeline towards the mountain. Towards us.

The princess was just underneath me.

I pulled with all my strength. Princess Laersa's hand grasped the ledge. I grabbed her hand and helped her climb up just as the dark mist reached the mountain.

Although it had no shape, it put on speed and lunged at us. Still holding on to the princess, I rolled backward, trying to get us both out of the fog's reach.

We flew apart, scrambling backward as fast as we could. The darkness lunged again, but hit an invisible wall. It tried again, but still could not break through.

I stared at the formless black cloud. It looked hazy, as if I was viewing it through a sheer curtain.

It hovered, just a few lengths away from us—could it see us through that magical barrier?—then soundlessly flew away.

Heart pounding, I let out the breath I hadn't even realized I'd been holding. "Oh, gods. That was close."

Princess Laersa moved to the magical barrier, feeling around the space. "Wow. I can't believe that it couldn't get through this."

Now that my fear had subsided, I could get a good look at our surroundings. The ledge had opened up into a wider tunnel that had little pinpricks of light set into its smooth walls. Curious, I followed the lights further in, finding a larger cave with a table and chairs, a chest on one wall, and an old, extremely large bed of straw. Another side of the cave contained a small room with a human-sized bed. From the look of the yellowed sheets and musty smell, the bed hadn't been used in some time.

I hurried back to Princess Laersa, who was still examining the magical barrier. "Princess, you might want to see this."

I led her back into the bigger cavern. Her eyes widened as she took everything in, and soon her curiosity had her poking around.

"It certainly looks like someone lived here, at one time," she said. "Do you think this is Joichan's cave?"

"It better be. I'm not in the mood to keep climbing tonight," I quipped. Then, more seriously, "I think it is. That strange shadow thing couldn't get through whatever magical barrier was at the entrance. And Pazho said all the spells Joichan had used on his cave were still active." I waved a hand at the glowing walls. "This, too, looks like magic to me."

The princess gave a relieved sigh. "Then we're safe here. For now, anyway."

"For now," I echoed. We couldn't stay in here forever. And we'd have to think about food, soon.

Which reminded me ...

"I left my pack outside." I stood at the barrier's edge, trying to locate the black fog. I couldn't see it, but that didn't mean it wasn't hiding nearby. My bag was by the rock where I had tied the rope, far enough away that I couldn't just stick my hand through the barrier to grab it.

"Perhaps you should wait until morning before retrieving it?" Princess Laersa joined me at the entrance. "Daylight will be here soon enough."

"A good point." I sighed. "So for now, we get some sleep. I'll get my bag in the morning. And then—we'll call Queen Jennica."

18

CHAPTER EIGHTEEN

I WOKE UP SNEEZING. My nose itched from sleeping in the oversized straw bed, while Princess Laersa took the private room with its smaller, human-sized bed.

Although from the sound of sneezing coming from her corner of the cave, she hadn't fared much better.

"If I ever meet this Joichan, I'll ask him why he doesn't maintain his home properly," she said. "*Ah-choo!* Even if he doesn't live here all the time, it's a lovely second home. If it was—*ah-choo!*—looked after, that is."

"Add it to the things we have to do after this adventure is over." I grinned. "The list is getting rather long."

Princess Laersa giggled. "I don't mind. It will be nice to have things to do, and discover. Palace life can be kind of dull sometimes."

I chuckled. "You mean you don't enjoy people waiting on you hand and foot, catering to your every whim?"

She shrugged. "That part is nice, I suppose. But since Father doesn't want it widely known that his own daughter can't shift, I don't get to meet a lot of people."

"Oh, that's right." My mirth faded. "I forgot about that."

"I'm glad you did." She yawned and stretched. "Why don't you go get your bag? I'll see if there's anything to cook with around here."

The magical barrier at the cave entrance filtered in the morning light. A quick glance around showed clear skies and a bright, sunny day. I stepped through the barrier, still wary, but nothing attacked me. I retrieved my bag and the rope, with one last cautious look around before going back inside.

I rummaged through my bag as I walked, finding a few squashed bread rolls at the bottom. "I'm afraid I don't have much for breakfast. What do you have left? We might have to go back down to hunt and look for food."

The smell of sizzling meat hit my nose. Princess Laersa stood in the cave's kitchen corner, which boasted an oven and a stove top set over an open flame. She had found a cast iron pan and was frying—fish, from the smell of it.

"Did you bring that with you?" I asked, confused. I didn't remember the princess stuffing raw fish into her bag back in the palace, but perhaps my memory was faulty.

She laughed. "Ew, no. No, I found it here." She indicated the pantry that stood nearby. "It has all sorts of food in it. The shelf I found this on was cold to the touch."

I eyed the fish, eyebrows raised. "Are you sure it's safe to eat? Who knows how long it's been sitting here?"

"It didn't smell rotten," the princess said in a practical manner. "And—I took a nibble of something else in the pantry, just to check."

Now I eyed Princess Laersa. "And you're still feeling all right?"

"So far. No upset stomach, no nausea, nothing's turned green and fallen off. But if something changes, I'll let you know."

I opened my bag again, to look at the two sorry-looking bread rolls. Closing my bag and tossing it to the side, I said, "You know what? I'll take my chances. That fish smells good."

She laughed. "I've never seen a pantry like this before. Some of the shelves have a thin layer of ice on them. Others feel normal, but nothing had mold on it. I couldn't see any evidence of rats or bugs, either."

"We'll have to ask Joichan where it came from."

The princess grinned. "Add it to our list. Now, shoo. Let me finish cooking."

While Princess Laersa worked, I poked around the area, looking for dishes and utensils. I supposed I could have just used the ones we brought with us, but honestly, I was curious about this place. And the person who had once lived here. The mountain cave was actually a nice, cozy home, with a beautiful view. Why would anyone want to leave?

We ate breakfast quickly, enjoying the brief respite from the heaviness of the previous day's events. I cleaned out my pockets, fishing out Denaan's soulstone cord, the key to the Red Antler Inn, and the blue ice dragon miniature. I put the necklace and key in the bottom of my bag for safekeeping, but just held the little dragon, admiring the handiwork.

"Oh, that's beautiful," Princess Laersa said. "May I see it?"

Hesitating, I handed it to her. While she examined it, I flexed my fingers, fighting the urge to snatch it back.

"This is how we'll call the queen?"

I nodded.

"How does it work?"

"Pazho said I need to concentrate on who I'm calling. It helps if I know the person, but I've never met Queen Jennica. I just know her through the stories Pazho would tell me about her."

"Ah. Interesting." Princess Laersa handed the little blue dragon back to me. I relaxed. "I look forward to meeting her." The princess looked at me expectantly.

I cleared my throat, feeling self-conscious. "Yes. Well. Let's see."

Holding the figurine up, I stared into its mesmerizing blue-green eyes. "Um. Queen Jennica. I would like to speak with Queen Jennica."

I could feel myself going cross-eyed from looking at the dragon so closely. I kept repeating Queen Jennica's name, hoping I didn't look too foolish in front of Princess Laersa. I could feel her interested, curious eyes on me, and it wasn't helping my concentration.

Perhaps it was a trick of the light, but the dragon figurine's teal eyes flashed once. I felt an answering heat in my tourmaline soulstone. I kept my eyes focused on the dragon.

And then I heard a woman's voice say, "Hello? Who is this?"

I nearly dropped the dragon.

Above the figurine in my hand, a translucent image of a beautiful woman appeared. Dressed in a gown of cobalt blue trimmed with silver lace, I would have guessed she was Queen Jennica even without the magnificent golden crown atop her long, black hair.

Somewhere behind the queen, a perky female voice said, "How on earth did unauthorized calls get through? That shouldn't happen ..."

"Um. Yes. Hello. Uh. Queen Jennica?" My suave way with words was coming back. "M-My name is Endri. Pazho and Denaan are my fathers. Pazho ... Pazho said you could help me. He ... He gave me a little blue dragon figurine to call you with ..."

Queen Jennica's face lit up. "Pazho and Denaan! It's been far too long. I've gotten so busy, I haven't been able to keep up with old friends. Not that that's any excuse." She looked at me quizzically. "But I didn't know they had a son."

"They adopted me, a few years back."

The queen nodded. "Well, I'd love to hear more about it sometime. But—you said you needed help? Where is Pazho? Or Denaan?"

"That's the thing." I told Queen Jennica about Pazho's investigation, and the recent events in Annlyn. I showed her Pazho's cracked ruby ring on my finger. "And now both of my fathers are missing, and Pazho had told me if anything happened to either of them, to come to Joichan's cave and call you. He said you would know what to do."

The queen frowned. "This is bad news, indeed. I don't know if I know what to *do*, exactly. But—"

A dark-skinned woman with curly lavender hair popped her head into the image. "But I might."

19

CHAPTER NINETEEN

"PARDON ME, JENNICA," THE purple-haired woman said to the queen.

"No problem, Farrah," Queen Jennica said. She moved to the side, allowing the new speaker some room.

"Well met, Endri," the purple-haired woman said. "I am Lady Farrah. I'm a long-time friend of Queen Jennica's, and I met your fathers years ago when we were on a mission to find Joichan."

Oh. Pazho had mentioned that the queen had traveled with a group of mercenaries, but I had never asked much about them, having been more interested in the shapeshifting Queen Jennica.

"This black cloud you mentioned. Can you describe it?"

I frowned. How does one describe a shapeless black mass? I explained it as best I could to Lady Farrah. Princess Laersa threw in her own insights.

Lady Farrah nodded at our description. "It sounds like something my intended and I encountered a few months ago. But not quite the same. And bigger. More powerful." Her expression turned thoughtful. "But how could that be?"

"Pardon me, my lady, but do you know what it is?"

"No, not exactly. It reminds me of a bit of nasty dark magic that was used to do a Fae King's bidding. It could possess others, and make them do things against their will. But I do not recall it being able to strip away people's essences."

"Essences?"

"I am part Fae and part human, which means I am of both worlds," Lady Farrah explained. "If you took away one part, say, just my Fae half, it would force me to become wholly human. Which means I would lose my inherent magical ability, among other things that my Fae heritage has gifted me with."

She touched her lavender curls. "I'd guess it's the same for you shapeshifters in Annlyn—take away your human self, and it forces you to become completely your animal self. No ability to speak, and no memory of your life as a human."

I shuddered. "How do we stop it and change everyone back?"

Lady Farrah frowned. "That I do not know. Pardon me a moment."

She turned away to talk to someone I couldn't see. Make that several someones—I could hear quite a few voices chiming in.

"It's probably best to see things first-hand," I heard Queen Jennica say.

Lady Farrah said, "But is that wise? Are you able to leave?"

"Yes. Coran's close to one now, and after that kidnapping scare I dismantled the spell that links us as soon as it was safe. I don't think we'll be repeating that spell in the future."

"But what about Beyan?"

Who's Beyan? Princess Laersa mouthed at me, but I just shrugged, unable to answer her.

A deep, serious male voice answered. "I'll be fine staying here with Coran. He's still too young to manifest any powers, but there have been ... hints." The unseen man sounded amused.

"So that's one thing settled," Queen Jennica said. "And, Farrah, you should probably come with me, since you've dealt with this Shadow before."

"Hey!" another male voice, this one more high-spirited, yelped. "I was there, too!"

This new person sounded so affronted, both Princess Laersa and I had to cover our mouths to smother the sounds of our giggles.

Lady Farrah said soothingly, "And I nearly lost you to it."

The serious man said, "It's all right, Rhyss. We can enjoy a nice, relaxing time back here in Castle Calia while the women go adventuring."

Lady Farrah added, "And you have an important job while we're gone—you need to sample the food for the wedding. Be thorough, please."

The high-spirited man said, "All right. But don't go getting killed—or enchanted, or anything else—while you're in Annlyn. After all, the wedding is in two weeks."

Lady Farrah laughed. "I'll do my best."

Princess Laersa and I exchanged an amused look, but Lady Farrah was returning to our call. I smoothed out my expression. I must not have done a good enough job, though, because Lady Farrah smirked at me. "I'm sure you heard all that."

"It was hard not to, my lady."

"Good. It makes things go faster." She pulled Queen Jennica back into view. "The queen and I will go to Annlyn. We'll leave shortly. Jennica, how long will it take us to get to Annlyn?"

The queen looked thoughtful. "When Father and I flew from Annlyn to Calia, it was just under a day's flight. I'd estimate our arrival sometime after moonrise."

I started to ask a question, but Princess Laersa beat me to it. "Your father, Your Majesty?"

"Joichan, formerly of Annlyn. I believe it's his cave you're staying in." The queen smiled.

I nearly fell out of my chair. No wonder Pazho had wanted me to contact Queen Jennica!

"Is that everything?"

Since I was still stunned with surprise, Princess Laersa took the liberty of answering for both of us. "Yes, Queen Jennica. As one royal to another, I look forward to meeting you and Lady Farrah in person." A funny look crossed her face, but it passed quickly. She finished, "And thank you for coming to our aid."

All I could do was nod.

"Don't thank us quite yet. Not until this cloud leaves Annlyn permanently," Queen Jennica said.

"And we get everyone turned back to their human selves," Lady Farrah added.

I nodded again, my throat tight. *Pazho. Denaan. I hope you're both all right.*

"Then we'll leave you now. We have much to prepare," said the queen. The two women said their goodbyes, ending the call. Princess Laersa and I watched as their translucent images faded away.

For a long moment, neither of us said anything. Then, from me: "That fog seems to favor the night. What will they do if it's prowling around outside when they get here?"

Princess Laersa looked out the front entrance of the cave, where deceptively cheerful sunlight shone. "I have no idea. Maybe it will forget about us and move on, and won't be here when Queen Jennica and Lady Farrah arrive."

"Maybe." I eyed Princess Laersa curiously. She was trembling, ever so slightly, and a silent, lone tear slipped down her cheek. "Princess? What's wrong?"

She sniffled. "I realized something, when we were talking to the queen. With my father incapacitated, I'm now Annlyn's leader. But—I can't do it. I'm not ready for this." More tears started streaming down her face.

Hesitantly, I put my arm around her. She moved in closer, letting me comfort her. "Oh, princess. You may not feel it, but I bet you're more ready than you think."

She swiped at her tears. "I'm a nobody. I can't even shapeshift."

"Neither can I." I smiled. "So we can be nobodies together."

She leaned her head against my shoulder. "There's nobody I'd rather be a nobody with."

We both laughed. Princess Laersa slipped her hand into mine and squeezed. "Endri. Thank you."

20

CHAPTER TWENTY

WE WERE BOTH RELUCTANT to leave the safety of Joichan's cave, even though the day remained bright and clear and I had retrieved my bag with no issues.

"The food in this pantry should tide us over for a day or two," Princess Laersa said, still marveling over its magic. "At the very least, until Queen Jennica and Lady Farrah arrive."

"And I'm not that keen on climbing back down unless we absolutely have to," I said.

"Good. We're staying in here, then," the princess said, and set about cleaning up the remains of our breakfast.

I sat at the table, pulling out the little dragon figurine.

"Are you calling Queen Jennica again?" Princess Laersa asked.

"No," I said. "This might sound odd, but—when we contacted the queen, did you feel any other magic in the area?"

The princess shook her head. "No, but honestly, I was too focused on what you were doing to pay attention to anything else. Why do you ask?"

I touched the teal tourmaline pendant that hung around my neck. "This is a new soulstone. Pazho and I created it right before ... before he disappeared. I haven't had a chance to try it yet. But when I called the queen, I felt it—respond somehow."

"Hmm. Interesting." Princess Laersa sat down across from me and stared at my necklace. "You said it's a *new* soulstone?"

I nodded, embarrassed. "My third. I haven't had much luck with soulstones in general."

"Did your other ones ever respond the same way?"

I shook my head. "No. The first one never took to me, even after years of trying. It just remained a dead jewel. The second one broke the instant I tried to use it." I grimaced. "I've been scared to try this one. Not that there's really been the time to do so."

"Why don't you try it now?" She played with a hammered gold bracelet around her wrist. "I'll try it too."

I took her hand, examining the piece of jewelry. It was simple, but the workmanship was exquisite. A circular citrine stone was set in the band. "This is beautiful. Is this your soulstone?"

She nodded. "My mother's, actually. Like you, I had several soul-stones over the years, and none of them worked. Many a jeweler lost his or her job because of that."

She slipped the bracelet from her wrist, examining it with the same care I had shown the dragon figurine earlier. "Father didn't want to keep many of her clothes or jewels after her death. This jewel is one of the few things I have left of hers. She used to wear it as a necklace, all the time. After she died, I had the pendant reworked into this bracelet."

I didn't know what to say to that. After all, I had no mementos from my birth family. Even the clothes I had worn when I first arrived at Pazho and Denaan's were gone, as I had long since outgrown them.

Something of what I was thinking must have shown on my face, because Princess Laersa suddenly clapped a hand over her mouth. "Oh, Endri! I'm sorry—I didn't think—"

"It's okay." I shrugged. "Even if I did have any keepsakes from my birth family, I'm not sure I would have held on to them."

An awkward silence fell between us. I flailed around for something to say. "Your hand. You're not wearing the bandage anymore."

Princess Laersa held up her hand. Several red streaks criss-crossed her fingers and palm, but the cuts looked like they had healed somewhat. "Oh, yes. It doesn't hurt as much anymore. I'll just have to be more careful in the future."

"What happened, if you don't mind my asking?"

The princess looked embarrassed. "I was admiring the new mirror Ambassador Allisandra gave to Father. When I touched it, I cut my hand." She shrugged. "The gilt frame must have been sharper than I thought, although I don't remember touching that part of it."

She cleared her throat. "Well. I think this new soulstone that your true father made you is beautiful. Let's try it, shall we?"

I smiled. "Let's."

The princess held her citrine-and-gold bracelet between her hands, looking like she was praying. I took off my tourmaline necklace, holding the pendant in one fist.

We both closed our eyes, concentrating.

Nothing happened, at least on my end.

I cracked open one eye. Princess Laersa had one eye open as well to survey my progress.

We both laughed.

"Well, that didn't work," I said ruefully.

"Wait," the princess said, before I refastened the necklace around my neck. "Didn't you say your necklace responded when you called the queen?"

"It did. You think we should call her again?"

"Not necessarily. Anyway, she and Lady Farrah should be mid-flight by now. It's probably not a good idea to bother them unless it's an emergency. But—if you touch the carving again while you're trying to transform, maybe that will trigger something?"

"I'll try it." But I doubted it would work.

Keeping my tourmaline necklace in one hand, I picked up the dragon figurine in the other. I closed my eyes again, feeling silly since I knew Princess Laersa was watching me.

Pazho had told me that shapeshifting involved what he termed "a deliberate use of instinct." Most shifters already knew what their second form was, since powers manifested early. The trick, then, was learning how to shift on purpose, calling forth your other shape and slipping it on and off like a coat or a tunic.

But since I didn't know what my second shape was, I had nothing to anchor my thoughts on when trying to transform.

Pazho had always instructed me to look inward to find my second self. But now, my mind kept wandering to the blue ice dragon figurine. I loved its proud stance, how it didn't seem overly aggressive, but you'd still think twice before picking a fight with it. I wondered what it would be like to fly, to feel the wind gliding over your scales, impervious to the chilly air. To be able to breathe ice.

The mountain cave was a bit cooler than being outside in Annlyn's desert heat, but not by much. My hands tingled and grew cold, although I didn't feel that sensation anywhere else in my body. Nor was it unpleasant. Just ... different.

Princess Laersa gasped. My eyes flew open.

"Endri," she said. "Your hands ..."

I looked down. The tingling feeling was beginning to fade, but my hands had a blue-green tinge to them, similar in shade to my tourmaline pendant and the scales of the little dragon figurine.

"Did I ... become anything?" I asked.

She shook her head sadly. "No. But your hands started to change color and your fingers looked like they were merging together."

"Oh." I looked down at my hands, wondering if I should try again.

"You were getting somewhere, I'm sure of it." Princess Laersa reached out to put her hand on mine. "Just keep at it, and—oh!"

When she touched my hand—the one clutching the dragon figurine—we both felt a jolt. A small yellow light flared across the table.

I put the carving on the table and flexed my hand, trying to rid myself of the shocked sensation.

"Ouch, that hurt," I said, shaking my hand out.

Princess Laersa was looking at her own hand in wonder. Unlike me, she didn't seem to be affected by the shock that had passed between us. "When we touched—my bracelet—it came alive all of a sudden." She held out her bracelet. The citrine now seemed to be glowing, as if a small fire had been lit within. "It's never looked like this before."

"Really? How does it feel when you wear it, now?"

She slipped it back on her wrist. After a moment, she said, "Invigorating. Like there's a bunch of energy, just waiting to be harnessed. I feel more alive, just wearing it."

"Hmm." I eyed Princess Laersa's bracelet. "Well. Why don't you try transforming?"

"Um. Okay," she said, suddenly shy. She turned a bit away from me, closing her eyes and placing a hand over the yellow stone in her bracelet.

I studied the princess while she concentrated on shapeshifting. For a long moment, nothing happened. And then, Princess Laersa *flickered*.

I'm not sure how to describe it, really. One minute I was staring at her—her long, dark eyelashes, mouth moving soundlessly, the cloud of her wavy black hair framing her heart-shaped face.

And then the next moment I saw something else entirely.

Princess Laersa was still there, but another image lay over her human face. A long snout, and a flash of purple skin. She kept her eyes closed, still trying to shift, but nothing more happened. The purple image flickered again and disappeared.

Princess Laersa's eyes fluttered open. She stared at me. "Well? Did anything ... happen?"

"Not a full transformation."

Her face fell.

"But."

The princess looked up at me, curious and hopeful.

"There was something." I explained what I had seen.

Princess Laersa turned thoughtful. "Purple skin? A snout? I wonder ..." She perked up. "Maybe I'll become a bird!"

I grinned at her excitement. "Let me know what it looks like up in the sky."

She smiled back. "Oh, don't worry. You'll be the first to know."

21

—·—

CHAPTER TWENTY-ONE

WE SPENT THE REMAINDER of the day resting or trying to transform. The cold, tingling sensation returned, but I didn't succeed in shifting.

Night fell outside, but there was no sign of Queen Jennica and Lady Farrah.

"They should be here by now," Princess Laersa fretted. She stood by the cave entrance, checking the moonlit sky for any sign of the Calians.

"I'm sure they'll arrive soon," I said from where I was reclining on the giant straw bed.

The princess suddenly gasped and recoiled from the entrance.

Outside, a dark haze had appeared, but it wasn't our expected visitors.

It was the black cloud.

Before, when we had seen it, it had been a shapeless mass. It still appeared that way—at first.

But now, it solidified into a figure. Tall, gaunt, and man-shaped, but still hazy around its feet and arms. Two crimson pinpricks appeared—beady eyes that fixated first on me, then Princess Laersa.

"Don't worry. We're safe," I said. I couldn't tell if I was trying to reassure Princess Laersa or myself. "It can't get in here."

The dark man reached out a long, black fingernail. Ever so slowly, it began to trace a vertical line down the magical barrier. Wherever its nail touched, the shimmery construct split and started to fray. A thin seam slowly opened.

The princess stayed frozen where she was, entranced by the creature's eyes.

"Princess Laersa! Get away from there!" I sprang up and started running towards the cave entrance.

The opening in the barrier was bigger now. The princess blinked, as if coming out of a trance. She began to back away.

The dark man lunged through the torn magical ward and clamped a gray, smoky hand over Princess Laersa's arm. She screamed as it pulled her towards it.

"Princess!" I leapt forward, trying to grab her back. My hand swiped empty air.

I rushed out of the cave in time to see Princess Laersa swept up in the air, trapped in grey mist. Red eyes appeared over her head, narrowed in a warning to stay back.

The princess, wrapped up in the darkness, was too far from the ledge's edge for me to reach without jumping. Even if I could reach them, I had no way of getting back to the ledge safely.

And even if I could reach her, if the dark man decided to drop us—it was a long way down.

But still. I couldn't let that *thing* take Princess Laersa.

So even as she yelled, "Endri, no! Don't!"—I jumped.

For a heart-stopping moment, I flailed about in the air. Had I misjudged the distance?

But then my right hand grabbed onto something solid. Princess Laersa's ankle.

The dark man screamed, an angry, inhuman sound. It seemed to be having trouble flying away with my added weight. It started weaving around erratically, trying to break my hold.

"Endri, are you crazy?" Princess Laersa yelled down at me. "How do we get back to the cave?"

"I'll figure something out!" I yelped. It was getting difficult to hold on.

The creature screamed again. Its hazy arm elongated and one of those pointed black fingernails came towards me, scratching my hand.

Whatever magic the creature possessed, it *hurt*. That simple scratch felt like the edge of a hot knife had been stabbed into my hand. I couldn't help it. I screamed.

The dark man pressed its nail deeper into my skin.

The blistering pain was making spots dance before my eyes. My hand slipped, and in that moment, the creature yanked Princess Laersa from my tenuous grip.

I started falling.

Princess Laersa began screaming. "En—!" But her voice cut off and her horrified face went still. The dark man's shadowy hand released its grip on her head as it lolled to the side. Her body went limp, and the black fog flew up and away with her still in its clutches.

With the wind rushing past me, I was all too aware that soon I'd hit the unforgiving ground below. There would be no way to survive a fall like that. I'd failed, both in keeping Princess Laersa safe and in restoring the citizens of Annlyn.

And yet, my mind kept wandering to another regret: that I would die before I ever learned to shift forms.

I thought of the blue ice dragon carving in my pocket. Not to call Queen Jennica—falling to one's death doesn't afford one the concentration needed to use magic. But just—what would it be like, to be able to fly like that majestic creature? Even if I fell from a great height, I would have no fear. For I would rise up with the air currents, and soar over the earth.

I braced for impact.

The air around me felt different, somehow. Cold and crisp, but fluid, like I was floating in water. And, I realized—how long had I been falling? Shouldn't I have hit the ground by now? Not that I wanted to, but—why hadn't I?

I raised a hand to touch my tourmaline soulstone, and then saw that I didn't have hands anymore.

I had claws.

Claws.

Wickedly sharp white claws, attached to sinewy blue, scaly arms that were about twice as long as my regular arms. I turned to look back, and my nose—now an elongated snout—bumped into my shoulder.

But what I saw nearly made me fall out of the sky.

The tip of one blue wing was unfurled in flight. I looked over my other shoulder. Same thing. Were those—my wings? I had never flown before, but I focused on one wing tip and thought about flapping and flexing it. The wing I was looking at did exactly that. I whipped my head around and looked at the other one. That second wing obeyed my mental command as well.

Woah.

Those were definitely my wings.

I laughed, delighted at my transformation. But what came out was a wheezy chuckle, deeper than I expected—for it was coming from a much larger chest now. I could see my breath, even though the night air wasn't that cold. And, wait—was that ice that came from my mouth?

I breathed out, and my eyes widened. It *was* ice! I was breathing *ice*!

I thought again of the ice dragon figurine in my pocket, my admiration of it, and my wish to become such a creature. I laughed again, thrilled at the ice particles that hung briefly around my head before falling away. I had become an ice dragon!

With that awareness, I quickly sobered. What was I doing, playing around while Princess Laersa was in danger? I needed to help her!

I shot up, flying a bit unsteadily. No matter. I'd have time to practice, once I saved the princess.

Back at the ledge where Joichan's cave was, I hovered in the air, looking around for the black cloud and Princess Laersa. But the fog was long gone. All I saw were twinkling stars, and the full moon. I had no idea which way the creature had taken the princess after I had let go of her.

I debated just picking a direction and flying, but my right wing suddenly buckled. I fell a few feet, landing hard on the ledge.

Oof. That was probably where the dark man attacked me.

As much as I wanted to find the princess, I knew I probably shouldn't fly any further until I saw how bad the injury to my wing—er, hand—was. But it rankled, knowing that Princess Laersa's trail was cold, and getting colder.

I tried to launch back into the air, but sprawled back ungracefully. My right wing now throbbed.

Okay, so I definitely had to attend to my wound. But how to change back?

My soulstone still hung around my neck. I touched a claw to it, intending to try to change back, when the light from above was suddenly blotted out.

Looking up, I saw a large, dark shape headed towards me. Had the black cloud returned?

But it didn't look like it. This dark mass was more distinct than the wispy form of the fog. And although there was someone accompanying it, it wasn't Princess Laersa.

The shape solidified into a beautiful golden dragon, the moonlight and the cavern's twinkling lights providing illumination so I could see the creature clearly. A woman sat upon the dragon's back. Her curly lavender hair billowed around her intelligent, ebony face.

"Princess Laersa?" the woman asked. I shook my head. "Ah. You must be Endri, then."

I nodded.

"I am Lady Farrah. And this—" she indicated the dragon "—is Queen Jennica of Calia."

22

─ · ─

CHAPTER TWENTY-TWO

THE DRAGON NODDED AT me in acknowledgment. Despite the fact that she was hovering mid-air with a person on her back, she still looked majestic. And dangerous.

I backed up to allow Queen Jennica to land. For a brief moment, I had forgotten that I, too, was in dragon form, and nearly bumped my head on the top of the cave entrance as I scrambled backwards. At the last second, I ducked. Surprised, I found I could move around the cave without scraping my body against the walls.

I had known the cave had a huge interior. I guess I hadn't realized how huge.

Queen Jennica landed on the ledge—much more gracefully than I had—and crouched down so Lady Farrah could disembark. Lady Farrah jumped down with ease, and I was surprised again by my visitors, this time at her attire—homespun brown pants and a cream linen tunic. *I suppose it's easier to ride a dragon wearing that than a full formal court dress.*

Lady Farrah made her way into the cave. Behind Lady Farrah, Queen Jennica shimmered and shifted, the golden dragon form collapsing inward to reform into a beautiful, dark-haired woman with a keen air about her.

"Endri, where is Princess Laersa?" Lady Farrah asked, after looking around.

I tried to speak, but a puff of fog came out of my mouth. Lady Farrah frowned, looking at her companion.

Queen Jennica regarded me. "Endri, can you shift back into your human self so we can talk?"

In all the excitement, I hadn't had a chance to try yet. I closed my eyes and concentrated, but although I waited for several heartbeats, nothing happened. I opened my eyes and lifted my wings in what I hoped looked like a dragon's shrug.

Queen Jennica frowned. "Perhaps I should have conversed with you before I transformed. Do you mean to say Pazho never taught you how to shift between forms?"

I didn't know how to answer that. He had tried, but since I could never become my second self before, I only knew the theory, not the practical application. I nodded, then I shook my head. The queen looked confused.

"I think you're saying you can't shift back?"

I nodded so vigorously that I caused a nearby cavern wall to shake. A few loose little rocks fell from the ceiling.

The queen's face broke into a smile. "Ah, I remember those days. I was fortunate to have my father talk me through my first shift—and several more after that. Perhaps I can help you."

I looked at her, hopeful. While being an ice dragon was a wonderful feeling, I didn't want to stay like this forever.

Lady Farrah wandered to another part of the cave, discreetly giving Queen Jennica and I some privacy for the shapeshifting lesson. I settled down, tucking my claws underneath me and drawing my wings around myself.

Across the room, Lady Farrah giggled. "You look like an overgrown cat, sitting like that."

Queen Jennica chuckled. "Cats and dragons do tend to get along well together."

She put a hand on my shoulder. "All right, then. Close your eyes."

I did as the queen said.

"Good. Now, you've already been a human. You know what that feels like—physically, mentally, and emotionally. Focus on those feelings, and your body will follow that and change."

I nodded, then stopped when more pebbles began falling from the ceiling again.

I closed my eyes and focused on the warmth of Queen Jennica's hand on my shoulder. Her human hand. My arms and hands were like hers, although perhaps a bit rougher and darker. My breath should be warm, not chilled, and should be coming from a much smaller chest. I flexed my feet, imagining smaller appendages with five toes, not five claws. Instead of a long blue snout, my face should be flatter, and—

Slowly, then with gaining speed, my body began to collapse in on itself. My wings grew tighter around my shrinking body. My long blue limbs and large white claws shrank down into smaller, human-sized arms, hands, and fingers. I opened my eyes and touched my face, feeling smooth skin instead of rough scales.

"Ah, very good." Queen Jennica sounded satisfied, as if she had been the one to shapeshift and not me. "Well met, Endri."

I bowed. "A pleasure to meet you, Your Majesty." I bowed in Lady Farrah's direction as well. "And you, Lady Farrah."

"I'm surprised Pazho never taught you how to shift," Queen Jennica said, echoing her earlier comment.

I bowed again to cover my embarrassment. "He did, Your Majesty. But until tonight, I never had a chance to actually try it."

"Until tonight?" Queen Jennica raised an eyebrow. "You mean, tonight was your first time ever transforming?"

I nodded, feeling the heat in my cheeks.

The queen smiled. "Then I am honored to witness it. It will get easier with time—and practice. And besides—" she winked at me "—dragons are the best creatures to turn into."

"I'm glad to hear it." I grinned, but my mirth quickly faded. "But I don't know how much time I'll have to practice. The black cloud came back, and it took Princess Laersa."

Both Lady Farrah and Queen Jennica looked at me sharply.

"But—Joichan's wards should be impenetrable," Queen Jennica said. "Unless the magic in here is fading?"

"It doesn't look like it," Lady Farrah said as she examined the area.

Queen Jennica turned to me. "Now that you can talk, Endri, please. Tell us everything."

I quickly outlined everything that had happened since Princess Laersa and I had talked to the two women earlier in the day. Queen Jennica's face grew dark when I mentioned the black cloud's return, and darker still when I spoke of how it had breached the magical ward at the cave entrance.

"I know the magic here is old, but that doesn't make it any less powerful or stable," Queen Jennica said, moving to the doorway.

Lady Farrah frowned. "Perhaps this black cloud really is King Balor's Shadow. I wish I could have seen it to be certain. If it is Balor's Shadow, and he's still tapping into the same magic that he had before, that kind of magic would be even more powerful than anything you, Joichan, or I combined could create," Lady Farrah warned.

"Then we'll have to outsmart it instead of out-magic it." The queen ran her fingers over the magical barrier. "Here's the tear. I might be able to repair it, but first I need to study this ward. Father and I have different approaches to magic."

"Do you think the dark man will return?" I asked.

Her lips thinned and her eyes flashed in anger. "I'd like to see it try."

23

CHAPTER TWENTY-THREE

QUEEN JENNICA'S SMILE WAS almost feral, a hint of her majestic dragon self. I recalled what my father Denaan had said, about how the kingdom of Calia had no need for a standing army ever since Queen Jennica took the throne. Now that I had seen her in dragon form, I had no trouble believing she was more than capable of protecting her country single-handedly.

While the queen focused on the magical ward, Lady Farrah approached me. "You said the creature attacked you."

I held up the back of my right hand, where a small, precise crescent moon shaped indent appeared. A small bead of dried blood pooled around the wound. I had largely ignored its dull throbbing as I recounted the night's events to the two women, but now that Lady Farrah mentioned it, it started to hurt again in earnest.

"May I?" At my nod, Lady Farrah took my hand, examining it. She tsked over the wound, flipping my right hand over and back, then looking at my non-injured left hand as well.

I sneaked a peek at my right hand. The indentation wasn't bleeding, but it had sliced through my skin deep enough that I could see a lumpy yellowish layer. The area around the open wound had turned a sick red-black, although it obviously hadn't scabbed over. I turned away, feeling nauseous, willing myself not to throw up.

Lady Farrah gave a brisk, unsurprised nod. "You're lucky you let go when you did."

"Lucky?" Maybe I had heard Lady Farrah wrong.

She ignored my doubtfulness. "Yes. You must always be careful with blood around magical beings. It calls to them—and, in some instances, binds you to them. And once you are bound, it is easy for them to possess you, or even kill you, if they are so inclined."

I shuddered. "I'll remember."

She poked at the wound's edges. I hissed at the sharp pain that flared up. "Sorry. I can heal you, but I can't promise it won't hurt."

I gritted my teeth. "I understand."

Lady Farrah rummaged through her pack, pulling out several paper packets. At my questioning look, she said, "Herbs. They don't take up that much space, and it's best to be prepared, just in case I can't find what I want while traveling."

"Oh." I had never seen a noblewoman travel so light, nor heard of one wanting to be ready in case she needed to heal someone. Then again, it wasn't like I encountered a lot of nobles—or royalty—that often. Perhaps this was just how it was done up north in Calia.

"Sit at the table, please, while I get things ready," Lady Farrah said. She bustled around the cave, gathering various items and depositing them on the table in front of me. Besides the herbs, she found a bowl, a pitcher of water, an unlit candle, and a small hand mirror.

While she did so, she continued talking. "I used to be a merce-nary-for-hire, along with my intended, Lord Rhyss. I specialized in healing, a bit of battle magic, and cooking." She smirked at that, although I didn't understand what was so funny about it. To me, cooking was a very valuable skill to have.

Lady Farrah sat down next to me, pouring some water into a bowl. Holding it between her hands, she whispered a quick spell to heat it. Once the water bubbled, she began adding in various herbs. "That's how I met Queen Jennica—although she was still a princess at the time. I don't do as much mercenary work as before, but old habits die hard."

A fresh, medicinal smell emerged from the bowl. Lady Farrah's hand hovered over the water, the pads of three fingers barely grazing the surface. She murmured another spell. I watched, fascinated, as the water in the bowl began to glow, as if lit from below. The light was so strong I had to resist the urge to look under the table to see if there was, indeed, a candle underneath. Although there was no possibility that candlelight could pierce through both an opaque wooden table and an equally opaque ceramic bowl, anyway.

The internal light faded. The water in the bowl turned thick, like a sludgy porridge. Satisfied, Lady Farrah pushed the bowl towards me, careful not to let any of the mixture spill out.

"Place your injured hand in this. Make sure your wound is completely covered."

I did as instructed, biting my tongue to focus on that pain instead of the sting of the herbal concoction against my deep open wound.

Lady Farrah snapped her fingers, and a small purple flame appeared at the end of her forefinger. She touched her finger to the candle, causing the wick to catch fire. She pressed her forefinger to her thumb, extinguishing the magic flame.

When she had the lit candle positioned to her satisfaction, she picked up the hand mirror and held it opposite the light. The mirror caught the candlelight and reflected it into the bowl.

At my quizzical look, she said, "I've been experimenting with mirror magic lately to see if it can intensify my spells. Mirror magic amplifies one's power, but at the same time, it's not a good idea to rely on it too heavily. There can be drawbacks to using mirrors, if you're not careful."

She paused, looking thoughtful. "I wonder if ice could act as a mirror? I know how reflective the lakes in Calia can be when they're frozen over in the winter. That might be something, in a pinch."

I nodded, as if I understood what she was talking about. My hand still smarted. But I soon forgot the pain as the light touched the bowl's contents and Lady Farrah's magic started working. Fascinated, I watched as the mixture seeped into my wound, weaving around the exposed tissue. The magic liquid pulsed several times, and the open wound began to seal itself.

"Just a little bit longer, and it should be—well, not good as new, but close to it," Lady Farrah said. "I advise you not to do anything too strenuous with that hand for a few days. Don't grip or carry anything. If that's your writing hand, don't write."

"I take it rock climbing is also a bad idea?" I asked wryly, thinking of the journey up to Joichan's cave.

Lady Farrah gave me a pointed look, as if she knew what I was thinking. "Yes. Don't do that."

"It's a good thing I can shapeshift now," I quipped. "Will this affect my ability to fly?"

"As long as you let it heal properly, no. But you'll notice your right wing will be a little weaker than your left one, for the same duration that you're letting your human self heal."

"In other words, don't stress out my hand or my wing while it's healing."

"That's right."

Lady Farrah stood up and joined Queen Jennica at the cave entrance. They began conversing in low tones. I sat in silence, watching the magic do its work. The constant throbbing pain had subsided, and I felt much better.

"How will I know when it's—oh!" I jumped in surprise as the mixture, apparently done healing me, rapidly absorbed into my skin. Nothing was left in the bowl other than my newly healed hand.

I examined my hand. It would be hard to tell the creature had ever injured me. The only indication was a small, faint, crescent moon shaped indentation on the back of my hand, outlined in a dull, dark red.

"How does it look?" Lady Farrah called to me.

"Amazing," I said, as I flipped and flexed my hand. "It looks and feels like the injury happened weeks ago, not just earlier tonight."

I walked over to the cave entrance to join Queen Jennica and Lady Farrah. Lady Farrah stopped her inspection of the broken ward to look at my hand.

"I like that particular spell, both for how well it heals and how easy it is to clean up afterwards," she said absently while she examined her handiwork. "And I'm pleased with how the mirror experiment worked out. It made the spell work much faster. But just remember, feelings can be deceptive. Go easy on that hand."

I laughed. "Yes, Lady Farrah." I turned my attention to the entrance. "How's the barrier, Your Highness?"

"Nearly done," Queen Jennica said, sounding a little strained. "It's not a particularly big tear, but the problem is how to fix it when all the magic in this cave is interconnected."

I blinked. "I'm sorry. I don't understand."

"It would be easier to repair the ward by taking it down completely and then casting a new one," Lady Farrah explained. "But when Joichan created the magic in this cave, he connected everything together. It makes the magic stronger, as all the spells feed into one another. But it also means if you remove one spell, you most likely will remove them all."

"Oh." Awkwardly, I waved at the ward. "Um, is there anything I can do to help?"

"You can rest that hand of yours while we finish here. And then we can discuss how to find your princess friend." Lady Farrah smiled, but I also knew she was politely telling me I'd be in the way.

I went back to the large sleeping area in the corner—the farthest possible spot away I could think of—and decided to practice shifting into my dragon form.

But the lateness of the hour, combined with my injury and the earlier excitement, overwhelmed me. In between worrying about Princess Laersa and trying to speed up my transformations, I fell asleep.

24

CHAPTER TWENTY-FOUR

"ENDRI. ENDRI."

I sat up, feeling disoriented as I looked around me, trying to find the source of the voice. When I found it, I immediately got to my feet. Princess Laersa stood in front of me, her face troubled.

"Princess Laersa?" I was now fully alert.

"Endri. I don't have much time. I'm back home, in Annlyn."

Her voice grew faint and distorted, as if she was speaking from far away, through a windy tunnel. Her image, too, flickered, like she was standing in a patch of sun that had suddenly been covered by passing clouds.

" ... Castle.... Darkness ..."

"Princess? Princess!" I reached out for her, in a blind hope that I could grab her and keep her with me. But with one last pleading glance, she disappeared from my view. My flailing hands touched only empty air.

I awoke with a gasp, breathing heavily. Lady Farrah was instantly by my side.

"Endri? Are you all right?"

Still groggy but feeling panicked, I said, "The princess ... Princess Laersa. I know where she is."

Lady Farrah raised an eyebrow. From her place at the cave entrance, Queen Jennica turned slightly, interested in our conversation.

"She's back in Annlyn. At the palace, I think."

Lady Farrah frowned. "How do you know this?"

"She appeared to me, just now, and told me. Maybe it was just a dream, but ... I don't think so. We have to go there. Now."

The two women glanced at each other, holding a silent conversation I couldn't quite follow. Then Lady Farrah turned back to me. "While I understand your concern for your friend, it's probably not wise to go back there. Not now, while it's still night out, and that darkness is at its full strength." She pointed at my hand. "And you need your strength. You're still injured."

"But if we wait, then who knows what could happen to Princess Laersa? Better to go now, when we're least expected."

"Then stay here, and Queen Jennica and I—"

"No! I have to go." Why couldn't Lady Farrah understand that?

Lady Farrah sighed. "Queen Jennica and I discussed some things while you slept. Now that you're able to shift forms ... you might be susceptible to the black cloud."

"If that's true, so is Queen Jennica." Although I knew I was being impertinent—Pazho would be so disappointed in me if he knew, and Denaan would put me on dish duty for the rest of my life!—part of me didn't care. Getting Princess Laersa back was the most important thing, even if I had to be rude to a hundred queens to do it.

"Yes, you're right," Queen Jennica said, her voice cold. "But I've also had years to perfect my shapeshifting ability, plus other magical skills at my disposal. I think I'll be able to hold my own. Besides, the black fog doesn't even know I exist. If anything, you'll draw its attention more than I will."

There was a long pause. I dropped my eyes. "I'm sorry, Your Majesty. Forgive me. I'm just so worried about Princess Laersa."

"It's understandable," the queen said, her tone warmer. "And wanting to help your princess is commendable. You make a good point—we should go now, and you should come with us. Get whatever you need, and let's go."

Okay, Endri. Take a deep breath, slow and steady, now. In. Out. That's it.

Queen Jennica dipped, her wings folding in close to her body, and I yelped in terror.

And whatever you do, don't throw up on the queen.

My musings fled as I held on to her for dear life.

I was riding bareback on Queen Jennica in her golden dragon form as she flew towards Annlyn in the night sky. Lady Farrah sat behind me, somehow maintaining both her balance and her dignity. Meanwhile, I had to keep biting my tongue from screaming nonstop.

Poor Queen Jennica could probably feel it every time I anxiously grabbed onto her scales. I hoped she wouldn't comment on it when she was back in human form. Flying was still a new sensation to me, and—as I was quickly learning—*riding* a flying dragon was much different than *being* a flying dragon.

I gripped a scale harder—sorry, Your Majesty!—and took in deep gulps of air, willing myself not to throw up. Vomiting on the queen of Calia would probably not help relations between Calia and Annlyn.

Plus, Pahzo would be so disappointed in me.

The dragon unfurled her wings, gliding towards the capital city's gates. She made a slow, wide circuit over the city, low enough for Lady Farrah and me to catch random glimpses of the quiet streets.

"I thought you said the citizens of Annlyn were roaming the city streets," Lady Farrah commented.

"I thought so too." I frowned, my airborne discomfort momentarily forgotten. "But I didn't see any animals out just now."

"Maybe they've all gone indoors to sleep?"

"Maybe." But I doubted it. "Although, if they've already begun giving in to their animal selves, there's no reason for them to suddenly act civilized and go back inside."

"And is that shield normally around Annlyn's castle?"

I turned to look, instantly regretting my choice. Fighting the queasiness, I squinted hard at the castle. Lady Farrah was right—there was a giant shimmering bubble surrounding the palace. In the moonlight, it looked like the castle was enclosed in a big, translucent pearl.

"No," I said, my stomach sinking from dread, or nausea. Quite possibly both.

"Hmm," was all Lady Farrah said. "How did you get in before, then?"

"The place was locked up tight, even without a shield. But Princess Laersa let me in."

Queen Jennica flew towards the open fields just beyond the city gates, landing next to the main road that led out of Annlyn. Lady Farrah dismounted gracefully.

Me? Not so much.

I tumbled off the dragon's back, just barely landing on my feet. My knees buckled underneath me, and I reached out blindly, not wanting to grab at the queen, but also afraid of falling.

Lady Farrah reached out and steadied me.

"Flying can be a bit disorienting at first," she said sympathetically. "Don't worry, you'll get used to it."

The large golden dragon shimmered, then shrank into the human form of Queen Jennica.

"He'd better," she said, but she smiled at me. "Now that you know what your second self is, you'll have to learn to like flying."

I smiled back. "I think it feels better being the one flying, instead of being the passenger."

"I would agree with that."

The three of us turned as one to look over Annlyn. The makeshift barricade that Princess Laersa and I had created still stood in the gated entrance. Beyond it, the city seemed eerily silent.

I looked up. The night sky was clear, and that prickling feeling of dread when the black fog was near was absent.

For now.

25

CHAPTER TWENTY-FIVE

"WELL, LET'S GO," QUEEN Jennica said. "The night's going by fast."

She strode forward, Lady Farrah by her side. I took a deep breath and followed the two women.

At the city gate, I moved a few wagons aside to clear enough of a small path for the others. "Should I move them back?"

Queen Jennica shook her head. "The only thing you'd want to keep out won't be deterred by some wagons piled up at the gate."

A chill crept down my spine. I glanced upward. Still clear.

"Well, we're back in the city. Now what, Your Majesty? Lady Farrah?" I asked.

"Let's head to the palace," Lady Farrah said decisively. "I want to take a look at that bubble around the building. My guess is, it's a shield of some sort. But is it keeping things out—or in?"

We made our way down the cobblestone streets, at first slowly and quietly. No one mentioned it, but I was sure that, as two shapeshifters and a Fae mage, we were a beacon to the black fog. I jumped at every little noise and dark shape. But as we continued walking, and nothing jumped out at us, we began walking faster, with less care to how loud we were.

Queen Jennica veered to the right to peek into one of the darkened homes that lined the main path. The door was hanging off its hinges, so it wasn't like she was breaking in, completely.

She poked her head through the doorframe, then disappeared inside. Lady Farrah made a small noise of dismay, but didn't naysay her friend.

We didn't have to wait long. The queen reappeared within a few moments, shaking her head in disbelief. "There's no one inside."

"No one?" Lady Farrah frowned. "Not even any sleeping animals?"

"No animals," Queen Jennica affirmed. "Sleeping or otherwise."

Lady Farrah entered the house next door to the one Queen Jennica had checked. I looked inside a home across the street, and then another one. All our investigations turned up the same conclusion: there were no people-turned-animals, anywhere.

"Where could they have gone?" I wondered, looking at the ground. In the dim moonlight, the cobblestone streets didn't give me any clues as to where the transformed people went.

"Who knows?" Lady Farrah said. "But this is a good thing."

I quirked an eyebrow at her. "It is?"

She nodded, her face troubled. "We have one question answered, at least. The shapeshifters of Annlyn are definitely not here."

We continued on in silence, each lost in our thoughts. I wondered where the others in the city could have gone, and if Pazho and Denaan were with them.

And if my fathers were too far gone in their second selves to change back into their human ones.

We were about halfway to the palace, when a brief shadow fell over the moon above. I looked up and over my shoulder, my blood going cold.

The black cloud was back. And it was heading towards us.

I quickened my pace, even as I called out, "Uh, Queen Jennica? Lady Farrah? That cloud? It's on its way here ..."

Lady Farrah looked behind her. "Oh, dear. Come on!"

She and Queen Jennica also walked faster.

A cold breeze passed over my skin. The night sky grew darker around us, even though I knew sunrise shouldn't be too far off. I glanced back again.

Bad idea. The dark fog was now even closer.

"Uh ... what now?"

Lady Farrah shot a worried look over her shoulder. "I have no idea. Run!"

The three of us broke into a run.

I felt the touch of cold again, although instead of a slight ripple, it now felt like a sharp, pointed fingernail scoring a thin line down my arm. And was that a laugh I heard on the air? Perhaps my anxiety was making me imagine things—which just made my fear grow worse.

The castle, encased in its milky white dome, loomed ahead of us.

"There's the castle!" I said, rather inanely. "Now what?"

"It was your idea to come back here," Queen Jennica pointed out, sounding out of breath. "Don't you have any ideas?"

"No!"

We had reached the castle. The doors were still shut, the portcullis still down. I didn't see the goat guards anywhere, not that they would have been able to help us. However, I did see a pile of shredded uniforms nearby, just outside of the bubble that enclosed the castle. *When they finally change back, that will be rather embarrassing,* I thought.

Lady Farrah put her hands out to touch the pearlescent bubble. There was a brief white flash and a crackling sound. "Ow!" She stepped back, shaking her stung hands. She looked at her hands, then back at the dome. And, for some odd reason, she rubbed at her cheek. "There's something strange about this magic. It felt like it was searching for something within me, but it couldn't find it."

The fog, knowing it had us cornered, swirled above us, biding its time. I saw two small red pinpricks of light within its dark depths, almost as if it had sprouted eyes to watch our every move.

"Let me try," Queen Jennica said. She turned to the dome, holding out her hands.

Lady Farrah's eyes grew wide. "Jennica, wait!"

Her warning came too late. The queen touched her palms to the barrier. Unlike when Lady Farrah had done so, the area around Queen Jennica's hands grew opaque. She tried to step back, but the dome held tight onto her hands.

I reached out, intending to grab the queen around her waist to pull her away.

"Endri, no!" Lady Farrah stopped me. "Stay back. We don't know if it will try to take you, too."

Above us, the dark cloud coalesced. Bursts of red light sizzled in its depths.

And then it dove at us.

26

CHAPTER TWENTY-SIX

QUEEN JENNICA SCREAMED, ALTHOUGH I wasn't sure if it was because of the black fog swooping down on us or because of the pearly dome that held her captive. I jumped in front of both her and Lady Farrah, drawing my sword. Although I knew my weapon wouldn't do much damage against a swirling gray mist anyway.

And I never did get those sword fighting lessons from Princess Laersa. So any damage I did would be from sheer luck.

But it would make me feel better, like I was being useful right now.

Maybe.

I held out my sword, like I could cleave the weird magical being that flowed towards us, and braced myself for its attack.

But that attack didn't come.

Instead, at the last moment, the darkness swooped slightly upward, and hit the castle's magical bubble just above where Queen Jennica stood. The shimmery white around her stuck hands changed to a sickly greenish grey, and she screamed again. The greenish grey glow pulsed and began to envelop the queen.

"Jennica!" Lady Farrah cried out. Purple flames appeared above her hands. She hurled it at the castle barrier, to no avail.

The queen screamed again as the black fog completely covered her. Within the mist, her form began to shimmer and shift.

"Your Majesty?" I said, unsure.

The mist began to spread outwards, growing bigger. Both Lady Farrah and I backed away, not wanting the dark cloud's taint to touch us.

Above us, the sky started to lighten into shades of orange and yellow, a sure sign that dawn was coming.

Queen Jennica's form kept growing, until she filled the entire courtyard around the castle. She shook herself all over, ridding herself of any remnants of the black fog that may have clung to her. It sighed, an eerie, mournful sound, then plunged into the pearly dome.

Standing before us was a large golden dragon—Queen Jennica in her second self.

"Jennica?" Lady Farrah whispered.

The queen turned her draconian head towards the sound. The dragon and the healer stared at each other for a long moment, neither one moving or blinking.

I was also now quite aware that I was pointing a sharp, shiny sword at a dragon. They didn't like those things, did they? Should I put it away? Should I try to hide it? Should I—

Then Queen Jennica opened her mouth, exposing two rows of very large, very sharp teeth. She bent her head towards Lady Farrah. I stared, mesmerized, until I realized—

"Lady Farrah, watch out!" I pushed her away, diving to the ground.

The dragon's jaws snapped shut just above my head.

I rolled, jumping up a few feet away. Lady Farrah now had a shimmery barrier surrounding her. The angry dragon queen was trying to break through Lady Farrah's ward, repeatedly smashing her snout against it.

Lady Farrah tried to reason with her friend. "Jennica, stop! It's me, Farrah! You know you don't want to hurt me. Whatever's taken over you, fight it!"

The dragon stopped for a moment, blinking as Lady Farrah's words reached her. I held my breath.

Then the dragon shook her head, like she was shaking off her friend's words. She snapped her jaws once, then tried to bite Lady Farrah's head off.

I gasped. Lady Farrah put more power into her ward, and Queen Jennica's open mouth bounced off the top of the shimmery shield. The dragon renewed her attempts to break through.

The ward was holding up, but barely. Lady Farrah staggered a bit with each blow to her shield. A few more hits from Queen Jennica, and Lady Farrah's ward would be destroyed.

I looked around frantically, trying to figure out how to distract the dragon.

The dragon snorted, angry that she couldn't get through Lady Farrah's shield. She looked around, her eyes alighting on me.

I gulped. Now that I had her attention, I didn't really want it.

The dragon snorted again, smoke trailing from her nostrils. She stalked towards me, each thunderous step shaking the ground.

I backed away slowly, facing the queen as I kept my hands out in front of me. Wasn't there something about never turning your back to a predator and not showing fear? Although I was sure the queen—and any other animal left in Annlyn—could sense my fear from miles away.

I couldn't go very far. A few more steps and I would back into the barrier around the castle, and—if Queen Jennica's condition was anything to go by—I probably shouldn't touch it. I could try to run, but the queen could easily fly and catch me. Besides, I couldn't leave Lady Farrah behind.

Something tangled in my feet, causing me to slip backwards and land heavily on the ground. I reached down to see what had made me fall. Tattered, dust-covered clothing came up in my hands—one of the former guards' uniform.

Above me, Queen Jennica paused, sniffing the air delicately as she fixed her huge golden eyes on me. She reminded me of a cat toying with its prey, savoring the sweet moment before the kill.

Behind her, Lady Farrah waved her hands to get my attention. She pointed at me, then at the ground next to her. Ah. If I was next to her, she could ward us both.

But first, I had to get to her side without being eaten.

Queen Jennica chose that moment to attack. Her head lowered towards me, smoke trailing from her nostrils as her mouth started to open.

At a loss for a better weapon, I threw the dirty clothing at the dragon.

They landed on the dragon's snout, covering her nostrils as she breathed in the dust from the clothes. Her face twitched, and she sneezed. And sneezed again.

The clothes went up in a puff of smoke as a bit of fire escaped her mouth. The resulting fall of ash caused another bout of sneezing. It would have been funny—a sneezing dragon is an interesting sight to see—if I hadn't been so afraid of getting incinerated by accident.

Lady Farrah motioned at me again, more frantic this time.

I ran towards Lady Farrah.

Queen Jennica, golden eyes watering, opened her mouth to snap at me in passing. Her hot breath brushed the top of my head.

Rays from the now fully risen sun hit the cobblestones of the palace courtyard.

The black cloud detached itself from the castle's barrier, shrieking. It caught Queen Jennica up in its shapeless form, dulling the shiny golden dragon's color under its dark mist. Disoriented, the dragon missed me, her jaws closing over empty air.

I reached Lady Farrah's side. She grabbed me to her and hastily constructed a new ward.

But she needn't have worried. Dark fog now completely covered Queen Jennica, and it seemed to have restricted her movements as well. She roared, frustrated that she couldn't get at me, or get free.

Darkness swirled around the queen, growing thicker. Queen Jennica roared again, so loud that it seemed the cobblestones danced under our feet from the vibrations. Lady Farrah even dropped her ward so she could clap her hands over her ears.

And then, an abrupt silence fell over the area.

Queen Jennica had disappeared, taken away by the black fog.

27

— · —

Chapter Twenty-Seven

For a moment, Lady Farrah and I just stared at the space where the dragon Queen Jennica had been. But she didn't reappear, and the black fog didn't return.

I waved my arms in the air where we had last seen the queen. Empty. "Where could she have gone?" I wondered.

"I don't know," Lady Farrah said. She surveyed the area, even though there was nothing to see. "I had no idea the Shadow—if that *was* the Shadow—could do that. The last time ..."

Her voice trailed off. I waited, but she didn't seem inclined to continue. Finally, I prompted, "The last time?"

She cleared her throat. "The last time I encountered the Shadow, it could possess people. Even kill them. But it never seemed able to physically take them. I mean, it's a shadow. It's not solid, it doesn't have substance."

She sighed, staring at the morning sky as if it held clues to where the queen had been taken. When she looked back at me, her eyes were bleak. "If it's able to move things physically now ... I'm worried that it's gotten stronger, somehow. Which it shouldn't be."

I swallowed hard. I hadn't known Lady Farrah for very long, but she seemed to be a very capable, knowledgeable person. I got the impression that few things fazed her. If she was worried about the black cloud ...

I indicated two nearby rocks that decorated the courtyard, inviting Lady Farrah to sit while I sank down on one of them. "I think you'd better tell me everything you know about this Shadow."

Lady Farrah sat as well. She stared at her hands, which had turned slightly red and swollen from her earlier shock trying to breach the pearly bubble. "A few months ago, my intended, Rhyss, and I had to go into the land of Faerie to find my father...."

She told me an amazing tale, then, about how she was tasked to discover who or what was behind the murders of many Fae, at a time when Faerie's Seelie Court was in shambles and they were scrambling to find a new ruler. This mysterious entity had also been responsible for wreaking havoc in the Gifted Lands.

It seemed that the Shadow had been behind the deaths and the chaos. It was a magical extension of the Faerie Unseelie Court's King Balor. He would split his self and send his Shadow forth to kill, possess, or destroy. When Lady Farrah and several others went into the heart of the Unseelie Court to save her betrothed and another Fae, they uncovered King Balor's plan to take over the Seelie Court, by aiding a disgraced Seelie noble who was intent on regaining her former glory.

Lady Farrah shook her head, remembering. "And here's a tip for you—if you ever encounter one of the Fae, know that they love to bargain with humans. And they will usually get the upper hand, so you must be careful in what you promise and how you word things. But if you can get the upper hand, even if it's to their detriment, they will respect you. And that counts for something."

"I'll remember," I promised. "What happened to King Balor?"

Lady Farrah shrugged. "He escaped. But he was weakened; we closed off the source of his power. Or so I thought."

"Oh." I looked down at the cobblestones, discouraged. A lone pebble lay by my foot, and I kicked it across the courtyard as hard as I could. I watched as it skittered across the ground, hitting the pearly bubble around the castle and slightly ricocheting off it.

"Hey." Lady Farrah's voice caught my attention, and I looked over at her. She gave me a slight smile, even though her eyes were sad. "We'll find Queen Jennica. And Pazho, and Denaan, and everyone else."

"I hope so."

"We can't lose hope, or the enemy will already have won," she said, standing. She held her hand out to me. "Come on."

I put my hand in hers and let her pull me up. "Where are we going?"

"For now, nowhere. We need to figure out a way into this castle."

But no matter what Lady Farrah tried, she couldn't break through the barrier. Direct magical attacks didn't work, nor did subtle, more complex spells. At one point she even drew out her bow and shot a few arrows—some with magic, and some with none—at the pearlescent dome. Nothing worked.

The growing heat of the day—combined with my lack of sleep from the night before—was making me drowsy. Despite the seriousness of the situation, I couldn't help but yawn.

Lady Farrah glared at me, several wisps of her lavender hair sticking to her forehead and cheeks. "If you think you can do better, please, be my guest."

"I thought you said I shouldn't touch the bubble."

She sighed in frustration. "At this point, I'm willing to try anything."

I snorted. "You may be, but I'm not. I'm the one at risk, here."

She nodded soberly. "True. But I'm out of ideas. Nothing I've tried has worked. If you're willing to have a go at it—"

"I am."

"—Then I'll see what I can do to protect you before you try to get through." She sighed again. "I wish I had done that with Jennica, before, but there was no time to think of things like that."

I stood there, unsure of what to say or do. *I'm sorry* or *It will be all right* both seemed paltry and pointless, and I didn't think it would make Lady Farrah feel better. So I just settled for an awkward nod, hoping that would somehow convey all the things I was feeling.

It seemed to do the trick. Lady Farrah smiled and nodded back, then put her hand on my arm. "Just stand still, here, while I cast the spell."

I nodded again, closing my eyes. Unlike Lady Farrah, I didn't need to concentrate on creating a spell, but I also didn't want to just stare at her while she worked her magic.

Lady Farrah murmured a long string of words under her breath. I could feel her magic coursing through her hand and into my arm. A chill spread over my body, but unlike the earlier touch from the black fog—the Shadow—this cold wasn't unpleasant. It actually felt like I was settling deeper into my second self, like my ice dragon form had woken up and hovered just under the surface of my human self.

Was Lady Farrah calling up my ice dragon self and making magical armor from it?

At my neck, my tourmaline soulstone sparked with cold. My hand flew to it, and I opened my eyes, surprised to see frost on my fingers.

In my pocket, an answering concentration of cold blossomed. I hissed at the sudden chilly sensation, but it quickly faded.

"What's this?" Lady Farrah murmured, her hand still on my arm. She removed her hand, flexing it to shake off the sudden stiffness in her fingers. "I didn't expect that to happen. You say you don't know any magic, but you're carrying something that has quite a bit of it."

Sheepishly, I drew the blue dragon figurine from my pocket. Holding it out, I could see that it, too, was covered in frost, even though the sun's heat should have melted that away in an instant.

"Maybe it's this? It's what I used to call Queen Jennica," I said. "My father Pazho gave it to me."

I placed the dragon miniature in Lady Farrah's outstretched hand. She flinched from the cold, but kept a firm grip on it as she turned it over and over in the sunlight.

She smiled. "I recognize this handiwork."

"Father said a man named Kye gave it to him?"

"Yes. He used to be a dragon Seeker, before he retired and turned the business over to his son, Beyan. But he liked to make carvings of all the dragons he had encountered during his travels."

"Father mentioned that," I said soberly, remembering that him giving me that carving was one of the last times I had seen him before he disappeared. I swallowed around the sudden lump in my throat. I hoped he and Denaan were all right.

Lady Farrah poked at the little dragon with an experimental finger. "And I particularly remember this little trinket. It was one of the first items Jennica and I tried to infuse with a calling spell."

"What? *You're* the one who put the spell on this?"

"One of the people, yes." She ran her finger lovingly over the dragon's outstretched blue wing, smiling at the memory. "We didn't quite know what we were doing, when we infused this little thing. It was able to contact others, but the magic it contained was a bit … temperamental. I think it was because we hadn't figured out a way to make Jennica's completely human magic compatible with my blended human-and-Fae ability yet."

Shyly, I said, "That 'little thing' unlocked my shapeshifting ability. Without it, I still wouldn't be able to transform into my second self."

Lady Farrah gave me a sharp look. "Really? What do you mean?"

I explained what had happened in Joichan's cave, when I had contacted Queen Jennica, and how the magic in the figurine had sparked something in my soulstone. "And then, when Princess Laersa and I tried experimenting with it, her soulstone also responded to it. Neither of us transformed fully, but we saw hints of what we might become."

"And then you were able to shapeshift later on?" Lady Farrah guessed.

I nodded.

She studied the frost-covered figurine, then turned and studied me. I fidgeted under her gaze, until I realized she was studying my blue-green tourmaline necklace, not me.

In either a self-conscious or protective gesture—I wasn't sure which—my hand flew to my pendant.

Lady Farrah raised her eyes to meet mine.

"There's more to you than I originally thought, Endri." A note of approval laced her voice. "And I've given you as much protection as I am able. So. Are you ready to break into the castle?"

28

CHAPTER TWENTY-EIGHT

I WASN'T, AT ALL, but I couldn't really object. So I just nodded, then stood there awkwardly.

Lady Farrah raised one eyebrow. "Well?"

I coughed, and meekly put out my hand. "Um. Could I have my carving back, please, first?"

She smiled and placed the cold statuette in my outstretched hand. "Of course."

I placed the figurine back in my pocket, breathing a small sigh of relief. I couldn't explain why, but I felt better once I had it back in my possession. Not that Lady Farrah would have done anything to it, but ... I just needed to have it near me.

I turned to face the pearly dome. Shimmering in the sunlight, it actually looked kind of pretty. Underneath, the stone of the castle walls rippled, looking a bit distorted under the changing light.

"You should be able to touch it without getting stuck, for a short time at least," Lady Farrah said. "I have a few spells ready in case something happens. When I touched it, I felt like it was searching for something. Let me know if you feel the same thing."

I nodded. Taking a deep breath, I carefully put my hand to the shiny barrier.

It wavered a little at my touch, the pads of my fingers making the barrier turn opaque compared to the rest of the see-through dome. At first, I didn't feel anything odd, besides some resistance to my hand trying to move through the barrier. Unfortunately, I couldn't just push through physically.

Of course it can't be that easy, I thought sardonically. *Otherwise there would be no reason to have this barrier here in the first place.*

I pressed my hand fully against the shimmery dome. Now I understood what Lady Farrah had been talking about. The magic of the barrier flowed into me, traveling up the length of my arm and into the rest of my body.

It felt like a slimy snake, slithering its way through me as it slowly and methodically searched for something.

And in an instant, I understood what it wanted from me.

My ability to change forms.

While Lady Farrah had magic, she was not a shapeshifter. It didn't want her type of magic. Or perhaps her magic was incompatible with it. Regardless, it had decided that Lady Farrah did not have anything it wanted.

But Queen Jennica definitely had.

Lady Farrah's protections helped, keeping the curious, questing magic of the barrier at bay. But it still felt odd, like a damp sheet clung to my skin. I shivered, resisting the urge to try to shake off the cloying, crawling feeling.

Instead, I closed my eyes and concentrated on the barrier. It was like a snarling, cornered animal, hungry and craving the magic it sensed I had. But it couldn't get at it—thanks to Lady Farrah—and it swiped at me, searching for any weakness to drain me.

I kept poking and pushing. The barrier's magic eagerly welcomed me in, hoping to eventually devour my newfound shapeshifting ability. Slowly, I leaned in, even though I hated the grasping sensation of the sinister magic that surrounded me. I would endure it. I had to find my fathers, and Princess Laersa.

Behind me, I heard a short yelp of surprise from Lady Farrah.

I opened my eyes and turned around. Lady Farrah was, indeed, behind me. But a thin, pearlescent wall of magic now stood between us.

It worked, I realized. Lady Farrah's form rippled, a bit blurry and shimmery through the castle's barrier. In a loud voice, I asked, "Can you get through?"

She flinched. "You don't need to yell, I can hear you just fine through this thing. It doesn't dampen sound, it just prevents entry."

In a more regular tone, I said sheepishly, "Oh. Sorry."

Lady Farrah nodded in acknowledgment, then put her hand out towards the barrier. Her fingers barely grazed the dome before she winced and stepped back, shaking her hand out as she had before. She massaged her right cheek, and I wondered at her subconscious habit. Was she aware that she was doing it?

She shook her head and pursed her lips, frustrated. "I don't think I can get in. You'll have to go without me. I'll wait here."

"Uh." I blinked, reluctant to explore the now obviously enspelled castle by myself. Lady Farrah had magic, strong magic, and the knowledge on how to wield it. I had an unruly new shapeshifting power that I had no idea how to control. "Um. Are you sure?"

She waved at me impatiently. "I can keep trying, but we'd probably waste the whole day with my efforts. Just go. If I can figure out a way to breach the barrier, I'll do so. But stop wasting time."

I nodded and turned away. My last glimpse of Lady Farrah was of her touching her face again as she moved her jaw experimentally.

Taking a deep breath, I faced the castle.

I figured I would have to go around the side of the building, to locate the hopefully-still-unlocked servants' entrance. But my mouth fell open as I got a good look at the metal portcullis and the large wooden doors beyond it. Both had been firmly shut against the outside world when I had been here last.

Technically, they were still shut. But now, both the portcullis and the double doors sported big, gaping holes in their centers. I examined the entryway. The silver metal of the portcullis had turned black around the edges of the hole, curling in on itself. The wooden doors hadn't fared any better—they were practically nonexistent. Only the smallest sliver of wood curved around the doorway, hinting that two doors had once stood here.

I shivered. No army, even wielding dozens of torches, could have melted through the metal so effectively. No, only some sort of powerful magic could have blasted through the castle's defenses like this.

I swallowed, picking my way carefully through the charred metal-and-wood doorway. Feeling apprehensive, I disappeared into the cool interior of Annlyn's castle.

29

CHAPTER TWENTY-NINE

RECALLING MY PREVIOUS VISIT here, I headed towards the throne room, where I had last seen King Tahrin. Perhaps Princess Laersa was with him?

I moved as quietly as I could, not wanting to attract the attention of any animals—or magical beings—that might be in the area. But as I continued through the hallways, I realized my caution might not be needed.

Just like the deserted streets of Annlyn, I seemed to be completely alone in the castle. The animals that had overrun the place were nowhere to be seen. Maybe they were sleeping, but I doubted they would all hide away in the castle's rooms to do so. More likely, they would just bed down where they were.

Wanting to be sure, I ducked my head in some of the rooms as I passed. Empty. As were the hallways. Some clothes from the transformed citizens still lay in haphazard piles on the stone floors, but their owners definitely were gone.

I reached the throne room. The broken wooden doors were still pushed open from when Princess Laersa and I had been here before.

And at the other end of the room, the twin red velvet thrones stood empty.

The king's sceptre still lay on the floor, abandoned. But now, the king's gold crown, its jewels winking in the dim light, also lay abandoned on the throne's plush red seat. I noticed a few scratch marks on the velvet, like a small creature had gouged the chair with its claws. Wherever King Tahrin had gone, he hadn't gone willingly.

The ambassador's mirror, hanging proudly on the wall, was the only thing not destroyed or tarnished in the room. It looked out of place compared to everything else.

I sighed in frustration. I would search the rest of the palace, of course, but it was becoming increasingly obvious that Princess Laersa most likely wasn't here. If she ever had been.

Impatient now for answers—any answers—and sure that I truly was alone, I went through the rest of the castle quickly. As I had suspected, the ground level was empty of any life. I found a staircase and went down to the dungeons. Also empty—although the abandoned dishes and indents in the dirt where people had once sat or lay gave me an uneasy feeling. The cells were still intact, and locked. I doubted the palace guards had freed all the prisoners in the last few days. So the prisoners hadn't escaped, but had been taken.

By magic.

I shook my arms and legs, as if I could rid myself of the creepy sensation crawling down my spine. Not wanting to spend another moment in the deserted dungeon, I hurried back up the staircase, passing the ground level to go upstairs.

I opened one of the doors, trying not to feel weird about poking into the private residences of the Annlyn royal family. *I'll beg for King Tahrin's mercy later*, I thought. *Given the circumstances, he can hardly get mad at me.*

And speaking of King Tahrin …

Before me was a large room decorated in bright, cheerful colors. Red and white diamond patterned tiles ran up the walls, while rich red and gold rugs covered the floor. A large ironwood armoire and matching bed dominated the area, an obvious hint that this was a bedroom.

On the wall across from the bed, a dark cloth covered a medium-sized object that hung there in a place of former prominence. Curious, I crossed over to it and tweaked the fabric away.

Under the cloth was a painting, set in a simple metal frame that seemed out of place compared to the room's opulence.

A lovely middle-aged woman, an older version of Princess Laersa, stared out at the room with intelligent and kind eyes. A slight smile played at her rosy lips, as if she was about to share a delightful secret with the painter. Around her neck was a thin gold chain, at the end of which hung a citrine pendant. I recognized the jewel as the one in the princess's bracelet. Once the queen's soulstone, it now was her daughter's.

I studied the painting, recalling Pazho's words. *He used to be much more forward-thinking, before the death of his queen. Now, he just hides away in his fancy palace, and he expects his people to hide themselves as well.*

For a moment, I felt sorry for King Tahrin, even though I was a commoner and he was a king. And I felt doubly sorry for Princess Laersa, who had to suffer because her neglectful father couldn't move past his grief.

Carefully, I placed the cloth back over the portrait of the late queen and left the room.

I opened a few more doors, doing a cursory glance in each room. I left them untouched once I was satisfied no one was present. After coming across the late queen's portrait, I was acutely aware that I was trespassing in a private area, even if no one was around to reprimand me for it.

Most of the other rooms in this hallway were smaller and plainer. An antechamber for the king's bedroom, and a smaller suite of rooms that looked like they had once belonged to the queen. I sneezed when I entered those rooms—the dust lay thick on all the furniture, clear evidence that the rooms hadn't been touched since the queen's death.

There was one more door at the far end of the hallway, before it turned the corner to go down the servants' stairwell. I reached for the handle, thinking the door would open as easily as the previous chamber doors had.

But this door was locked.

I tried the handle again. Still locked.

I hesitated. Should I try to force my way in? I looked up and down the hallway, even peering around the corner. I didn't see anything nearby—and so far, it didn't even seem like anyone was even in the palace anymore—but I didn't want to attract any attention.

Any magical *attention*, I amended mentally.

Hearing rustling inside the room, I froze. Holding my breath, I carefully pressed my ear against the door, trying to determine exactly what I was hearing.

The swishing movement sounded again. It was a bit faint, as if the person—or creature—was on the far side of the room. It didn't sound like they were coming any closer, either, but staying where they were.

I swallowed. Now that I knew there was someone—or something—on the other side of this door, I didn't particularly want to search this room. But I had to be thorough, so I could report my findings to Lady Farrah.

I ground my teeth. If only the mage had been able to breach the barrier with me. I would feel a lot better right now, with her calming presence beside me.

Speaking of calming ...

I slipped my hand into my pocket, running my fingers over the smooth edges of the little dragon figurine. Just knowing it was there, having that link to my newfound shapeshifting ability and to my fathers, helped ground me.

The figurine grew cold at my touch. My tourmaline pendant also flared to life, a small bit of ice blooming at my neck. My hand—the one curled around the carving—felt stiff and thick, and I withdrew it from my pocket to look at it.

My normally tan, smooth hand had turned blue and leathery. My fingernails, usually short and neat, had lengthened into sharp talons. I wiggled my fingers—claws?—a bit, marveling at how I could partially retract my new talons.

And, I thought, grinning wickedly, *at least I have a small bit of protection now against whatever is inside there.*

Gazing at my transformed hand, I wondered if any of my second self's other abilities were available to me.

I blew out an experimental breath towards the doorknob. My breath frosted mid-air, encasing the handle in a thick layer of ice. Underneath the ice, I could see cracks forming in the doorknob, blossoming out from the handle's center.

Could it really ...?

I flicked my thumb and forefinger at the doorknob. The ice solidified along the cracks, and the door handle shattered. My dragon hand, sadly, changed back into my smaller, human one. The chamber door swung open slightly before me.

I pushed it fully open, bracing myself for whatever I would find on the other side.

At the window, gazing out over the castle grounds, stood Princess Laersa.

30

---·---

CHAPTER THIRTY

SHE TURNED WHEN I entered the room.

This last bedchamber, I assumed, belonged to Princess Laersa. Unlike her mother's untouched and dusty rooms, this one looked lived in, smaller but cozy. Unlike the heavy golds and reds of King Tahrin's rooms, the princess had decorated her bedroom in airy blues and whites. I smiled to myself. It looked like just the sort of place my second self would be comfortable in.

A wooden vanity table stood at one end of the room, boasting a large, oval-shaped mirror. The glass sparkled, as if a servant had just finished polishing it. Perhaps it was the angle of the sunlight hitting it that made it appear overly bright to my eyes.

"Princess Laersa!" I rushed forward, arms out, but stopped myself from reaching out and grabbing her up in an embrace. She didn't move towards me, either. For a long moment, we just stared at each other.

Finally, I dropped my hands to my sides and said lamely, "You're all right! I hope?"

She tilted her head, studying me. "Pardon me. Do I know you?"

I blinked. "It's me, Endri. I've come to rescue you."

She put a hand to her head. "Forgive me. Now that you say it, I vaguely recall your name and face. But I have such a headache, it's hard to think straight at all."

"Of course," I nodded, trying not to feel hurt that she didn't remember me. I mean, it hadn't been *that* long since we'd seen each other last. "I thought I saw the black fog do something to you as I fell. What happened?"

She frowned. "I'm not sure. I lost consciousness when that shadow man touched me. When I woke up, I was here, in my room."

"You didn't try to leave?"

She raised one eyebrow. "How could I?"

"Well, why didn't you just unlock the door?"

"Oh, I didn't think of that."

I blinked in confusion. Trying the doors would have been the first thing I—or really, anyone—would have done. I was surprised that Princess Laersa *hadn't* tried it. I looked around the room, but wherever the entrance was to the hidden passageways, it was well-concealed. "Or you could have gone out through the tunnels."

Her brow furrowed for a moment, then she shrugged delicately. "I suppose I could have. But when I woke up, I saw that pearly shimmery thing outside, surrounding the castle. Maybe the shadow man put it up to keep me trapped. I didn't know what it was, exactly, and I didn't want to take any chances."

Now it was my turn to frown. While I didn't know Princess Laersa that well, I hadn't gotten the impression that she had a passive personality. Maybe she was more unnerved by the night's events than she wanted to admit.

"Well, I'm here now. As is Lady Farrah, just outside."

"Lady Farrah?" Princess Laersa's tongue tumbled over the name, as if she was just saying it for the first time.

"Yes. She couldn't get through the barrier around the castle. But she's waiting for us, so we should get going."

"Of course." The princess surveyed her bedchamber.

"Do you need to take anything with you?"

"Hmm? Oh, no. Let's go." But she just stood there, unmoving.

"Should we take the tunnels? Although it doesn't seem like there's anyone but us in the palace anymore."

"Oh, that's not correct." She shook her head. "The Graenir ambassador is still here as well. Poor thing."

As if on cue, a knock sounded at Princess Laersa's chamber door. "Your Highness? Are you all right?"

"I'm fine, dear Allisandra," the princess called out. "You may come in."

Ambassador Allisandra entered, cautiously looking around before lowering the heavy golden candlestick she held upraised in one hand. "I heard noises in here—I thought perhaps you were in trouble."

"Oh, no, my ambassador friend. I was just having a discussion with my rescuer, here."

Allisandra gave me a careful once-over. "I remember you. You and the older gentleman accompanying you had an audience with King Tahrin right before I did."

"Yes," I said. "Endri, at your service. And the gentleman you mentioned is my father, Pazho."

"It's good to meet you—even better if you can help us leave. Both the princess and I have tried to get through that magical barrier surrounding the castle, but it's got us firmly trapped in here."

Thinking of how I was able to breach the barrier, I said, "I think I can get you both out. Let's go."

The princess shook her head, as if to clear it. "Dear Endri, would you mind leading the way? I'm afraid the recent excitement has left me more exhausted than I want to admit. My head is all foggy."

"O-of course, Your Highness." I took her outstretched hand. It was stiff and cold, which was surprising considering it was midday outside. It was cool inside the palace, but not that much cooler. Her hand felt nearly as cold as the icy doorknob I had broken earlier.

"Princess Laersa, are you unwell?" I asked as I led her and the ambassador out of the bedroom and down the hallway.

"Perhaps I might be," she said. "I haven't felt quite myself since the black cloud took me."

Ah, that explained her odd behavior. "Don't worry, princess. We'll get you somewhere safe so you can rest and get better."

"Thank you, dear Endri. You seem like a dependable sort. I'm sure I can rely on you."

My chest swelled at her words of praise, even as my mind clouded in confusion. Hadn't we escaped to Joichan's cave together? Hadn't she watched me risk my life to try to save her from the shadow creature? What else did I have to do to prove I was reliable to her?

Next to me, the ambassador swiped at her sweaty brow. "I hope this safe place is also nice and cool."

Poor Allisandra. She definitely wasn't used to the Annlyn heat. Her blond braids clung damply to her face and neck, and her silk blouse was damp with sweat and sticking to her.

"Would you like to change?" I said. "I'm sure we can find you a change of clothes here in the palace before we leave."

"That would be nice," Allisandra said. She peeled part of her blouse from her chest, and I noticed a thin raised line outlined against her neck, underneath her shirt. "But I couldn't take anything from the princess's rooms. Do you know where the servants' quarters are?"

I looked at Princess Laersa, expecting her to chime in. But she stayed silent, touching her temple with her free hand. She must have been nursing quite the headache.

I sighed. "If we find something, ambassador, then we'll stop so you can change. Does that sound good?"

Allisandra nodded, and both women let me lead them down the corridor.

For the most part, I navigated the palace hallways successfully. There were a few times that I lost my way and we had to retrace our steps, but it didn't happen too often. Princess Laersa, claiming a headache, didn't tell me the correct paths to choose. Despite her lack of assistance, we did find a servants' area that had some plain linen clothing the ambassador could use. Princess Laersa and I waited outside while Allisandra changed.

The ambassador stepped out of the room, her arms open wide to show off her new clothing. "Well? What do you think?"

"It looks good," I said. "You look like you're from here."

Kind of. Allisandra's fair hair would still cause her to stick out in a country of mostly dark-haired people. And I noticed that she had picked another high-collared shirt. Whatever that raised line on her neck was, it was hidden now. Perhaps she was self-conscious about a scar?

We left the servants' area and continued walking through the palace. Eventually, we found ourselves near the throne room.

Princess Laersa pointed. "There's the exit!" She started to walk faster, passing me. The ambassador followed.

"He's not here," I blurted out without thinking.

The princess paused, turning back to give me a quizzical look. "Who's not here?"

"King Tahrin," I said, waving at the throne room's entryway.

Princess Laersa blinked. "Oh." She sounded slightly confused, as if wondering why I was telling her this. "Well, I'm sure we'll find him later. Let's go."

She continued down the hallway, exiting through the destroyed front gate into the Annlyn sunshine.

31

CHAPTER THIRTY-ONE

OUTSIDE, PRINCESS LAERSA, AMBASSADOR Allisandra, and I stood before the shimmery barrier, trapped on the castle side, while Lady Farrah gazed at us from the city side.

"How are we going to get through?" I wondered.

Lady Farrah said, "The wards I placed on you should still be active, Endri."

I looked at the princess and the ambassador. "But what about them?" I paused as an idea occurred to me. "If I'm touching them, my ward should protect them as well, right?"

Lady Farrah frowned. "In theory. I didn't specify that in the spell, which would have ensured that."

"I guess there's only one way to find out."

With Princess Laersa on my right and Ambassador Allisandra on my left, we held hands and stepped through the barrier together.

Please hold, I silently pleaded to my wards. *Please hold*.

As before, the magic of the barrier prodded at me, trying to find any weak spot. But fortunately, the wards held.

Until they didn't.

We were halfway through the barrier when I felt Lady Farrah's magic falter. The ward, already spread thin trying to protect three people, shattered.

The insidious barrier magic rushed in, flooding my body and constricting my chest. I doubled over, wheezing and coughing.

"Endri!" I heard Lady Farrah cry out. And then, "Ow!" She must have tried to reach into the barrier to grab me, and failed.

And then I could breathe again. I looked up to see Ambassador Allisandra's free hand out, holding the barrier magic at bay. Whatever she had done had made it loosen its grip on me, but from the sweat running down her forehead, I knew she wouldn't be able to hold her ward for long.

"Hurry, hurry!" she panted.

I pushed forward, although all I wanted to do was fall to my knees and rest. A few more steps, and the three of us were away from the barrier's clutches. Now that we were safe, I did fall to my knees, trying to catch my breath.

A hand reached down to me. Feeling stronger, I grabbed it and let Ambassador Allisandra help me stand.

"Are you all right?" she asked me, concerned.

"Because of you, I am," I said. "Thank you."

The ambassador smiled. "Any time."

From a few steps ahead, Princess Laersa's cheerful voice floated back to us. "Hey! Aren't you coming?"

We walked through Annlyn's capital unchallenged. Princess Laersa kept up a steady, unflagging pace down the cobblestone streets as Lady Farrah, Ambassador Allisandra, and I trailed along behind her.

At the front gates, Princess Laersa stopped short at the sight of the blockade. Even though there was a narrow path for us to get through, the area was still a bit cluttered. She sniffed in disapproval. "What is all this?"

"It's the blockade—or, what's left of it." I kept my voice carefully neutral.

"Blockade? Why would this gate need to be blocked? How did it get here?"

I gave the princess a funny look. "We put it here, together. Don't you remember?"

She frowned, then touched her forehead in a gesture that was quickly becoming way too familiar. "I must have forgotten."

As the four of us picked our way through the overturned carts, heavy wagons, and random barrels and boxes, I said, "Are you sure you're all right, princess?"

She paused, considering. "I thought so, but ..." She massaged her temples. "I'm having trouble remembering."

Outside the city's gates, the princess paused again. "Which way do we go, again?"

I refrained from commenting on her memory issues. Instead, I pointed towards the tree line, and the mountain beyond. "That way."

For someone who claimed she didn't know where we were headed, she marched with surprising confidence into the forest. Soon she disappeared from view.

"She's a bold one, I'll give her that," Ambassador Allisandra said.

Lady Farrah clicked her tongue and shook her head. Sighing, she started forward.

I put a hand on her arm. "Wait, Lady Farrah."

The noblewoman didn't say anything, but merely raised a curious eyebrow at me. Allisandra, also curious, stayed where she was and waited for me to speak.

"I know I said earlier that I don't know Princess Laersa very well, but now I'm beginning to worry." I spoke in a low voice, even though the loud rustling sounds ahead told me the princess was well out of earshot. Or at least, making so much noise that she wouldn't be able to overhear my conversation with Lady Farrah and Ambassador Allisandra. "I'm surprised she didn't remember us putting together the barrier at the gates. Or which way Joichan's cave is. If that black fog is indeed the Shadow you've encountered before, I was wondering—is forgetting things common for its victims?"

Lady Farrah frowned thoughtfully in the direction that Princess Laersa had gone. "The last time ... when the Shadow possessed someone, they couldn't recall what happened while the Shadow was working through their body. That's when the headaches would hit them, but they would feel fine once they stopped trying to remember those moments under the Shadow's influence.

"But the Shadow's victims *only* had trouble remembering what they did while possessed. They could easily recall things that happened before, or after, as long as the Shadow was not in control of them at those times."

"Huh." I mulled over Lady Farrah's words. "So, since Princess Laersa can't seem to remember *anything*—should we be worried?"

"I'm not sure. It's possible she's in shock, and this is just a way of dealing with everything. If so, it should be temporary, and she'll be back to her normal self soon."

"I hope so." I pursed my lips. "And if it's not? Temporary, I mean."

Lady Farrah blew out a breath, her expression grim. "Then we have much more to worry about—new things from the Shadow. And its master."

Our conversation finished, she headed into the trees. Ambassador Allisandra gave me a sympathetic smile before she, too, started after Lady Farrah and Princess Laersa. I sighed noisily and threw my hands up in the air, exasperated, before following.

The three of us easily caught up to Princess Laersa, who wasn't even trying to hide the sounds of her passage through the forest. Not that we had to worry about the black fog—*yet*, I thought, as I eyed the position of the sun in the sky nervously—but there were other things in the area that we didn't want to notice us.

Like the gryphons in their cave, somewhere in the area. Which Princess Laersa also didn't remember, when I brought it up to her.

We were near the river, a good indication we were about halfway to our destination. I insisted on a brief rest, at least for Lady Farrah, Allisandra, and me. The lavender-haired noblewoman and the blond ambassador were both made of surprisingly stern stuff. Neither of them had complained about the walk one bit. But I could tell Lady Farrah's energy was flagging, probably a result of all the magic she had expended earlier. Allisandra seemed to have recovered faster from her magic use at the barrier, but she didn't protest when I suggested we stop.

Lady Farrah gratefully sat down on a fallen log near the water. The ambassador started examining the area plants and trees, no doubt curious at the landscape which was so different from her home kingdom's. Princess Laersa paced back and forth impatiently.

"Aren't you tired at all?" I wondered. I was getting antsy just watching her—not conducive to a much-needed break.

"Not really," the princess said.

"How is your headache?"

Her right hand flew to her head, as if she had forgotten she had been in pain earlier. "Oh! Better. But still there, a little."

I patted the ground next to me. "Sit and rest. That might help."

She did as I suggested, but was still so fidgety that it made me anxious again. Finally, I jumped up. I held out my hands to the three women. "I'll refill our water skins, then we can get going."

Lady Farrah and Princess Laersa both handed me their water skins, but Ambassador Allisandra said, "Oh, there's no need for that. Let me help you."

We headed the few feet to the river. Kneeling, I bent over the water as Allisandra handed me an empty water skin to refill. Once I was finished, I exchanged the full one for another empty one. I was careful as I refilled each one. The water didn't look particularly deep here, but we didn't have time to spare for a detour if I accidentally fell in. Which would be bad, since I couldn't swim. Besides, I didn't want to finish our walk to Joichan's cave looking and feeling like a drowned rat.

The ambassador walked away, holding three newly refilled water skins.

"Endri."

Princess Laersa's unexpected voice made me jump, and I nearly did fall in the water. As it was, I dropped the water skin I was holding, and for a few frantic moments, scrambled to get it back before it floated away. Once the water skin—and I—were secure, I looked up. "Yes, Your Highness?"

The princess shifted her weight from one foot to another, looking slightly annoyed. "Are you done yet?"

I held back a sigh. "I have one more water skin to fill, and then we can get going."

"Oh, good."

I expected her to walk away, maybe go talk to Lady Farrah or Allisandra, but instead she hovered near me, on the edge of the water. Just waiting for me to finish, I supposed. Well, the sooner I was done, the sooner we could leave.

I leaned back out over the water, then froze, unsure that what I was seeing was true.

With the angle of the sun overhead—and slightly at our backs—I could see my distorted shadow in the moving water of the river. A medium-sized darkened blob to reflect my head and shoulders, and a smaller one to my right where my hand and part of my arm extended, holding the last water skin.

But where Princess Laersa stood, there was no shadow at all. The area that should have been darker in the river sparkled a clear, deep blue-green, a twin to my tourmaline soulstone.

"Hurry up, Endri."

Princess Laersa's words snapped me out of my musings. I filled up the final water skin, taking my time so I could observe the princess and our surroundings without being too obvious.

Maybe it was just a trick of the light. Maybe I hadn't seen what I thought I had seen. I was still exhausted, after all, and my eyes had that gritty, heavy feeling that signaled a lack of sleep. That must be it—my overly tired eyes.

But as we left the river and continued towards the mountain that housed Joichan's cave, I made a mental note to ask Lady Farrah about it.

And to keep an eye on the princess.

32

— · —

CHAPTER THIRTY-TWO

THE MOON HAD RISEN by the time the four of us reached the base of the mountain. We started up the path towards the cave.

Lady Farrah eyed the moonlit trail. "I don't suppose this goes all the way to Joichan's cave, does it?"

"Unfortunately, no," I said.

The lavender-haired woman sighed. "It's never that easy." She side-eyed me. "You sure you can't transform into your dragon self at will yet?"

Ambassador Allisandra looked at me sharply, but didn't comment.

"I can try." My fingers crept around the ice dragon figurine in my pocket, which was quickly becoming my magical security blanket. "But I can't guarantee anything."

"I wish Jennica was here." She blinked a few times, and I realized she was trying to hold back tears. "Well, I guess that leaves us two options. We'll either have to climb once this trail ends, or I can try to levitate us up to the cave. But that's quite a distance."

I could hear the ragged weariness in her voice. Hastily, I said, "I can try shapeshifting. I could use the practice, anyway."

"All right." There was a faint note of relief in Lady Farrah's voice. "And if it doesn't work, or you can't stay in your second form long enough, then we can try levitation."

"Agreed."

We started up the path in silence. Any energy Lady Farrah and I had regained from our earlier rest was definitely now gone. I couldn't wait to get back to Joichan's cave and rest. From the way Lady Farrah moved and sounded, I guessed she was feeling the same way.

The ambassador also seemed tired, or perhaps she was just lost in her thoughts. Being so far from home—and getting caught up in some strange goings-on in a strange land—must have weighed heavily on her.

Princess Laersa, on the other hand, seemed to have boundless energy. Despite not resting at the river, and the hours we had spent walking here, she acted completely unfazed and not tired at all.

Finally, to break the quiet, I commented to Allisandra, "I'm sorry you got caught up in all this. When all the transformations started happening, why didn't you leave Annlyn?"

The ambassador shrugged. "Honestly? I didn't know what was happening around me, at first. And then, once I realized everyone was changing—it didn't seem safe to go into the streets. Not to mention, I couldn't be sure if my horse at the stable was truly a horse, or some poor shapeshifting soul I had captured and forced to take me to Graenir. It just seemed like a better idea to hide in the palace and hope for the best."

That didn't seem like a good idea to me, but perhaps, as an ambassador, she was bound to certain rules.

Lady Farrah stopped walking and looked up. "Well, I guess it's try-and-see time."

We had reached the end of the walking path. Now that we were higher up the mountain, and away from the trees, we could see the nighttime sky in all its glory, with the moon and stars winking down at us.

But that also meant we were more exposed. I looked up and around, wary.

Lady Farrah noticed my caution. "What is it?"

"Nothing, for now," I said. "It's just ... the last time Princess Laersa and I were here, that black cloud was after us. If I can't transform, and we have to climb ... I don't like being such an easy target."

"Of course." She tilted her head, considering. "I can try to either ward us from attack, or cast a spell so we aren't so noticeable. But if I do that, I don't think I can *also* levitate any of us to get to the cave. It would have to be one or the other. And we'd only get one chance at it, before I completely drain my magic reserves."

"Right. So it's ice dragon or nothing. Got it. No pressure." I gripped the figurine in one hand, while touching my tourmaline soulstone with the other. "Uh, you three might want to back up a little."

Lady Farrah and Ambassador Allisandra both heeded my warning, moving back a few paces away to give me room. Princess Laersa stayed where she was, just by my side. Fine for my human self, but uncomfortably close if I became a dragon and knocked her off the mountain with a flailing wing. *That would be hard to explain to her father. Assuming we can even find and turn King Tahrin—and everyone else—back.*

I cleared my throat and gave Princess Laersa a pointed look, but she still didn't move. Ah, well. It wasn't like this was going to work, anyway.

Turning away slightly, I put the three women firmly out of my mind. Instead, I concentrated on the magic flowing through me, bolstered by my tourmaline and the carving. I didn't have much sense of what it felt like to become my second self—before, it had all happened so suddenly that I hadn't had time to really study what was going on with my body as it transformed. Eventually I would have to be aware of how that change felt.

But instead, I focused on how it felt to be an ice dragon. How it felt to be in a larger, wider body, one that was built for power and flight, not speed or limited strength. The sensation of soaring through the air, the wind rippling over my scales. How my dragon form carried an undercurrent of constant coolness to it, a welcome relief in Annlyn, the warm, southernmost country in the Gifted Lands. And that ever-present—but not unpleasant—tickle in my throat, signaling the chilly breath I could call forth almost without thinking.

Although—thinking about that made me feel itchy. Not in my throat, though—along my shoulder blades.

And now that I was aware of that feeling, it wouldn't stop. I was reluctant to let go of either of my magical lifelines, but, *my gods,* was my back itchy.

Releasing my hold on the dragon miniature, I flexed my back slightly and then reached over to scratch one of my shoulder blades.

Or, I should say, tried to scratch. But I couldn't quite reach it. My arms were the wrong length, and where my shoulder blade had been, a large blue wing now protruded from it.

I straightened my arm, bringing it in front of my face so I could look at it. My smooth tan skin was now a leathery, pale blue. And scaly.

Examining my other arm, I saw the same transformation had taken place.

I laughed, the sound deep and wheezy since it was now coming from a bigger chest. My back was still itchy, but I had no good way of scratching it. I reared up a little and shook myself all over.

Lady Farrah reached out, hastily grabbing Princess Laersa's arm. Allisandra backed up even more.

"Huh?" The princess, who was still standing nearby, blinked in confusion as Lady Farrah drew her away from me.

Magnificent blue wings unfurled at my sides, one swishing through the air where Princess Laersa had just been. The itchy feeling faded from my back.

"Oh," I heard the princess say.

That's a rather disappointing, lackluster response, I thought. Although only a small part of my mind registered what Princess Laersa said. The majority of my attention was on the fact that *I actually did it! I transformed into an ice dragon!*

I blew out an experimental breath, marveling at the pale-colored air that shot from my mouth. Small ice crystals formed instantly, even though the night air in Annlyn was, as usual, too warm for ice or snow.

"Endri!" Lady Farrah spoke loudly to get my attention.

I turned my scaly head in the direction of her voice. Seeing my singular attention, she gulped, but that was the only sign of discomfort she showed. "Endri. Can you understand me?"

I nodded, much slower than I would have in my human form. This dragon head was not only large, it was heavy.

"Good. Do you think you can carry all three of us up to Joichan's cave?"

That I wasn't sure about. I opened my mouth, wanting to say that, but no sounds would come out. At least, nothing a human could understand. Lady Farrah waited patiently. Princess Laersa seemed remarkably unaffected at the sight of me, in my ice dragon form, trying to talk.

Since I couldn't speak human language, I shook my head. *No.* Then I nodded. *Yes.* I gave Lady Farrah a beseeching look, hoping she understood.

She didn't. Her brow furrowed and she said, "So ... does that mean you can? Or you can't?"

Could dragons shrug? I attempted it, but my back structure didn't work that way.

I could tell from Lady Farrah's expression that she still wasn't sure what I was trying to convey. "Hmm. Well, are you at least willing to try it?"

That I could answer. I nodded.

"All right, then." She stepped closer, waving at me to crouch down. I obeyed, lowering myself as close to the ground as I could without toppling over. I still wasn't used to this new body.

Lady Farrah climbed on my back with surprising ease—or maybe not so surprising, considering her arrival on Queen Jennica's back—and then held out a hand to Princess Laersa. "Come, princess."

But the princess shook her head. "I don't think there's enough room for all of us."

"I agree," Allisandra said. "Perhaps for two of us, but not all three."

Lady Farrah frowned as she surveyed my back. "I suppose you're right. I'll go first, and if anything goes wrong ... well, let's just hope nothing goes wrong."

That didn't sound like a vote of confidence to me, but then again, I wasn't risking as much as Lady Farrah in this test flight. I felt the noblewoman's hands tighten on my back. "Whenever you're ready, Endri."

I backed up a few paces—nearly to the mountain edge—and looked up. Crouching low, I tensed.

And then I sprung.

33

— ◦ —

CHAPTER THIRTY-THREE

I LEAPT GRACEFULLY INTO the air, my powerful hind legs giving me added momentum as my blue wings unfurled, propelling me to a greater height. A long, triumphant plume of frosty air shot from my mouth, a lance of pure ice piercing the night sky before melting away in the balmy Annlyn air.

That was how I imagined my flight going, anyway.

The actuality was rather disappointing.

Lady Farrah, sitting astride my back, added an unexpected weight that I wasn't accustomed to. In addition, my human mind was unsure how to gauge distance in my much larger dragon body. I moved back a little too far, and as I jumped into the air, one of my feet slipped off the edge of the mountain path.

Taken off guard, I swayed slightly, trying to find my balance while flying. Lady Farrah yelped and her hands dug into my scales, a sudden sensation of sharp nails. I hissed at the pain.

"Sorry." Even though she was apologizing, she didn't sound sorry. "I nearly fell off, there."

Since human speech wouldn't come from my new throat, I settled for a low sort of growl, soft enough that I hoped Lady Farrah wouldn't mistake it for hostility.

The noblewoman giggled. "Are you *purring*, Endri?"

The thought of me purring like an overgrown blue cat made me snicker. My soft growl ended in an icy snort.

The grip of Lady Farrah's hands on my back eased a bit. "Are you feeling more steady, Endri?"

I nodded—a little too vigorously, as I felt Lady Farrah's hands tighten on my back again—and then held myself still. Well, as still as I could be, hovering mid-air. Nearby, Princess Laersa watched Lady Farrah and me, her expression curiously unreadable.

Lady Farrah patted my back. "Good. Let's go, then."

I gave my wings an experimental flap, feeling pleased with myself when I floated a few inches higher. With renewed confidence, I flapped my wings again, enjoying the sensation of air lifting me.

We glided up the mountain face, and soon we were outside Joichan's cave. I landed on the ledge, making sure my claws were firmly gripping the rock before I crouched down to allow Lady Farrah to climb off my back.

She put a proud hand on my shoulder. "Good job, Endri. You picked up flying—and shapeshifting—quickly."

I snorted a puff of cold air.

"No, really," Lady Farrah said, correctly interpreting my snort as laughter. "It took Jennica much longer to figure it out. And she wasn't learning it under duress, like you. *And* she also had Joichan to help her. So, really. You're doing quite well."

I gave her a skeptical side-eye. It was unexpectedly much easier to do so in dragon form than in human form.

"I know you're going for intimidating, but you actually look kind of funny." The noblewoman giggled, then waved me away. "Go get Princess Laersa and Ambassador Allisandra so we can all settle into Joichan's cave and rest for a bit."

She sighed. "And then we have a lot to talk about."

I nodded once, then stepped off the ledge and flew back down to where Princess Laersa and the ambassador still waited on the mountain path. Flying down went much faster—or maybe, like Lady Farrah had said, I really was learning how to be a dragon quickly.

I landed on the rocky path a few paces away from Princess Laersa and Allisandra. The princess stood near the mountain's edge, gazing out at the night sky. Perhaps she was keeping a lookout for the black fog?

Hearing my talons clicking against the gravel, she turned to me.

"Ah, you're back." She sounded surprisingly serene, considering full night had fallen, the black cloud could return at any time, and she was standing in the unprotected open. "Shall we?"

I snorted, thinking, *I really will never understand her.* But I obligingly lowered myself closer to the ground so she and Allisandra could climb onto my back.

Princess Laersa placed a hand on my back, readying herself to jump up.

Involuntarily, I hissed and recoiled with sudden anxiety.

The princess removed her hand and looked at me, head tilted in curiosity. "Endri? Are you all right?"

I think so? Oh my gods—I'm not sure. But I couldn't say any of that, so I just nodded slightly and stayed low, an unspoken invitation to Princess Laersa to continue.

She paused, but then reached out to me again. I ground my teeth, fighting against the new wave of unexplained panic. My mind was confused, wondering at my body's strong reaction. I wanted to run, to roar, to hide—anything to get rid of this crippling anxiety that threatened to drive me insane. But the rational part of me kept thinking, *There's nothing to fear here. What is wrong with me?*

After the princess settled atop my back, Allisandra scrambled up after her. The unsettled feeling was now crawling over every part of my body, and it took all I had to focus on the next thing I needed to do.

Step back once, then again.

Was my claw shaking?

Turn slightly so I was facing the right direction.

Why did it feel like my heart was going to burst from my chest?

Shift my weight slightly onto my hind legs, so I would have power behind my jump into the air.

Oh my gods, I couldn't breathe. Black was beginning to creep in the edges of my eyesight. Maybe I couldn't handle more than one passenger at a time?

Calm down, Endri. Calm down. You can do this. You've done it once already, and you were fine.

I leapt forward, my takeoff into the air much more graceful than my original flight with Lady Farrah had been. My wings found the air currents that would take me higher, lifting me with ease.

I began breathing easier. Maneuvering around in my dragon form really wasn't that hard. I was definitely getting the knack for it.

We were climbing steadily up the mountain face, towards Joichan's brightly lit cave, where Lady Farrah waited on the ledge.

Now, all I had to do was figure out how to shapeshift faster and on purpose, and I would be all set.

Nearly there. Just a few more moments, and I could land, let Princess Laersa and Allisandra off my back, and then shift back into my human self.

And get rid of this nervous feeling that would not go away.

Surely, since I had the flying thing down, the shapeshifting thing would be—

We had reached the ledge. I was about to land, when Princess Laersa gripped my scales a little harder than she had been previously holding on. Pain flared along my right wing, concentrated in the spot of my mostly healed injury.

A thundering roar ripped from my throat as I screamed, the panicked feeling rising up full force, and lost control of my body. My wings fell limp at my sides.

The last thing I saw was Lady Farrah's horrified face as she watched me drop like a stone.

34

Chapter Thirty-Four

Something soft tickled my face. I tried to brush it away, but it kept returning.

Twitching my nose, I groaned and turned over on my left side in an attempt to get away from whatever kept brushing my cheek. But it hurt when I did so—and my right side wasn't much better. The ground underneath me felt hard and unyielding, and the air was colder than it had been earlier. But I didn't feel a breeze.

Groaning again, I opened my eyes. The rock walls of Joichan's cave met my bleary gaze. Confused, I turned again, laying on my back.

Princess Laersa's face hovered above my own, her long black hair sweeping over my face randomly as she moved around.

"Princess Laersa?" My voice came out hoarse, and I realized I was extremely thirsty. "What ... what happened?"

"Oh, Endri. I'm glad you're awake. You were out for a while. A few hours, at least." Her voice—like her expression—was fairly neutral, as if she was discussing the weather, and not the fact that I had apparently been unconscious.

"A few *hours*?" I smacked my lips together, wishing there was water nearby. Princess Laersa just looked at me. Since she didn't seem inclined to do anything—besides stare at me—I spoke up. "Um. Could I get some water, please?"

"Of course." She stood up and surveyed the cave.

"The kitchen area is over there." I propped myself up on one elbow and waved a weak hand. "There should be cups and a pitcher on the side table."

"Ah, yes." She crossed the room as I lay back down. I could hear Princess Laersa rummaging around the cave, pouring some water, and then her light footsteps as she returned. She knelt down next to me, holding up a cup. "Here you go, Endri."

She helped me sit back up so I could take a careful sip. The overwhelming anxiety I had felt earlier was gone, replaced with a deep weariness. I felt a little queasy, but the water didn't affect my roiling stomach, so I downed the rest of the water.

Feeling a little bit better—and more awake—I asked again, "What happened?"

The princess took my now empty cup. "Would you like some more?" At my impatient head shake, she resettled herself, sitting cross-legged on the ground. "All right, then. What do you remember?"

"We were nearly to Joichan's cave," I said. "Then ... I started falling."

She nodded. "Yes, you did. There wasn't much Allisandra or I could do, except hold on and hope we didn't fall off. Or get crushed, if you fell on us. But Lady Farrah reached out, and shouted a spell of some sort. We stopped falling, and then began to rise up slowly until we were level with the ledge outside. Lady Farrah backed up, still holding us in her spell net, and brought us inside the cave."

"Huh." I looked around. "Where is Lady Farrah?"

"She's sleeping in the other room. Casting that spell—whatever it was—took a lot out of her. But don't worry, she said she would be fine once she rested a bit."

"That's good to hear. I ... I owe her a lot." Indeed, without the noblewoman's quick thinking, I could have easily gotten hurt, or even died. Not to mention the fall would have definitely harmed Princess Laersa and Ambassador Allisandra.

"I'm sure she knows." The princess glanced towards the front of the cave, where it was still dark out. "But for now, you should get some sleep."

I nodded, wincing at how much my head hurt when I did that. Princess Laersa helped me stand, then assisted me as I dragged myself over to the huge straw bed in the corner, where I had slept before. I yawned, feeling the weariness settle over me. "What about you?"

"I'm not tired just yet. But I'll go to sleep soon." The princess walked away, but instead of going back to the kitchen to drop off the dirty cup, she went to the front of the cave, stopping just shy of the magical barrier. The last view I had of her before sleep claimed me was of her staring into the distance.

A rustling sound woke me up. I groaned softly and sat up, looking around the cave through bleary eyes.

I must not have been asleep for that long—it was still night beyond the cave entrance. And, still standing where I had seen her last, was Princess Laersa.

As I watched, with horror creeping into my tired mind, the princess ran a long fingernail down the length of the magical barrier. It was eerily reminiscent of when the shadow man had done the same thing, but from the outside, trying to get in. A rip in the ward followed Princess Laersa's fingernail.

The princess had her back to me, with all her concentration on her task.

"Princess?" My voice echoed off the cave walls. "What are you doing?"

She whirled around at the sound of my voice.

I gasped as I got a good look at her face, and the rest of her body not covered by clothing.

Her brown eyes were sunken, and her formerly shiny black hair was dull and limp. Her skin, usually as tan as my own, was an odd greenish-gray color.

Worse, it looked like her flesh was falling from her body.

No, not falling off.

Melting.

Her dark eyes suddenly flashed red.

I screamed.

The princess opened her mouth, letting forth an inhuman wail. I wanted to clap my hands over my ears to muffle the sound, but I was also paralyzed by my fear.

Abandoning her task at the cave's ward, she took one step towards me. And another.

Then she sprang at me.

Aside from my meager shapeshifting abilities, I had no magical talent. And as I was still in the large straw bed, I had no weapons at hand.

Except for the straw I was sitting in.

I grabbed a fistful of straw, ready to fling it at Princess Laersa, even while I threw up my opposite arm to protect myself.

Then I heard a shout to my right. I didn't know the language, but I recognized a spell when I heard one.

A stream of purple fire hit Princess Laersa from the side.

And then another spell joined it, a yellow blast of energy. Ambassador Allisandra had also thrown some magic at the princess.

The colored flame engulfed Princess Laersa, making her already melting skin fall off even faster. I winced at the horrific sight.

"Lady Farrah! Ambassador!" I yelled. "Stop! You're hurting the princess!"

"That's. Not. The. Princess." Lady Farrah's spell didn't let up.

Ambassador Allisandra also renewed her magical attack.

The princess—or whoever she was—burned up in front of us. I would have expected her—it?—to turn into ashes on the spot, but instead she shriveled in on herself, becoming a mound of liquidy goo on the cave floor.

With the princess now gone, Lady Farrah ended her fire spell.

But above the ooze that had once been the princess, a semi-transparent dark person-shaped form rose up.

It hissed at the three of us, its red eyes shining with pure hatred.

35

CHAPTER THIRTY-FIVE

I GASPED. I HAD seen that face and form before.

The dark man.

The shadow.

It hissed again. Its hazy hands moved in a quick blur, and green light flared.

Lady Farrah yelled something and jumped in front of me. Nearby, I heard the ambassador yell something similar. Allisandra's hands were a blur as she weaved a complex spell, holding them out as if she was pushing the dark man away from her.

The green light arced through the air, directly at Lady Farrah's face, but then stopped just a hair's breadth from her nose. The spell bounced off the invisible wall, falling to the floor where it went off in a small shower of green and gray sparkles.

The creature hissed again, then darted towards the cave entrance.

And the hole it had created in the ward.

Lady Farrah swore as she ran forward, sending another blast of purple fire after it, but she was too late. The creature had been too quick, and it was now beyond her spell's reach.

"Should we go after it?" I asked, even as I was grabbing my boots and jacket.

Lady Farrah opened her mouth to speak, but whatever she was going to say was cut off by a low moan to my right.

I turned, my stomach clenching. Ambassador Allisandra was lying on the floor, curled up in pain.

I rushed to her side. Lady Farrah joined me a moment later.

"Ambassador, are you all right?" I asked.

Her voice came out in a whisper. "I ... didn't get my ward ... up fast enough. Ugh ... whatever that ... *thing* ... threw at you, I got ... hit by some of it."

Lady Farrah's face was grave. "Let's get you to the bedroom, where you'll be a little more comfortable. I'll look you over and do what healing I can."

Allisandra coughed weakly. "I just ... need rest."

"Of course. Can you stand?" At Allisandra's slight nod, Lady Farrah looked over at me. "Help me get her up."

Gingerly, we helped the ambassador stand. With Lady Farrah supporting her on one side and me on the other, Allisandra moved with slow, careful steps towards the bedroom in the far corner of Joichan's cave.

As the bedroom had primarily been used by the women of our group—first Princess Laersa, then Lady Farrah, and now Ambassador Allisandra—I hadn't been in this room yet, only seen it in passing. When I entered, I gave a little gasp. "It's so ... small!"

"Compared to the rest of the mountain cave, yes," Lady Farrah said, as we maneuvered Allisandra around the bed. "But don't forget, Joichan is a shapeshifter. Even if he didn't use it much, I'm sure it was nice to have at least one human-sized room and furnishings."

"Oh, that makes sense." I had forgotten the history of the man—and apparently dragon—who had once lived here.

I stepped back, allowing Allisandra to climb into the bed with a little help from Lady Farrah. The lavender-haired lady frowned. "Are you sure you don't want me to try any healing magic, Ambassador?"

"No, no, I'll be fine." Allisandra closed her eyes. "I just need sleep, please."

"Very well." Lady Farrah bustled out of the room, waving at me to follow her. After I had cleared the entryway, Lady Farrah quietly shut the door behind me. We walked a few paces away from the bedroom, keeping our voices low.

"What should we do now?" I asked. "Should one of us go after that shadow creature?"

Lady Farrah shook her head. "It's too late now. The trail will have gone cold. Besides, I don't relish the idea of being alone to face that thing."

I grimaced, secretly relieved. I didn't like the idea of facing that thing alone either, but if it had to be done, I would do it. Not happily, of course, but I would do it.

Lady Farrah sighed. "You may as well rest, for now. We can't leave the ambassador here alone, not while she's hurt." She threw a troubled glance towards the closed bedroom door. "I wish she hadn't turned down my offer of healing. Not only would it help her recover faster, it would ease my mind over what, exactly, is afflicting her. As it is, I can only guess."

"I've never known anyone to turn down healing before," I said. "Then again, I haven't been in many situations when healing magic would be needed. But I can't imagine why anyone would *not* want to be healed."

The noblewoman shrugged. "It's rare, but it happens. Usually my aid has been refused when the person is too far gone, and they know my magic won't make a difference. Graenir is a mysterious country;

they might have certain beliefs or customs that make the use of healing magic taboo."

"Maybe." I frowned. "But Ambassador Allisandra didn't seem to have a problem using magic. Like at the castle earlier, or defending herself just now and taking down Princess Laersa—or whatever that thing was."

"Who knows how the citizens of Graenir think? This is my first time encountering anyone from there."

"Likewise." I fell silent, thinking of the recent magical battle with the creature pretending to be the princess. "Speaking of magic—what was that creature wearing Princess Laersa's face? *Was* it the princess, possessed? Or was it something else?"

The thought that we may have killed the actual Princess Laersa made my stomach churn. So I felt a small measure of relief when Lady Farrah said, "It was not the real princess. It was a simulacrum, meant only to last for a day or less. But realistic enough to fool us into thinking it was the true Princess Laersa, and not a construct."

A lump of embarrassment formed in my throat. "I can't believe I didn't figure it out."

"Don't feel bad. It was a very well done construct; it would have fooled anyone."

"It explains so much, though. Why the princess couldn't seem to remember anything—"

"She knew who you were, though."

Remembering our conversation in the princess's chamber, I said, "Not until I gave her the information. But it was enough, I think."

A worry line creased Lady Farrah's forehead. "Which means whoever created the simulacrum not only took the time to animate it, but also pulled a few memories from the real Princess Laersa."

I immediately understood where Lady Farrah's train of thought was going. "Which means that whoever created the fake princess had access to the real one."

"And possibly still has access."

I looked towards the cave entrance. "How was it able to get in here? I thought the ward would stop anything with evil intent from entering."

Lady Farrah frowned. "The ward on this cave is old, and it's already been weakened once with a magical attack. And, if you invite the evil in, the ward can hardly protect you then, now can it?"

I hung my head. "I am so sorry, Lady Farrah."

She put a comforting hand on my shoulder. "You couldn't have known. It was a very good likeness." She bit her lip, thinking. "Out of curiosity, what else did you notice, but just dismiss?"

I thought back to my time spent with the false princess. "Besides her memory loss? Well, she acted so formal with me. I know she and I haven't known each other long, but from what I could tell, she's just more—free, I think, with people she likes and trusts. The real Princess Laersa strikes me as someone very inquisitive and bold, but when I found the false one in the palace, she hadn't even tried to open her door. She just waited for me to come rescue her. And—there was one more thing."

I paused, wondering if the sudden dread that had come over me in my dragon form was worth mentioning. When I didn't continue, Lady Farrah said encouragingly, "Yes?"

"When I was bringing her and the ambassador up to the cave—the minute she touched me, I felt anxious. Afraid. I wanted to run and hide—which seems like a silly feeling for a large ice dragon to have. It took all of my self-control not to throw off my riders and fly away."

Lady Farrah nodded, as if she had been expecting this. "It makes sense—you were in your animal form, and so your instincts would have been sharper than usual. Your dragon self sensed danger, and it was only because you were rationalizing against your fear—as a human would—that you didn't give in to that instinct."

"Oh." I blinked in surprise. "I never would have thought of that."

"I think, as you shapeshift more often, you'll find that some of those good traits—like an animal's instinct—will seep into your human side." She chuckled. "And of course, the opposite is also true. You'll have to curb any bad animal habits that come up as well."

She paused, considering. "Most animals have more raw power at their disposal than humans do, perhaps because they're not fighting against that innate instinct. Humans often rationalize their power away, or channel it into other things. I wonder if people would be much stronger if we just followed our instincts as well?"

Lady Farrah looked at the cave entrance, where the tear in the ward was plainly visible. "I'll have to repair that, eventually. I'm not looking forward to it. Maybe if Allisandra recovers quickly, she can help me."

"I can stay nearby in case the ambassador needs anything," I offered.

"Thank you. I'll relieve you in a bit. But for now, I need to make a call."

36

CHAPTER THIRTY-SIX

LADY FARRAH STEPPED OUT on the ledge, probably to get a little bit of privacy to make her call. Before she created her calling spell, however, she threw a spell net of some sort at the cave entrance. A shower of light purple sparks glittered in the night, and then settled over the doorway.

Probably some sort of temporary ward, I thought, and then turned away to survey the cave.

The liquid mess that had formerly been the false Princess Laersa was still in the middle of the floor. Except now it had congealed into some sort of sticky glob. Disgusting. I didn't even want to think about what the simulacrum had been made of.

Sighing, I rummaged through the cupboards, looking for a bucket and a shovel so I could scoop up the construct's remains and throw it out of the cave. I briefly debated burning the mess, but since it hadn't burned up in the magical attack, I doubted it would burn at all.

I eventually found what I needed and turned back to the goo. Kneeling down, I gagged when I got a good whiff of it. It smelled like burnt and moldy bread—not a pleasant combination. I turned my face away, trying to get a breath of fresh air.

It was around this time that I realized it was extremely quiet in the cave. I wasn't expecting any sounds from the bedroom—Ambassador Allisandra should be fast asleep by now.

But I couldn't even hear a low murmur from Lady Farrah's conversation outside. Looking over, I could see her standing on the ledge, palm upturned as she spoke earnestly with the image of a man—most likely her intended, I guessed. But I couldn't hear a word of what she was saying.

Hmm. That spell net must have been more than just a temporary fix for the ward. It must have muffled the sound, too.

I shrugged. Whatever she and her betrothed wanted to talk about, it was none of my business. I turned back to the mess I planned to clean up. My current business was distasteful.

I put my sleeve to my nose, breathing shallowly in an attempt not to pass out from the smell. My cleanup efforts were slow going—I had to stop several times to avoid passing out from the odor—but I eventually got it done.

By the time I scooped the last of the pungent goop into the bucket, Lady Farrah had finished her call and walked back inside.

She wrinkled her nose as she came closer. "Oh, that is horrible. I wonder why we didn't notice it before?"

"I'm not sure, but it's getting worse." I stood, indicating the bucket. "You have great timing. If you'll excuse me?"

Lady Farrah waved me away, just as eager as I was to be rid of the bucket's smelly contents. I practically ran out of the cave, tipping the bucket over the ledge. I felt bad for any animals that happened to be down below. They were going to get a nasty surprise.

My thankless task finished, I walked back inside. Lady Farrah sat at the table, her head down on her folded arms.

"Is everything okay, Lady Farrah?" I asked.

She startled at my voice, then sat up straight and yawned. "Yes, yes, it's fine, Endri. Thank you for asking."

I sat down at the table with her. "How did they take it back home when you told them what's happened?"

Lady Farrah's grim countenance said it all, before she even spoke a word. "King Beyan is, understandably, distraught. He was ready to come down here himself, if he thought it would help. Rhyss had to talk him out of it."

She chuckled, and her face softened at the mention of her intended. "Never thought I'd see the day when Rhyss would be the voice of reason."

I chuckled too, even though I didn't get the joke. Lady Farrah had an infectious laugh.

"I did mention that the Graenir ambassador was with us," Lady Farrah continued. "I asked Beyan to contact his in-laws, Joichan and Melandria, who are currently living in Graenir as Calia's ambassadors. I thought Joichan and Melandria could give us more insights into Graenir customs, so there will be no more accidental breaches of etiquette." She grimaced. "And doing that research for me will give Beyan something to do while we work on getting Jennica back."

"I look forward to what your friend the king has to say," I said sincerely. I always found learning about the other kingdoms fascinating, perhaps because I had never really traveled outside of Annlyn. Maybe if—*When!* I chided myself. *Think positively!*—this whole craziness was resolved, I could travel around the Gifted Lands more.

And besides, I thought, brightening. *I have wings now. That should make getting around the Gifted Lands* much *easier.*

"So now what?" I wondered.

Lady Farrah sighed and looked towards the closed bedroom door. "We just wait, for now. Once Allisandra wakes up—and hopefully feels better—we can figure out our plans from there."

"All right." I waved at the large straw bed in the corner. "Would you like the bed?"

Lady Farrah looked at the dragon nest and shuddered. "No, thank you. I'll be much more comfortable here."

And with that, she put her head back down on the table.

I shrugged and climbed into the straw.

37

Chapter Thirty-Seven

I OPENED MY EYES to see several rays of sunlight streaking across the cave floor. Lady Farrah was already up and moving about.

Yawning, I sat up and stretched, then got out of the big straw nest to join her. "Did you sleep well?"

She grimaced. "I lied. It was not more comfortable sleeping at the table." She turned her neck this way and that, trying to stretch out the stiffness.

"Sorry to hear that. Do you know if Ambassador Allisandra is awake yet?"

As if she had heard me, the bedroom door opened. The ambassador stood in the doorway, looking much better than she had the previous night.

"Good morning, everyone," she said cheerfully.

"You look well," Lady Farrah said. "How are you feeling?"

"Good as new," the ambassador said. "And ready to take on that creature who so rudely put me under last night. Where shall we start?"

Lady Farrah frowned. "I suppose we could return to Annlyn, to see if there are any more leads." But she sounded doubtful.

I bit my lip, thinking back to Pazho's investigation. "Before Pazho—and the rest of Annlyn—disappeared, he went into the hills north of the capital to investigate something. One of our neighbors reported seeing a bunch of animals in the area, obviously transformed, without their soulstones. So they had no way to shift back."

The ambassador raised an eyebrow. "That sounds promising."

"I agree," said Lady Farrah. "Do you know where, exactly, Pazho went to investigate?"

"Hmm ... Mistress Laina—that's the neighbor who came to Pazho for help—said it was where Fan the shepherdess would bring the sheep to graze." I paused, trying to picture the area in my head. "I thnk I can find it. If I remember right, that should be near Lake Vitrum."

"Good. Let's have some breakfast, and then let's get going."

"So. How do you propose we get there?"

Lady Farrah and Ambassador Allisandra both looked at me as if I had grown two heads. "By flying, of course," they said as one.

"Of course." I sighed. "Easy for you to say. You're not the ones still trying to master your shapeshifting ability."

The three of us were standing on the ledge, surveying the land in the morning sunshine. In the distance, Annlyn's capital city looked peaceful and quiet, although the shimmery bubble still surrounded the castle. Beyond Annlyn, Lake Vitrum sparkled invitingly, nestled in between the gentle hills.

"Is it really that difficult?" Ambassador Allisandra wondered.

"Yes. No. I don't know." I touched my tourmaline soulstone. "It still doesn't come as easily or naturally as I'd like."

"You're getting better at it each time," Lady Farrah said encouragingly. "And if I may suggest something ..."

Something about her tone told me I wouldn't like her suggestion. "Yes?"

The lavender-haired woman coughed delicately. "You seem to do well when you transform under pressure."

I blinked. "Meaning?"

"Meaning, when you're in a stressful situation, you're able to change into your dragon form with no problem. Maybe because you're not thinking too hard about it."

Ambassador Allisandra clapped her hands. "A brilliant idea!"

I glared at her. "So I should learn to transform by jumping off this ledge?"

"Or we could push you." Even though her eyes twinkled, I couldn't quite tell if she was joking or not.

"I think I'll take my chances with jumping." I eyed the distance from the ledge to the ground. Even if I fell to the mountain path and not the longer distance to the forest floor, it was still a long way to fall. I turned to Lady Farrah. "Perhaps, just to be safe, we could—"

But I didn't get to finish my thought.

Without warning, the ledge underneath my feet crumbled, the rocks tumbling down the mountainside.

And I was now following those rocks down the same unfortunate path.

I heard Lady Farrah give a shout, and felt her magic surround me. A ward appeared, like I had tried to ask her for before I fell. But unlike the last time she had aided me, the ward did not slow my descent.

And the rocky mountain path was approaching fast....

Why didn't Lady Farrah's magic work? Maybe she was still exhausted? But I didn't have time to puzzle that out now. Not when I was about to meet a brutal and quick end right below Joichan's cave.

I grabbed my soulstone and closed my eyes. In what was part hasty shapeshifting and part desperate prayer, I poured every bit of concentration I could muster into my tourmaline pendant.

The jewel warmed under my touch, and then frosted over.

And suddenly I was no longer clutching my soulstone with long, smooth fingers. Instead, I was delicately holding it between two long, sharp claws.

I opened my eyes. The rocky ground was just moments away.

With effort, I pulled myself back into the air. My serpentine belly barely grazed the path as I shot upwards.

Now that I was securely aloft, I flew back to the ledge where I had left Lady Farrah and Ambassador Allisandra behind.

Tears streamed down Lady Farrah's face as the ambassador put an arm around her, trying to console her. "Endri! Thank the gods you're all right! When you fell—and my magic couldn't save you—I thought for sure we had lost you."

Since I was now in dragon form, I couldn't respond. So I flapped my large blue wings to show her I was all right.

Ambassador Allisandra patted Lady Farrah's shoulder. "It could happen to anyone, Lady Farrah. Exhaustion can be hard on a mage."

I hovered near the ledge. Lady Farrah placed a hand on my scales, shaking her head as she climbed atop my back. "I've cast harder spells on less sleep. Perhaps my spells have been less powerful when I've done that, but they've never completely failed."

She held a hand out to the ambassador. Allisandra took it, clambering up behind the noblewoman.

"Who knows why things choose to fail when they do?" Allisandra said. "If you need to rest, I'm happy to take over any spell casting. My magic might not be as powerful as yours, but it's good for basic tasks."

With both women securely on my back, I pushed away from the ledge and started flying towards the hills north of Annlyn.

Lady Farrah's response to the ambassador was drowned out by a sudden roaring in my ears. I breathed in the morning air as deep as I could, trying to calm myself. At least I could now recognize the stirrings of panic within me. My breathing began to even out, and the roaring sound subsided.

I felt better, but I still didn't know why I felt anxious at all. What had caused that primal fear instinct in my animal self to flare up again?

38

—·—

CHAPTER THIRTY-EIGHT

I WAS ABLE TO keep my anxious feeling at bay for the rest of the flight to the hills surrounding Lake Vitrum. Fortunately, it was also a short flight.

A small bit of the morning mist still clung to the ground as I landed in the grassy field. I crouched down, letting my passengers dismount. First Allisandra, then Lady Farrah, jumped down from my back, both women wandering a little way off to explore the area.

Instantly my anxiety subsided. Perhaps my dragon self really hated ferrying passengers.

Concentrating on shifting forms, the air around me shimmered briefly. Soon my human self stood with the two women.

I walked over to where Lady Farrah was studying the ground. From her intensity, I surmised she had found something fascinating.

I looked at the area she was examining, then back at her, uncomprehending. "Do you see anything interesting?"

"Actually, yes." She pointed at something invisible—to me, at least—on the ground.

I blinked, confused. "Um ... whatever it is you're looking at, I'm not seeing it."

She chuckled. "I forget that not everyone spends all their time in the wilderness."

Oh, that was right—Lady Farrah had told me that she used to work as a mercenary-for-hire, and had traveled all over the Gifted Lands. "I suppose hunting and tracking are useful skills, in your former line of work."

"Exactly. If you don't hunt, you don't eat." She turned her attention back to the ground. "And what I see here are footprints. Lots of them. Some are from animals I recognize—here's a few rabbits, this one's a fox. Some of these bigger ones, I'm not sure, but they're definitely from different animals."

I crouched down and looked more closely at the area Lady Farrah had indicated. Now that I knew where to look—and what to look for—I could see the animal prints. I wouldn't have been able to identify what kind of animal made them, unlike the noblewoman, but at least now I knew what I should be searching out.

The ambassador came over to join us. She, too, bent over to examine the ground. "It's interesting, to be sure, Lady Farrah. But what does it mean?"

"From the last time I visited Annlyn, I remember your people were able to shift into all sorts of animals, not all of them native to the southern part of the Gifted Lands. I couldn't see them, of course, as I lack the ability to transform. But that's what Pazho told my friends and me." At my nod, Lady Farrah continued. "Some of these tracks may be from regular animals that live in these hills. But I would guess that many of these others—" she pointed at the larger tracks "—are non-native animals, which would make them shapeshifters."

Allisandra also nodded. "An astute observation." She frowned as she studied the prints a little more closely. "But look—these animal tracks all start moving in the same direction."

She was right. In the area we were examining, the myriad of animal prints were a jumbled mess, indicating that the shapeshifters had milled about here for a while. But further on, the tracks all sorted themselves into several straight lines—still a little muddled, so perhaps the animals had been following one another. But they all seemed to be going to the same destination.

As one, the three of us all looked up to see where the tracks would eventually lead.

Lake Vitrum.

I frowned. "I mean, that makes sense. Animals have to drink water, after all."

Lady Farrah shook her head. "Of course. But not every single animal, all at the same time."

She pointed a few paces ahead of us. "See how every single footprint starts heading towards the lake? There's no more chaotic jumble of tracks, as it is here. Which suggests to me a summons of some sort, and not natural animal instinct."

"Well, then." I shrugged. "Let's go check it out."

"Wait!" The ambassador startled us with her outburst. Lady Farrah and I both turned to look at her. "Are you sure that's wise? What if that shadow creature is out there, waiting for us?"

"We can't just abandon the people of Annlyn," I said. "We have to find them."

Allisandra colored slightly. "I understand. But, with all due respect, they're your people, not mine. If something should happen to the ambassador of Graenir while we're here ..."

The sad thing was, I did understand. Annlyn's leadership was already in shambles—which the ambassador had no doubt witnessed firsthand. The last thing my home kingdom needed was an international incident. But I was also disappointed in this sudden show of kingdom politics. Allisandra hadn't seemed like the type of person who would put her position above other people's welfare.

"You're already involved," Lady Farrah pointed out. "And by extension, so is Graenir. As is Calia."

"But you're here with the express permission of your sovereign," Allisandra countered. "My leaders don't know I'm here."

I sighed inwardly. If this was truly such an issue with the ambassador, we should have just left her in the cave. Or better yet, the castle.

Lady Farrah frowned. "You have no way of contacting them? Not even a calling spell?"

Allisandra shook her head. "We don't use those. And unfortunately, I left my only means of communication with them back in the palace."

I sighed. I didn't relish the idea of traveling all the way back to the palace to retrieve whatever device Allisandra was talking about. Even if it would be a short flight by dragon back. But I couldn't see any other way around it.

Lady Farrah said, "It's a bit of a roundabout way to do it, but let me call Rhyss and Beyan back in Calia. They can relay a message to our ambassador in Graenir. Besides, they'll be excited to meet you."

"All right." Allisandra sounded doubtful.

Lady Farrah held one of her hands up, muttering a quick spell. Almost instantly, a man with messy brown hair and tired brown eyes appeared. His golden circlet lay slightly askew on his head, and I got the impression he had been neglecting his appearance in his obvious worry. I recognized him as King Beyan, from when Princess Laersa and I had first called the Calian nobles. When the King saw Lady Farrah, he perked up.

"Farrah! It's good to see you again—but so soon? What news?" His voice was hopeful.

Lady Farrah smiled sadly. "I didn't mean to get your hopes up. I wish I could tell you Jennica is with me, but she's not. Not yet."

The man deflated.

"I'm calling because I had a favor to ask you."

"Of course. And speaking of favors, I did that research you requested."

"Terrific. We can talk about that in a minute. First, let me introduce my companions to you. This is Endri of Annlyn, Pazho and Denaan's son."

The man nodded. "Yes, I remember you. Well met, Endri. I hope you find your fathers soon."

"Thank you, Your Majesty," I said.

Lady Farrah indicated the Graenir representative. "This is Ambassador Allisandra, of Graenir."

King Beyan shifted slightly. I could have been wrong—it was such a small move—but I thought I saw his back stiffen. "Well met, ambassador."

Allisandra merely nodded back.

Lady Farrah said, "She has yet to tell the Graenir leaders what is going on here in Annlyn. If it's not too much of a hassle, could you contact Joichan again, and relay a message through him?"

"Of course. What should I say, and to whom should I send the message?"

Allisandra glanced at Lady Farrah, then addressed King Beyan. "Please tell the king and queen that Ambassador Allisandra is safe and well in Annlyn, and will assist the Calian noblewoman and Annlyn native in their mission to recover the lost citizens. Should something happen to me, I do not want them to hold Annlyn—or Calia—responsible."

King Beyan nodded once, in acknowledgment. "Thank you for that. I will relay the message."

He looked over at someone just out of our sight, and then turned back to us, a smile on his face. "Farrah, I believe someone here would like to say hello."

A tall, red-haired man stepped in. "Hello, Farrah."

Lady Farrah beamed. "Hello, Rhyss."

I touched the ambassador on the arm and motioned to the side with my head. With a question in her eyes, she followed me away from Lady Farrah.

"It's her betrothed," I explained. "I thought perhaps we should give them some privacy."

"Ah," Allisandra said in understanding. "Of course."

While Lady Farrah continued her conversation, Ambassador Allisandra and I set off for the lake.

39

CHAPTER THIRTY-NINE

"I MUST CONFESS, I still feel largely in the dark," Allisandra said as we walked.

"About what?" I gave her a quizzical look. "I'm pretty sure you got here right as all the madness started. You should know as much as either Lady Farrah or I do about all of this."

She shook her head. "Not about that. But really, more about Annlyn, and how your kingdom's power works."

I shrugged. "I'm probably the worst person you could ask about that. I just came into my power a few days ago, whereas most of the people in Annlyn manifest their abilities when they're younger. At least ten or twelve, if not sooner." I smirked. "And as you know, I only seem to transform under pressure."

Allisandra smiled. "Well, for just coming into your ability, you're doing quite well."

"Thank you."

She pointed at my tourmaline soulstone. With its bright blue-green color, it looked like it could have been pulled directly from the surrounding landscape. "I noticed most everyone in Annlyn has something like that. I know your kingdom is famed for its jewelry, but I find it amazing that all of your people, regardless of status, are able to afford such pretty, precious items."

"I suppose they can be expensive, if one is willing to spend that kind of money. A lot of times, they're passed down in families." Such as Princess Laersa's bracelet. Oh gods, I hoped she was doing okay, wherever she was.

We had reached the shores of Lake Vitrum. The animal tracks we had seen earlier all led here—even looking, oddly enough, like they disappeared into the lake. But the deep, calm blue of the lake didn't reveal any secrets it may have held within its waters. Instead, true to its name, the surface was as smooth as glass, reflecting the outline of the hills beyond and the clouds in the sky above.

I wanted to study the tracks more, even though it was probably better to wait for Lady Farrah, who would be able to make more sense of what we were seeing. But Ambassador Allisandra wanted to continue our earlier conversation.

"Ah, that makes sense." She studied my necklace, a little too closely. "Is there any special significance behind the jewels?"

I gave her a sharp look, but Allisandra merely laughed. "It was hard not to notice the menagerie that suddenly appeared in Annlyn a few days ago. Besides, King Tahrin mentioned that your kingdom was full of shapeshifters."

He did? That seemed quite unlike him. Perhaps he had had a change of heart after his talk with Pazho. Or, more likely, she had overheard our conversation with the king.

Something about the ambassador's comment struck me as odd, but I didn't have time to ponder it before she continued. "I figured the jewels everyone wore were connected to their ability to change forms. So, if the jewels have been handed down, does that make them more powerful?"

"We call them soulstones—at least, the gemstones that have been tied to us through magic. And I'm not sure. My father Pazho—you met him, we were leaving together when your arrival was announced to King Tahrin—would know more. He's quite a learned scholar, and has helped several people with their shapeshifting."

I chuckled, remembering the countless hours he had tried to help me. "He spent years trying to teach me. Ironic, really, that I finally figured it out after he was gone."

"Pazho." Allisandra looked thoughtful. "Yes, I remember him. What kind of animal is he?"

"A large grey wolf."

"Interesting. Thank you."

Rapid footsteps made us both turn to see Lady Farrah hurrying towards us. Her face was drawn in concern.

"Lady Farrah, is everything all right?" I asked.

"Yes, thank you, Endri." But her expression didn't lighten.

"Your intended is well?"

"Yes, he is. Thank you for asking." Lady Farrah looked down at the sand, where the lake water lapped at the remnants of various animal tracks. "This looks promising."

"Promising? I thought it looked more like a dead end."

"I think we should take a closer look at this," Lady Farrah said, ignoring my complaint.

"There are prints as far as I can see," Ambassador Allisandra said, shading her eyes to look down the shoreline. "I can go check."

"I'll go with you," I said.

"Actually, Endri, I could use your help here," Lady Farrah said quickly.

I turned to her, eyebrows raised. Lady Farrah was the most capable person I had met in a long while. I couldn't imagine what help she could possibly need, but I merely said, "All right. Ambassador, will you be all right by yourself?"

"Of course. If I run into any trouble, I'll call out." With that, Allisandra walked away, skirting the west side of Lake Vitrum.

When she was out of earshot, Lady Farrah grabbed my arm. In a low voice, she said, "Walk with me, and make it look like you're studying the sand."

I nodded, confused about her sudden intensity.

The noblewoman made a show of pointing out a track here or there. Anyone watching from a distance would have thought we were, indeed, studying the ground.

But in that same quiet tone, Lady Farrah said, "Beyan wanted Rhyss to talk to me so I would have an excuse to stay behind and talk to them privately. You couldn't have known, but when you took the ambassador away, it was a big help.

"When Beyan contacted his father-in-law Joichan, Joichan told him there is no Graenir ambassador. Their isolationist policies—even more stringent than Annlyn's—meant that they've pulled back from all contact with any of the kingdoms in the Gifted Lands. Joichan is the first ambassador they've allowed in their borders for close to one hundred years. They've certainly never sent any representatives to other countries. Also, there is no king in Graenir—something I didn't even know. The queen was widowed ten years ago, and has been ruling Graenir by herself ever since."

"Allisandra did say she hadn't been back home in a while," I said.

"But she would be remiss in her duties as Ambassador if she didn't know such a basic fact about her home kingdom. And that doesn't explain the rest of it. Tell me, have you had any odd feelings lately? Like you did about the false Princess Laersa?"

I frowned, remembering. "Well, when we were flying over here, I did feel anxious. But I thought maybe it was just because I'm still getting used to carrying passengers."

Lady Farrah shook her head. "Always trust your animal instinct. It will be much more true and pure than your human instinct, although you should listen to that as well."

I hung my head. "I'm sorry. And after you told me that, too. I—I'm still trying to understand my second self."

She put her hand on my arm. "Don't be sorry. I should have realized it sooner, too. When my magic failed. Like I said, even at my most tired, that's never happened. So much was happening, but when I think back—I think something, or some*one*, was blocking my magic from working.

"Which also made me wonder about the ledge crumbling underneath you, the way it did. Again, a lot was going on—but I vaguely recall the feeling of magic being used in the area. And it wasn't coming from me."

I took in a deep, shaky breath. "What do we do now?"

"Be watchful, and wary. When the time is right, we'll confront Allisandra with what we know."

A footstep crunched on the ground nearby, causing us both to look up. Ambassador Allisandra stood just behind us, a calculating smirk on her normally open and friendly face.

"Or you could ask me about it now."

40

CHAPTER FORTY

ALLISANDRA WALKED TOWARDS LADY Farrah and me, her movements slow and deliberate. If she could shapeshift, I imagined her second self as a cool, calculating leopard, stalking its prey.

Us.

My hand rested on my sword hilt, ready to draw. Lady Farrah tensed, ready to cast a spell.

"My friends, why so nervous? It's just me." Even Allisandra's voice had changed, from her normal friendly tone to something deeper and more sinister. "You know who I am."

"Do we?" Lady Farrah challenged. "It seems that you are not who you claim to be."

Allisandra shrugged. "A minor detail. I was hoping I'd have a little more time, but unfortunately you've found me out. No matter. It doesn't change anything."

"Who. Are. You?"

The false ambassador laughed, her voice starting in a girlish high pitch and ending in a man's lower register. Her face morphed and shifted. Allisandra's pretty, open features disappeared, replaced by someone still as beautiful, but ethereal and otherworldly in his beauty.

Emerald eyes regarded us coldly. The man raised a pale hand, brushing back his long hair with equally long fingernails painted black as midnight. Two matching strands of black hair ran down either side of his face, standing out starkly against his otherwise blond locks.

I had no idea who Allisandra had become, but next to me, Lady Farrah hissed in recognition.

"King Balor."

My eyes widened, remembering Lady Farrah's story. King Balor was the Unseelie Fae leader that Lady Farrah and her intended, Rhyss, had encountered recently. The same man who had split his soul, using his Shadow to possess and kill other Fae.

His Shadow.

I had thought that perhaps a different, unknown mage had been behind the dark cloud that had plagued Annlyn. But if King Balor was standing before us....

"I'm touched you remember me," the Fae king drawled. "It's lovely to see you again, Lady Farrah. I'm so glad to see you're all right, especially after our last meeting."

"Spare me from Fae double talk and trickster ways. Lying, especially from a ruler, is unbecoming."

King Balor shook his head in mock sadness. "You mean you're not happy to see me alive, and well? I must confess, when I learned that you and the rest of your friends had survived the—cave-in, shall we call it?—I was quite surprised. And now, here we are. How did you survive the grotto collapsing, anyway?"

Lady Farrah's glare alone could have killed King Balor on the spot. "I don't believe you need to know."

"That's too bad. I was hoping I could have my curiosity satisfied. I wasn't lying, you know. I am happy to see you alive. It will make killing you now that much more satisfying."

I drew my sword, holding it out ineffectually before me. If I survived this whole ordeal, I would definitely have to find someone to train me in fighting.

Lady Farrah acted instantly, throwing me behind her with one hand as she shouted and threw up a ward with the other.

The light purple barrier shimmered into place just as the now exposed King Balor threw a spell at us. The ward barely protected Lady Farrah and me from getting hit. King Balor's magical attack hit Lady Farrah's shield, exploding in a shower of green and yellow sparks.

The ward rippled in response as Lady Farrah shuddered from the force of King Balor's magic. The noblewoman took a deep, steadying breath, and the ward stilled and strengthened.

King Balor just laughed, lazily flicking his slender fingers at us. Another spell slammed into our magical shield. The ward held, but the fine sheen of sweat on Lady Farrah's face betrayed her calm, determined expression.

Would we be able to withstand another blast like that?

"It's so cute, really, that you think your little shield will be enough to stand against me," King Balor said, almost sounding bored as he examined a perfect black nail. Slowly, he put his finger to his neck. From underneath his shirt collar, he pulled out a leather cord.

His fingernail traced a line down the length of the cord, where a perfectly round object hung. A little smaller than a closed fist, the white pendant had an odd black feathery seam down the middle.

Even though I definitely was not an authority on magic, something about the necklace struck fear into my body. Lady Farrah's eyes narrowed.

"Lady Farrah," I whispered. "What is that?"

"If it's what I think it is, it's nothing good."

"That's right, you haven't had a chance to see what my lovely can do." King Balor ran a loving finger down the side of the sphere. "Perhaps we should show you."

He ran his finger over the object again, but this time it seemed like he was prodding it, willing it to awaken.

The feathery seam I had noticed on his pendant earlier started to move.

No, not move.

Flutter.

Short little tendrils along the black seam quivered, and then the white sphere began to split apart.

And then I realized what I was seeing.

I gasped, horrified.

In King Balor's hand lay a large eye, attached to the thin leather cord around his neck. The now open eye was a mesmerizing shade of hazel, changing from brown to green to gold in the light. Black eyelashes framed the hazel eye—the thin black seam I had mistaken for a decorative line.

The eye blinked once, then again, as if it was just waking up. It darted around as it took in its surroundings.

I shuddered. But even though I found it grotesque—after all, it was a random, disconnected eyeball—I couldn't look away from it.

King Balor smiled at Lady Farrah's sudden intake of breath.

"Oh, you recognize this, but not me?" King Balor said. "My dear Lady Farrah, I am almost insulted."

"It was a bit overshadowed by the other things going on," the noblewoman said flatly. "I only know of it because Lady Hahna mentioned it, before she died."

The Fae king laughed, as if Lady Farrah's comment had been extremely witty. "Overshadowed, you say? Yes, I can see that."

"Endri," Lady Farrah said in a low voice.

"Yes?" My own voice betrayed my fear.

"If something should happen to me, I want you to run. Don't stay and try to help me. Just go."

"But Lady Farrah—"

"No buts. Just do as I say. Got it?"

King Balor stroked the pendant again, and the hazel eye looked up at him. The Fae king gave it a fond glance. "Well, you've seen what my Shadow can do. Now, I think it's my Eye's turn."

The ward around us strengthened, nearly opaque as Lady Farrah poured all her magical energy into it.

As one, both King Balor and his Eye turned their gazes on Lady Farrah and me. A sickly green mist began oozing from the hazel-colored iris, reminiscent of the black fog that had plagued Annlyn. The green mist seeped down onto the lakeshore, growing thick all around us. Within moments, it had surrounded us in our little protected bubble, so dense that I couldn't see the king or Lake Vitrum, although I knew both were right near us.

The fog lapped at our shield, eating away at it.

"What is that?" I said, panicked.

"I don't know, and I don't want to find out." Sweat poured down Lady Farrah's face, and her voice was strained.

Every way I turned, I just saw green mist. And within moments it would break through our shield.

Outside our now prison, I could hear King Balor's laugh, oddly distorted through the mist. Or maybe it sounded strange through my heart pounding in my ears.

Lady Farrah whispered urgently, "Endri, I can't hold this back much longer."

"What do we do?"

"*I* will redirect this shield to you, to give you time to escape. *You* will run."

"I can't leave you behind."

"You're ... going to ... have to," she said grimly, her breathing labored. "Ready?"

"No!"

"Now!" The shield around us shrunk rapidly, staying just large enough to encompass my body. At the same time, I felt myself propelled forward by some unseen force—a magical push from Lady Farrah, I guessed. I wasn't pushed far enough to get beyond the fog, but it looked to be thinner where I was. I was standing about knee deep in the lake, although thanks to Lady Farrah's shield, I couldn't feel the water against my legs.

Behind me, I could hear Lady Farrah coughing as she breathed in the foul green fog.

I turned, but I couldn't see her through the mist.

Should I go back? But she told me to run....

From within the green fog, over Lady Farrah's coughs, I heard King Balor give a shout. "Where is he? Where did he go?"

There was a loud smack, and Lady Farrah's coughing suddenly stopped.

Oh, gods....

As if she was standing right beside me, I heard Lady Farrah's voice echo in my head. *Endri. Run.*

Taking a deep breath, I plunged deeper into Lake Vitrum.

41

CHAPTER FORTY-ONE

I KEPT WALKING UNTIL the water was well over my head. Perhaps the ward was weighted in some manner, because my feet stayed firmly on the bottom of the lake, when I should have been floating—or drowning—by this point.

Looking up, I could see sunlight rippling on the lake's surface. Back the way I had come, the light was slightly darkened, tainted by the green fog.

I didn't really have a plan, other than to not be visible once the eerie mist on the lakeshore dissipated. But I had no idea how long that would take. Since Lady Farrah's shield seemed to be watertight—and for now, also airtight—I could hide under the lake's surface until King Balor left.

But who knew how long that would take. Or how long Lady Farrah's ward around me would last.

Submerged in the water, I couldn't hear what was happening above ground. King Balor could still be in the area, searching for me. Or was he more likely to leave immediately, to put whatever evil plan he had into action?

And if he had gone, had he taken Lady Farrah with him?

I forced myself to take a deep breath, then another. Fretting about what was happening on the surface wouldn't help me any. I just had to wait here for a little while, then I could head back to the surface to see what, if anything, I could do.

I was still in a relatively shallow part of the lake, where sunlight could still penetrate the water. Further on, the water looked darker as the lake grew deeper. Lady Farrah's ward sparkled and glowed with a soft lavender light that reminded me of her wild, curly hair.

Looking down at the sandy lakebed, I paused.

All around me, the animal prints that we had seen leading into Lake Vitrum were pressed into the sand. Surprisingly, the water hadn't eroded the tracks; they looked as intact as if they had just been made. And all the tracks, in neat, even rows, led deeper into the lake.

I glanced up again. The light closer to shore still looked tainted. Besides, I hadn't been down here very long.

Perhaps I could at least peek above the surface, just to see what was happening. Even though Lady Farrah had told me to leave her behind—something which I was still reluctant to do—I knew she would want to see what I had just discovered.

If she's still even there.

I gave myself a mental slap. *Don't think that way!*

I headed back towards land, intending to just take a quick look around, and then duck back down under the water. But when I reached a shallower part of the lake, where I should have easily risen above the water, I found I couldn't break through to the surface.

Confused, I tried to walk forward again. But my head bumped into something solid and unyielding, even though the gentle waters of Lake Vitrum rippled above me.

I reached out, trying to punch my hand through the water and into the air.

"Ow!"

I pulled my hand back and shook it out, glaring at the water's surface above me. It looked like water, and was as wet as water. But my bruised fist told a different story—the top of Lake Vitrum was as hard as stone.

My breath started coming in shallow gasps. Was I going to die down here? And what about Lady Farrah?

I beat my fists against the lake surface, but no matter what I did, I couldn't break through the wall of water. And all I had for my efforts were two bloodied hands.

I tried using my sword to stab through the surface, even though it was not magical by any means. That didn't work either. When I checked my weapon, I thought that the tip looked a little dulled from the attempt. Great.

Get a hold of yourself, Endri. Calm down. Think.

So. I couldn't get back to land, for some reason. A magical reason, of course, although I didn't know exactly how or why I was trapped. And here I would stay, until I could figure out how to break the spell or Lady Farrah's ward failed me and I drowned.

Neither thought was very comforting.

Since I couldn't leave this cursed lake and get back to Lady Farrah, the only other thing I could do was carry on our investigation.

I'm so sorry, Lady Farrah. I hope you're all right. Please be all right.

My heart heavy, I turned and followed the animal tracks that led deeper into the lake.

The water around me grew darker as I moved further away from shore. Down here, in the depths of Lake Vitrum, the sunlight could no longer break through. Without the faint glow from Lady Farrah's ward, I would not have been able to see anything. Even with it, I could only see about two or three tracks ahead of me.

Time also seemed to have lost meaning down here in the dark depths of Lake Vitrum. Even though the shield kept the water at bay, I was quite aware of the lake's oppressive pressure.

Just focus on the prints, Endri.

One step. Then another. And another, and another. I kept my head down, solely concentrating on following the line of animal prints. If I let my mind wander—thinking of King Balor, Lady Farrah, and being at the bottom of Lake Vitrum—it would break apart.

I recognized some of the smaller tracks—rabbits, pigs, cows—but some prints were abnormally large or oddly shaped in comparison. *What kinds of animals made those prints?* I wondered.

Just keep going ...

But I couldn't. Something was in my way. Something quite solid and large.

I looked up, wondering what new, impassable magic I had encountered. But it didn't look like another wall of water. The light from the shield caught on something golden and—scaly?

Looking to my left and my right, I saw the same gilded, textured wall on both sides.

I went left and followed the golden wall, curious to see where it led.

And then I choked back the scream that threatened to rip from my throat.

Set in the golden wall was an equally golden giant eye.

Backing up a few paces, I took in the eye and its surroundings. A large golden dragon, the back half of its body disappearing into the darkness of the deep water, regarded me.

For a long moment, the creature and I just stared at each other.

The dragon seemed familiar. True, I hadn't encountered many, but I had a hunch—"Queen Jennica?"

She didn't move, or blink, or anything.

"Uh. Dragon?"

Still nothing. I reached out a tentative finger and poked the creature, but it didn't flinch.

Was the dragon dead? Possibly. But the creature was posed in such a way as to make me think not. Its wings were partially unfurled, and one limb was extended, as if it was reaching for something. Caught poised in a moment of action, instead of its body and muscles limp from death.

A shimmer caught my eye. I stared at the dragon, harder.

A faint sparkle, similar to my ward, lay over the dragon's body. While I didn't know much about magic, I would bet my newfound shapeshifting ability that this creature was under a magic spell that clung to it as tightly as Lady Farrah's shield was clinging to me.

My blood ran cold. It didn't matter if it was Queen Jennica, or a completely different, unfamiliar dragon. The creature wouldn't hurt me.

It couldn't hurt me.

It was frozen.

42

CHAPTER FORTY-TWO

I SWALLOWED HARD. I was pretty sure I had found Queen Jennica of Calia, but in this suspended state, she was in no position to help me.

But would I be able to help her?

I looked around, but—besides the golden dragon—it was just darkness and shadows as far as my eyes could see.

What I wouldn't give for a light down here. I wished Lady Farrah was here—I was sure she would be able to call up a magical light.

I patted my pockets, knowing as I did so that the effort was pointless. I hadn't brought any flint or wood with me to create fire. I just had the clothes on my back, my tourmaline soulstone, my sword, and—

My fingers closed around the dragon figurine.

I ran a finger over the curve of the wing, thinking. True, I couldn't conjure a mage light. But perhaps I could try something else?

I drew out my sword, twisting it this way and that in the dull light of Lady Farrah's shield. The sword caught a bit of the glow, reflecting the light. It extended my sight a little further, but not by much. The blade, while serviceable, hadn't been polished for quite some time, sitting in the palace's storage.

Oh, gods. I should have thought of this sooner.

All right, then. My sword was helpful in amplifying some of the light. But was there a way I could bolster it more?

My mind wandered back to my carving. Of an ice dragon. Which I was.

And—wasn't ice reflective? I thought I recalled Lady Farrah saying something about that.

It was worth a try. Besides, it wasn't like I had a ton of other ideas. Or options.

Shifting into my second self was becoming easier each time I did it. The challenge now was to not transform fully. Lady Farrah's shield clung fairly close to my skin, and I didn't know if it would change with me if I were to grow several sizes larger than my current form.

I could feel my body reknitting itself, eager to settle into my dragon form. It would be so easy to just let that instinct take over, but, with effort, I held myself back. I didn't know if it was a good idea to change into an animal form down here. Although I had only seen one creature so far—the dragon Queen Jennica—I worried that whatever magic held her captive would overtake me as well, if I completely shifted.

I didn't need to transform fully into an ice dragon. I just needed some of the abilities.

My right hand felt funny. Looking down, I saw that I no longer had a hand—it was a scaly blue claw, complete with sharp talons at the end. The blue scales continued up my right arm, but my left hand was an odd mix of tan and blue, a sign of an incomplete transformation.

For the first time, I was glad I was down here alone. I must have looked a sight, with the right side of my body in dragon form, and my left side still human.

But had I changed in the way that mattered most, right now?

I coughed a little, as an experiment. My breath came out cold, small icicles hanging in the air for a brief moment before falling to the ground, encased in my shield.

I smiled. Perfect.

Holding up my sword, I breathed again, making sure to completely cover the blade. Ice coated the weapon, adding an extra sheen to it. I turned it this way and that in the light, my smile growing wider when the glow from Lady Farrah's shield caught on the icy blade and illuminated the area more than it had before.

Holding my makeshift "torch" aloft, I surveyed the area.

And gasped.

I had stumbled upon what looked like the entirety of the missing Annlyn shapeshifters. Besides the frozen dragon form of Queen Jennica, I saw animals of all sizes. And they all stood motionless, suspended in time.

I moved my light around. A family of foxes. A bear, and a tiger. A pair of snakes. Even several birds, paused in mid-flight, although I had no idea how they could have flown underwater.

My sword light caught on pale grey fur.

"Pazho!"

I rushed over, kneeling down to look more closely at the animal. Sure enough, it was a stately grey wolf, and as I looked into its eyes, I recognized the second form of one of my fathers.

I reached out to touch the wolf. Even though I knew Pazho was frozen and probably couldn't feel my hand upon his back, my heart still broke when there was no reaction from him. Tears sprang to my eyes. "Father, I'm glad I found you."

Sniffling, I looked around. A bulky elk stood nearby, and I smiled through my tears at seeing Denaan's animal form. It was small comfort, but I was glad to know my fathers had found each other down here in their magical captivity.

"Now, to get you—and everyone else—out of here."

Easy to say, but not so easy to do.

How *was* I supposed to get all these frozen animals back up to the surface? How had they gotten down here in the first place? There hadn't been any tracks leading from the capital city into the hills, but I knew the creatures had gotten here somehow.

Queen Jennica had been caught up in the black cloud before it had disappeared with her before my eyes. The fog had visited Annlyn several times, the first time to force the kingdom's people to shapeshift. It had probably come back to take them away after the transformations had been completed. And, recalling the tracks Lady Farrah had found, it had left the newly changed animals in the hills until, for some inexplicable reason, the animals had felt compelled to walk into Lake Vitrum.

I blew out a breath, frustrated. Perhaps I could carry some of the smaller animals, but I wouldn't have the energy to go back and forth for all of them. And, of course, I wouldn't be able to carry the larger animals, like Pazho or Denaan. I definitely would not be able to carry Queen Jennica.

Never mind the fact that I wasn't a strong swimmer, either.

To give myself more time to think, I walked among the shapeshifters, looking for Princess Laersa. Not that I would have known what kind of animal she would have transformed into. I also wasn't sure if she had been able to shift—she had seemed close, back in Joichan's cave, but to my knowledge, she was still trying to figure it out.

I frowned, trying to remember. What had Princess Laersa looked like, as she had started to transform? Oh, that's right. Her skin had turned purple—something that was unusual and striking enough that it would be easy to pick out.

But although I was surrounded by creatures as far as my eyes could see, I didn't find any with purple feathers or skin. Maybe I wasn't searching hard enough.

Or maybe Princess Laersa wasn't down here.

43

CHAPTER FORTY-THREE

As I WANDERED AROUND the frozen menagerie, I realized that the area was growing brighter. I looked up, but it wasn't from the sun—I couldn't see any light coming from above.

And it wasn't my icy sword. Even though it was still reflecting my ward's magical light, it hadn't intensified in any way.

I looked around me, uncomprehending for a moment. And then it hit me.

The shimmery magical binding I had noticed on Queen Jennica also held the other animals in place. The magic sparkled in the glow of my sword's reflected light, like I was standing in the middle of a field of tiny mirrors. Those multiple reflections were the cause of the much brighter area.

I looked down at my right hand—now dragon claw. My injured wing—which corresponded to my human shoulder—still felt a bit stiff, but not as bad as I would have thought. I had been able to fly here, with no issues. Well, unless you counted my reaction to Allisandra.

I frowned as fragments of memory came to me. Something about mirrors.

In King Tahrin's throne room, there had been a large, elaborate mirror. Gifted to him by Ambassador Allisandra, whom I now knew to be King Balor of the Unseelie Fae. King Tahrin had wanted to learn more about mirror magic from the false Graenir ambassador, his daughter had told me.

Whether or not Graenir was skilled in mirror magic, I didn't know. That could have been a lie Allisandra had told King Tahrin to gain his favor.

But Lady Farrah had said mirrors could amplify someone's magical power. Which was why she had been experimenting with it. And her experiment had been successful, if my mended wing was any indication.

And there was something else Lady Farrah had said. That animals, operating on pure instinct, had more raw power than humans did.

I didn't know what King Balor's ultimate goal was, here in Annlyn. But I could guess at his immediate goal—to steal power, whether it was King Tahrin's throne or—

I looked at the watery tableau of frozen animals before me.

—Or the magic of our shapeshifters.

All around, the water sparkled in the glow of my makeshift light, like part of the magic that bound the people of Annlyn had seeped into Lake Vitrum. If that were true, then I would have expected the animals to break free from their binding at any moment. But they were still firmly held in place.

Unless the water itself was part of the binding?

Gods, I wished Lady Farrah was here. Her knowledge of magic would be so useful right now. I hoped she was all right.

Thinking about Lady Farrah brought her talk about mirrors back to my mind. I didn't know how mirror magic worked, except for the amplification part that the noblewoman had mentioned. And even then, I didn't know the exact details of it.

A field of tiny mirrors....

If anything could amplify power, it would be this odd, watery prison.

With its floating, sparkly fragments of mirrors all around.

Even as realization dawned on me, disappointment followed hard on its heels. Great, I was suspended in a liquid mirror at the bottom of Lake Vitrum. I still wouldn't know how to free everyone around me.

The purple ward around me flickered.

And that was my only warning that something was amiss.

I barely had time to take in a big gulp of air before Lady Farrah's shield dissipated in a sudden shower of sparks. No longer held at bay, the water rushed towards me. It hit me with unexpected force, nearly knocking the breath out of me.

Precious air bubbles floated up from my face. As it was, I wouldn't be able to stay down here for very long.

There was nothing for it. I'd have to swim to the surface, and figure out a way to get back to this deep part of the lake later. After I got more air.

I kicked off the bottom, desperate to get out of here. I figured the momentum would help propel me to the lake's surface, although I didn't know exactly how deep I was. I'd just swim for all I was worth, and hopefully make it to the top in time.

That was the plan, anyway.

Part of me cooperated. I could feel the buoyancy in my legs and most of my body, trying to rise upward. But one part of my body felt like a lead weight, keeping me tethered to the bottom of the lake.

My right hand and arm. The part that had shifted into my ice dragon form.

I tried to swim upwards, again. Since only a small part of me had transformed, surely the rest of my non-shifted body could compensate, and I'd still be able to float? But the more I tried to move, the more my right side wouldn't let me.

I could feel the panic rising, however. *Stay calm, Endri.* Frantically, I ran through my options.

Transforming fully into either my dragon or human form would take time, but which would take more? I didn't think the animals around me were dead, which meant that perhaps if I became a dragon, I would be able to breathe down here? It was a thin thread of hope to gamble my precious air on. And if my guess about the animals' breathing was right, did that extend to humans as well?

But what if I transformed into a dragon, and then fell victim to whatever had trapped the other animals down here?

I was running out of time. My lungs burned, wanting air *now.*

My dragon form seemed like the safer bet.

I just hoped my guess was correct, or I wouldn't live long enough to regret it.

I closed my eyes, willing myself to complete my shapeshifting. My body eagerly complied as I released the mental gates that had held it back from transforming.

Now in full ice dragon form, I floated a few feet above the field of animals. My lungs involuntarily expanded, wanting air to fill my now massive form. If changing was the wrong choice, it was too late now. A flood of water rushed into my nostrils.

But I didn't drown.

I breathed in again. And again. Somehow I was able to breathe down here, even though Lady Farrah's ward was broken and water surrounded me.

All right, then. Good. That was one worry taken care of.

In my larger body, I could take more of the animals to the surface with me. I had never tried swimming as a dragon before, but how hard could it be?

The mild stiffness that had plagued my hurt wing came back, more intense this time.

Glancing at my talons, I realized that the other fear I had had—that the magic that had frozen the other animals would affect me once I became a dragon—was now coming true. The parts of my body that I could see—my talons, my tail—shimmered with the same magical glow I had seen surrounding the others.

The stiffness started to grow worse, more intense as it spread throughout my body. I flexed my claws, dismayed at how little movement I had in them in just mere moments. Soon I'd be trapped, just like the other creatures here.

Well, I'd fight it as long as I could. I thrashed around, hoping to throw off some of the sparkly magic that clung to my scales like a second skin.

But the stiffness kept spreading. And the magic didn't fall off, as I had naively hoped. I swiped at my tail with a sharp claw, thinking I could tear the magic from my body. That didn't work, either. All I succeeded in doing was creating a thin red line across my blue scales.

Some frantic part of me thought, *Well, that was stupid. Isn't it seven years' bad luck, to break a mirror?*

To break a mirror.

The sparkles around me grew brighter. I felt like I was falling into a mirror, myself.

And a mirror could be broken.

In a last, desperate attempt to not succumb to the binding magic—which was beginning to look rather futile—I blew out a large, icy breath. The water around me instantly froze, ice coating the animals below.

I kept breathing out, twisting every which way, trying to blow ice in all directions.

And when I was surrounded on all sides by ice—and nearly frozen myself by magic—I hurled myself, with all my strength, at one of the ice walls.

A dull thump sounded, and the air—water?—around me vibrated with an intense force.

And then Lake Vitrum shattered.

44

CHAPTER FORTY-FOUR

EVERYWHERE I LOOKED, ALL I could see was silvery-white.

I was floating, although I was no longer submerged in the depths of Lake Vitrum. But I wasn't in the air above the lake, or anywhere near Annlyn, at least as far as I could tell.

Was I dead?

Maybe.

I flexed my wings experimentally. I still had feeling in them, and although I was floating, it wasn't my wings that were keeping me in the air. It was like a giant hand held me in its palm, and I relaxed into the calming sensation.

But my body hurt way too much for me to be dead. Unless one takes their physical pain with them into the afterlife.

That would be a pretty crummy afterlife, if that were the case, I thought.

Residual stiffness, either from the magic or my injured wing, laced through my body. A myriad of thin red lines streaked my blue scales. Fortunately, the cuts had stopped bleeding, but they still stung something fierce.

If I wasn't in the lake, or outside of it, where was I? Perhaps I was back in Annlyn's capital? But as I looked up and down and around, I realized this didn't look like any place that I was familiar with.

Where in the Gifted Lands was I?

A faint sound teased at the edge of my hearing. I couldn't quite make out what the sound was. Concentrating, the sound solidified into a woman's voice, and the indistinguishable words became something I could understand. "Endri. Endri."

I gasped as I recognized the voice. "Princess Laersa."

The princess kept calling my name. I nearly called out, then I stiffened, not wanting to get taken in again. The last time I thought the princess was trying to reach me, it turned out to be a deadly doppelganger. I wasn't going to be so easily fooled again.

But the voice kept saying my name, over and over. And I realized, even if it was another magical construct made to fool me, I couldn't turn my back on the voice. Not if there was the slightest chance it could be the princess.

"Princess Laersa?" I called out, a bit tentative. And then I blinked, surprised. I must be dead, or dreaming. How was I able to use human speech while still in dragon form?

Or was it a result of the magic here, wherever here was? Was the magic in this place so potent it was able to alter even the natural boundaries of animal to human communication?

"Endri?" The voice was still faint, but now held a thread of hope. "Are you really here? Oh, Endri, please help me."

I looked around frantically, but I didn't see Princess Laersa anywhere. And I couldn't pinpoint which direction her voice was coming from.

"Princess Laersa? Where are you? Where am I?"

"I'm—"

I couldn't quite make out what she was saying. It sounded like she had suddenly moved farther away, and had muffled her voice in the process.

"What did you say?"

"This is—"

I still couldn't hear everything. A chill ran down my spine. This place, wherever it was, had to be magical in nature.

It had to be magic that was hiding her from me. Perhaps that same magic was stopping her from telling me the information I needed to know to help her?

I just had to pick a direction. "Princess, I'll come to you. Keep talking so I know which way to go."

"Oh, Endri. If you—"

And then whatever was holding me aloft disappeared. I started to fall, and even though I spread my wings wide and tried to fly, I found I was unable to. It felt like an invisible boulder had fallen on my body, and no matter what I did, I couldn't shake it off.

I screamed as I fell.

"Princess!"

I hit the ground, hard. Groaning, I turned on my side, waiting for the pain of impact to subside.

"Endri?"

I looked up at the feminine voice. Queen Jennica, now back in her human form, looked down at me.

I groaned again as I tried to sit up.

"No, no, stay where you are." Queen Jennica knelt down beside me, concern on her face. "Are you all right?"

"I—I think so?" I took stock of myself. The jarring from hitting the ground was ebbing away, although I'd probably have a nasty body-length bruise for a while. My right arm throbbed, a sure sign that the injury was flaring up again. And both of my arms and legs stung. "Yes, I'm all right. For the most part."

"Can you stand?"

I flexed my legs and my toes. "Yes."

The queen held out a hand and helped me get up. I brushed myself off, hissing in pain when some sand got in a cut on my hand. I noticed that, like Queen Jennica, I was now back in my human form. I shivered as a slight breeze passed by, wishing I had brought a coat to cover my short-sleeved tunic.

Not that it would have mattered. It would probably have been left behind at the bottom of the lake when I transformed.

"You're covered in cuts," the queen said. "What happened?"

That was a good question, but as I took stock of myself, I realized she was right. The red lines I had noticed on my wings in that strange, silvery-white dream world were still with me, appearing as long slashes criss-crossing my now human arms. I lifted my pant legs. Cuts covered both of my legs as well.

"To create these?" I asked, indicating my arms. "Or in general?"

"Both. And, also, where are we?"

A serene male voice answered her. "You, my dear queen, are on the shores of Lake Vitrum."

As one, the queen and I said, "Pazho!"

Pazho stepped forward, and we embraced. Tears sprang to my eyes as I breathed in his scent. And then I started coughing and laughing all at once. "Father, you smell like wet dog."

He shrugged, a twinkle in his eyes. "What did you expect?"

I kept laughing, wiping at my tears. "I'm glad you're back."

Another, deeper voice, piped up. "What about me? Don't I get a hello?"

"Denaan!" My other father scooped me up in a hug as Pazho greeted Queen Jennica.

"How did you—?" I started to ask, but Denaan shook his head.

"We should be asking you that, Endri. When I saw you down there, walking around—well, I can't speak for everyone else, but I thought my heart would burst out of my chest, I was that proud."

"You were able to see me? I was so afraid—" And then the second part of what he had said registered. The tears came flooding back. "You were?"

Denaan smiled. "It was endless torture, being trapped in my elk form down there for gods know how long. The only thing that kept me going was knowing that you were still free."

He swept an arm out, indicating the shores of Lake Vitrum. "Somehow, you saved us all."

45

--·--

CHAPTER FORTY-FIVE

"ALL" INCLUDED QUEEN JENNICA, my fathers Pazho and Denaan, and the entirety of Annlyn. The dazed citizens milled
around, marveling at their newly transformed back-to-human
bodies. Some seemed more confused than others, and I wondered
at how long they had spent trapped in their second selves at the
bottom of the lake.

I smiled at my father's praise, but as I surveyed the area, I
sobered. There were still a few people who weren't here. "Not all."

Pazho turned to me, raising an eyebrow. "Hmm?"

"Princess Laersa isn't here. But I don't think she was down there
to begin with. And Lady Farrah isn't here anymore. He must have
taken her. Unless she somehow left on her own." I frowned. "But
then I would have expected her to wait, or to come after me."

"He? Who are you talking about?"

I shook my head, coming out of my musings. "Let me fill you in
on what's been happening."

Quickly, I told Pazho and Denaan about everything that had
happened since they had disappeared. Queen Jennica filled in some
of the details regarding her and Lady Farrah's involvement, but she
fell silent when I explained what had happened at the palace.

At the mention of King Balor, Queen Jennica hissed in anger. "That's the 'he' you were referring to?"

I nodded.

Her eyes flashed. If she could have breathed fire in her human form, I'm sure she would have. "He's got some nerve. If—no, *when*—I meet him, he's going to regret showing his face in the Gifted Lands."

Pazho put a calming hand on her shoulder. "My dear Jennica, that might not be the best thing for diplomatic relations between the Fae and humans."

"I'll show that King Balor a thing or two about *diplomacy*." The way she said it left no doubt in any of our minds about her idea of diplomacy when it came to the Unseelie Fae king.

I finished the rest of my tale, including the odd event with floating and hearing the princess calling out to me after I broke through the icy Lake Vitrum. "I wondered if perhaps King Balor was using the lake as a giant mirror to siphon the magical power from the people of Annlyn. I'm not sure how it would work, though. And now, here we are. Minus Lady Farrah and Princess Laersa."

Denaan nodded, but Pazho frowned. "How did you get all those cuts on your arms?"

I shrugged. "I don't know. Queen Jennica asked me the same thing. They just appeared after I got out of the lake."

"Hmm," Pazho mused. "Your Majesty, how much do you know about mirror magic?"

Queen Jennica frowned. "Not that much, I'm afraid. It's not something widely taught in Calia. We rely more on spell components and memorization. I'd watched Farrah experiment a bit with it, but I never tried anything myself."

"Do you know any of the fundamentals?"

She paused, thinking. "Using a mirror can bolster a failing spell, or intensify a good one so it works faster or better. What about you, Pazho? What do you know about mirror magic?"

Pazho tilted his head in thought. "There's an old story, here in Annlyn. About the magician and his daughter ..."

Denaan snapped his fingers. "I remember that tale! It always scared me. Makes my skin crawl now, just thinking about it."

I looked between my two fathers. "What story? What are you talking about?"

"As I said, it's an old story. So old, some doubt its veracity." Pazho's voice took on the lecturing quality he used when he had been teaching me how to use my soulstone. I smiled despite the seriousness of our situation, glad to see his time in captivity underwater hadn't changed him. "But there was once a mage who lived here with his wife and daughter. They were unable to have more than the one child, but they were happy and content, until their daughter became ill. None of the healers could help her, and the mage's skills couldn't cure her. The daughter died, and the mage and his wife were understandably distraught.

"The wife eventually moved beyond her grief as best she could, but the mage became obsessed with bringing his daughter back to life. Which, of course, he could not. In the course of trying to save his daughter, he had experimented with all kinds of magic, including mirror magic. Now, with his daughter gone, he thought perhaps he could take a bit of his wife's essence, contain it in a mirror, and use that bit of his wife's essence to create a copy of his daughter.

"But when he tried it, instead of taking just a bit, he captured all of his wife's essence. He lacked the skill or knowledge to free her or restore her, and he worried that breaking the mirror would kill her outright.

And so her body perished while her soul was trapped in the mirror. Thus, he lost all he loved when he tried too hard to hold on."

For a moment, none of us could say anything in response to this disturbing story. Then, finally, Queen Jennica asked, "Did the wife eventually die in the mirror? What happened to it?"

"I believe her soul couldn't move on while it was trapped in there, suspended between life and death. There are variations on the story's ending, but the one most told is that the mage eventually sold or gave away the mirror, overcome with guilt over seeing his beloved wife trapped in it every day."

"Wretched man," Queen Jennica muttered. Privately, I agreed.

"From what you said of the lake, Endri, I think your guess that it was functioning as some sort of conduit for King Balor's power was correct," Pazho said. "It did function like a giant mirror. When you broke it, you probably got cut up a bit."

"Yeah," I said ruefully, examining my sliced arms. I frowned. "Something about your story, though ... Princess Laersa said King Tahrin wanted to learn more about mirror magic. And you said the king never stopped mourning the death of the queen. And everyone else is here, but Princess Laersa is not...."

My voice trailed off. Pazho's sudden frown matched my own. "Finish your thought, Endri."

A new voice sounded. "No. Let me."

46

CHAPTER FORTY-SIX

As ONE, QUEEN JENNICA, Pazho, Denaan, and I turned to face the newcomer.

"Your Majesty!" Pazho, Denaan, and I bowed deeply. Queen Jennica dipped her head slightly, a nod of respect from one sovereign to another.

King Tahrin waved a hand at us, indicating we should rise. "I ... I need to thank you, boy. For releasing us from that watery prison that would have eventually been our grave."

"It was no trouble, Your Majesty," I said.

"You're being too kind," the king said gruffly. "It was a lot of trouble, and I'm afraid there is still more trouble to come."

We all stayed silent, waiting for his explanation.

King Tahrin sighed heavily. "That old story ... it was brought to my attention several months ago, and I couldn't let it go. I—I put out a notice, secretly, for assistance in learning mirror magic. I offered to teach some of Annlyn's own secrets in trade. Not that shapeshifting can be taught, if one does not possess the innate ability, but ..."

Pazho raised an eyebrow. "Despite your adamance against letting outsiders know about our abilities?"

The king hung his head. "Yes. Despite that."

He sighed again, and when he looked up, there were tears in his eyes. "I hoped to succeed where the mage of the tale had failed. When Ambassador Allisandra came to court, bearing that mirror as a gift and the knowledge of how to use it, I couldn't believe my luck. I thought perhaps, if I could use a part of Princess Laersa's essence, I could bring my wife back...."

"And in doing so, you put all of Annlyn at risk."

"Pazho!" Denaan nudged his mate, trying to get him to be quiet. This was the king, after all. Even I was shocked at how Pazho had talked to him.

But the king just nodded sadly. "You are right, my old friend. I was a fool, and have now not only lost my wife, but the one good thing I have left of her—my only daughter."

"We'll get her back, Your Majesty," I said with more confidence than I felt. I took a deep breath, remembering the silvery-white world I had found myself in after leaving Lake Vitrum. "I wonder if Princess Laersa is in a mirror."

The king narrowed his eyes at me. "How could that be possible? The spell—I mean ..."

When he didn't continue, Pazho speared him with a look. "What spell, Your Majesty?"

The king deflated. "The ambassador said she could help me collect some of Laersa's essence with the mirror she brought to court, but the spell on the mirror had yet to be completed. Until that time, she said it was unstable."

Queen Jennica pursed her lips. When she spoke, her voice was cold. "I think we need to have a long talk, King Tahrin. But not here. And hopefully, once we get the answers we need, we can save your daughter."

"And your friend, too."

"Yes," Queen Jennica said. "Recovering Lady Farrah safely is a matter of both personal and political concern."

Her not-so-subtle threat hung in the air. I expected King Tahrin to bristle and bluster, but instead, he just nodded soberly. "I have put both my personal life and my kingdom's welfare at risk through my stupid and selfish actions. You have whatever aid you need from Annlyn to recover your friend."

"Good. And thank you." Queen Jennica brushed her hands together, as if to say, *Now that that's taken care of.* "All right, then. First thing—let's get these poor people back to Annlyn. And then, King Tahrin, we need to know all you know about Allisandra and her mirror. Hopefully, that will give us an idea of how to go after Princess Laersa and maybe even Farrah."

"Ahem." King Tahrin coughed pointedly. "Last I recalled, I was still the ruler around here."

Queen Jennica gave him her sweetest smile as she dipped a mocking half-curtsey. "Then, by all means, Your Majesty. Please lead."

He arched an eyebrow at her, and she met his gaze unblinking. After a moment, he laughed. "My wife would have liked you. We'll be friends, you and I." It wasn't quite a declaration of alliance between Annlyn and Calia, but perhaps it was a start.

King Tahrin clapped his hands together, getting the attention of the crowd. "My people! Now that we are restored to ourselves again, let us head back to Annlyn to recover, take stock, and repair our fair capital!"

A ragged cheer went up from the dazed crowd. Several guards began to gently corral people, and the king disappeared into the throng, offering encouragement.

Queen Jennica nodded in approval. "That's heartening to see. A good leader can admit when he's wrong."

A good leader wouldn't have put his own selfish wants above the good of his people. But I didn't say the words out loud.

The crowd started moving. Queen Jennica, Pazho, and Denaan started following. I hesitated, taking one last look at the deceptively still waters of Lake Vitrum.

"Endri," Pazho called to me. "Are you coming?"

I nodded and hurried after them. When I joined them, Denaan was saying, "It was just the oddest thing. I was in the middle of making the evening meal for the Red Antler, and I went into the garden to get some fresh herbs. A shadow fell over me, and suddenly my body wasn't my own anymore. I transformed into my elk form, and then I felt compelled to leave Annlyn. To come here, to the hills."

"I felt much the same way," Pazho said. "It's frightening, to be aware that you are doing things you don't want to, but be unable to fight it."

"Oh, that reminds me," I said. I tugged Pazho's silver ring from my finger and offered it to him. "I found your soulstone, Pazho. But Denaan, yours seems to have disappeared. Piedra gave me the cord, but I couldn't find the pendant."

Speaking of my cousins, where were they? I looked around, but didn't see a pair of hummingbirds anywhere. Perhaps they had flown ahead to Annlyn.

Denaan shook his head sadly. "I vaguely remember clawing at it and shaking it from my neck. I suppose I'll have to get a new one."

"How was everyone here able to turn back without their soulstones?" I wondered, waving at the crowd of people ahead of us.

Pazho slipped the ring back on his finger, giving a deep sigh of relief. The ruby winked in the sunlight. "Thank you for returning this, Endri. It's nice to have it back, even though it looks like I'll have to be parted from it again for a time for repairs."

He ran a finger over the cracked jewel, and I smiled at the familiar habit. "It's not necessary for one to have a soulstone to transform, but it does help. And since we use them so often, they become a part of us. Losing a soulstone feels like losing a limb, in a spiritual sense. But one can learn to adapt and transform without one—Queen Jennica's father Joichan is a perfect example of that."

"Oh, that's true," the queen said. "He spent years up in that mountain cave in solitude, and he didn't have his soulstone until I brought it back to him. But he still was able to shapeshift."

"So our soulstones don't really mean anything?" I thought of the years of lessons with Pazho. I touched my tourmaline pendant. "Did I not need this?"

"They mean something," Pazho said. "After all, once we use them, we create a magical bond with them. But ultimately, it comes down to the resolve of the shapeshifter." He smiled at me. "That's why I knew, one day, you'd be able to shift. And I'm so proud you proved me right."

I basked in my father's praise. "You were the only one. There were a lot of days—all of them, really—that I thought I'd never be able to shift."

Pazho clapped me on the back, but our good feelings faded somewhat when King Tahrin fell back to join us. "My guards have everything well in hand. Even moving this large of a group, we should be back to the capital in a few hours. I just hope that, in our absence, nothing has been altered at the palace."

I told the king about what I had seen at the palace, the second time I was there. He frowned at the mention of the pearlescent barrier surrounding it. "That 'ambassador' must have done something. But what about the mirror she gave me? Is it still there? Is it still intact?"

I nodded. "Yes, and yes."

"Good." He put a hand on my shoulder, stopping me from moving forward. A frowning Pazho also stopped, ready to interfere in case King Tahrin acted against me.

The king noticed Pazho's expression. "My old friend, I owe you an apology. If I had listened to you before, perhaps we wouldn't be in this situation. And now, I'm not afraid to admit that this is wholly my fault."

He turned to me. "You somehow freed us all, despite how impossible it seemed. You don't know how much I despaired, for my daughter and my kingdom, while I was trapped down there in Lake Vitrum. If you can save my daughter, then anything you ask for, if it is within my power to grant it, is yours. Just—please. Save my daughter. Bring my Laersa back to me."

47

CHAPTER FORTY-SEVEN

BY THE TIME THE citizens of Annlyn straggled through the ruined gates of the capital, the sun hung low in the sky. But there was still enough light to see the sorry state the city was in: broken doors and windows, ruined market stalls, piles of dirt and dung in the streets.

Around me, I could hear murmurs of dismay.

"Our fair city ..."

"How could we have caused so much destruction in such a short time?"

"Just looking at this makes me want to give up. This will take forever to clean!"

And then:

"Oh, gods. What is *that*?"

"The palace ... what's wrong with it?"

For beyond the city's destruction, at the far end, the castle loomed, proud and impressive—and with that shimmery, pearlescent barrier still around it.

King Tahrin pitched his voice to be heard above the crowd's dismayed murmurs. "My people! Do not lose heart! Together, we will restore our city to the beautiful oasis it was before! For now, return to your homes, rest, and enjoy the reunion with your loved ones. Tomorrow, we rebuild!"

A ragged cheer went up at his words, but it sounded obligatory and half-hearted to me. I couldn't help but wonder if Princess Laersa would have inspired more heart from the people of Annlyn. From what I had seen, she worked alongside her people, something that endeared her to them more than her royal status ever would.

King Tahrin turned to Queen Jennica. "I would offer you a place to stay at the palace, as befitting your station, but as you can see, the palace seems to be out of commission at this time."

Pazho said, "The queen is welcome to stay at our humble home, for as long as she requires."

"Thank you, Pazho," Queen Jennica said. "But before I settle in for the night, I'd like to take a look at the shield that covers the palace." She pursed her lips. "Again."

"Again?"

We began walking towards the palace, followed by a few soldiers, servants, and courtiers.

Queen Jennica recounted what had happened when she had last encountered the barrier. "Once I touched it, I realized it was a trap, to capture my human self. But I couldn't fight it off. And then I couldn't control myself—my animal instinct took over."

"How did you manage to get through, then, Endri?" Pazho asked me.

"Lady Farrah warded me," I said. "When I left the castle, it was with the ambassador and the construct pretending to be Princess Laersa. I don't think it would have affected the construct. The real princess would have been with King Balor, and I'm sure he would have kept it from harming her."

"And King Balor created the barrier. So as Ambassador Allisandra, he could pass through it with no problem." He tapped his chin in thought. "With King Balor gone, I wonder if the spell around the castle has weakened?"

"It would be better if it had just left with him," I grumbled.

Pazho chuckled. "If only it were that simple."

We had reached the castle, stopping in front of the shimmery shield to study it in the fading light.

"No one should pass through this barrier until we have determined how to dismantle it," King Tahrin announced. A general murmur of agreement arose from the crowd. People milled around, talking or looking curiously at the shield.

Recalling the last time, I was careful not to touch it. But as I stood near it, I realized something had changed.

"Pazho," I said.

My father must have heard the urgency in my voice, because he broke off his own study of the barrier—and trying to get Pazho to stop investigating something was no easy feat—and came to where I was standing. "Endri? What is it?"

I raised an outstretched hand towards the shield. My fingers hovered just shy of actually touching it. "Something is different. Before, it acted hungry, like it would swallow me whole. Or at least, one of my forms. Now, it feels—still hungry, but also fragile."

The shield suddenly rippled. I gasped as Pazho pulled me back.

I caught a glimpse of a moving shadow on the other side of the barrier.

"Francis!" King Tahrin sounded annoyed. "While I commend you for wanting to return to your post, a bit of warning would have been nice. And this magic could have hurt you!"

"Sorry, Your Majesty," Francis said, embarrassed. Whether it was from being caught at disobeying the king's orders, or from being caught holding his torn uniform, I wasn't sure. Then again, it could have been from the fact that he was facing a sizable crowd—one that included his sovereign and several Annlyn nobles—in nothing but a thin pair of worn breeches.

"Wait," I said. "Francis, did the barrier do anything to you when you passed through it?"

The guard frowned. "It stung a little, like it was poking at me while I walked. And I'm ticklish. But other than that, not really. A small part of it felt a bit familiar."

I scrutinized the guard through the barrier. "Do you have your soulstone?"

He shook his head. "I can't find it. I thought it would be with my clothes, but it's not here."

Francis bundled up his uniform and disappeared into the castle. I stared after him, thinking. *The barrier was now a little fragile. And ... familiar.*

I waved at Queen Jennica to join Pazho and me. "Pazho. Your Majesty. I wonder ..."

"Yes?" Pazho prompted, when I didn't continue right away.

"If this shield is connected to King Balor, then it stands to reason that it is connected to the 'mirror' of Lake Vitrum, where everyone was imprisoned. And to the king's mirror magic in general. Does that sound right?"

Both Pazho and Queen Jennica nodded.

"I never felt any 'familiarity' when I went through the barrier the last time. But I have my soulstone with me." I touched my tourmaline pendant. "If Francis felt that part of the barrier was calling to him—"

"Then perhaps this barrier is comprised of everyone's soulstones," Queen Jennica said. "Endri, that's brilliant."

"But Francis didn't get his soulstone back when he went through the barrier," Pazho pointed out. He frowned. "At least, he said he couldn't find it. He wasn't very helpful, honestly."

"It's all right. We don't need him," I said. "But I do think we need the majority of Annlyn to help. As many people as possible."

Pazho waved a hand at the crowd around the castle. "Is this group not sufficient?"

"Maybe. But just to be safe, let's get all the other shapeshifters over here."

Queen Jennica nodded and went to talk to King Tahrin. Soon, several runners were dispatched to gather the people throughout the city.

In what seemed like no time at all, the courtyard flooded with the citizens of Annlyn. Although the people looked weary—after all, they had just escaped a watery prison and walked half a day home, only to return to utter destruction—a sense of determination permeated the air. Knowing that they might be able to get their soulstones back, something that was such an intimate part of each shapeshifter, had buoyed their spirits.

Although not everyone would be able to get their original soulstones back. Sadly, I remembered Pazho's cracked gem.

King Tahrin said, "Everyone's here, Endri. Now, what would you have us do?"

I looked out at all the expectant faces. And swallowed nervously. All these people, with hope in their eyes, waiting for me to instruct them.... Gods, I hoped I wasn't wrong about this.

I cleared my throat. Loudly, I said, "Everyone, spread out and find a spot in the barrier for yourself. Don't touch it until I tell you."

The gathered crowd dispersed, until the shield that surrounded the palace was itself surrounded by a wall of people. Courtiers and commoners alike mixed, with shorter people ducking under their taller counterparts to make sure every inch of the shield was covered. I heard giggles and talking, and the whole thing seemed almost festive.

When I was sure everyone was settled, I stepped up to the barrier. Pazho and Queen Jennica moved slightly to make room for me.

"All right, everyone. On three. One—"

A collective sigh sounded around me. There was some last-minute rustling as people readied themselves.

"Two—"

I met Pazho's eyes as I raised my hand. Gods, I hoped I was right, or I would be responsible for single-handedly annihilating all of Annlyn.

"Three!"

As one, everyone placed their hand on the barrier. It buckled under our collective magical weight.

"When you find that small, familiar feeling, hold on to it! Call it to you! That is your soulstone!"

The shield rippled again, more violently this time.

Then, in a shower of sparks, the barrier dissipated. A cheer went up again, much happier than the one at the gate had been.

And in the glow of sunset, a myriad of shining gemstones appeared in the sky, looking like colored stars before falling down into the eager, waiting hands of their shapeshifting owners.

48

CHAPTER FORTY-EIGHT

"THERE IT IS. DO whatever you think is fit. Break it, burn it, I don't care. Just get my daughter back."

King Tahrin waved a hand at the shiny mirror hanging on the wall, then slumped back in his throne, exhaustion and sorrow evident in every line of his body. Now that the shield had been taken down and the citizens of Annlyn had been safely restored to their homes, the monarch had relaxed somewhat, allowing us to see glimpses of his personal turmoil.

Not that there were many of us to witness it. I stood in front of the ornate mirror in the palace's throne room, looking it over uncertainly. Nearby, Pazho and Queen Jennica talked in low voices. They had decided to accompany the king and me, since they both had magical insights that might prove helpful.

Denaan had decided to go to the Red Antler Inn to cook, even though we had all just arrived. "That King Balor sounds like a nasty sort to tangle with—and I've already tangled with him once. I'd rather not get in the way of all you magically inclined folk. My time will be better spent feeding whoever wants to come by the Red Antler."

I nearly offered to help him, even though King Tahrin had made it clear I was needed to find his missing daughter. Denaan's generous offer had attracted a long line of people before we had barely cleared the castle's portcullis. But my duty to the princess and the king had to come first. Besides, we had found my hummingbird cousins among the crowd at the barrier, leading to a quick and happy reunion. When Denaan had announced that he was going to the Red Antler, they had immediately volunteered to go with him.

Although the shimmery barrier was now gone, and we had seen no new signs of King Balor, we also had not seen any signs of Lady Farrah. While it would be good for Annlyn if King Balor had, indeed, left, I didn't know what that would mean for the noblewoman.

Beyond the throne room, the hallways were busy with servants cleaning the palace and setting things to rights.

But now, however, I sighed, nowhere close to unlocking the mirror's secrets. "I wish Lady Farrah was here."

Queen Jennica put a sympathetic hand on my shoulder. "As do I. She's much better at the whole adventuring thing than I am."

"I wouldn't say that, my dear queen," Pazho said. "You're getting a lot of practice in."

Queen Jennica chuckled. "That I am."

Her smile faded as she, too, studied the mirror. She must have had the same luck as I did, for she turned to King Tahrin and asked, "When the ambassador—or I suppose I should say, King Balor—gifted you this, did she have any instructions as to its use?"

King Tahrin shook his head. "Not really. Allisandra said she had enchanted it prior to her arrival in Annlyn. She mentioned needing to complete the spell, through some sort of a ritual, but we didn't do anything before ... everything happened. I do remember she didn't want me to touch it. She said no one should touch it, until she had a chance to finish the spell. And she only took her gloves off after she had attached the mirror to the wall."

I leaned forward, studying the mirror more closely. It looked overly bright, too polished, but a small stain marred the object's perfection.

"What's this?" I reached out to touch the glass.

Next to me, a slender hand shot out, grabbing my wrist before I could do so.

"Don't touch it," Queen Jennica warned. She also peered at the dark red spot, about the size of the tip of my finger, that stained the mirror's right hand corner.

It looked like—was that blood? Seeing that, my own blood ran cold. "Did this mirror break at any point?"

Even as I asked, I doubted it. The mirror appeared to be in perfect condition. And, if it had broken, I doubted the king would have had time to have it repaired before the Shadow forced everyone to shift.

"No, it's still intact," the king confirmed. "And I'm not sure where that stain came from."

My heart sank, remembering my conversations with Laersa. "I think I know."

King Tahrin, hearing my voice shift, gave me a sharp look, but I continued on. "Your Majesty, did Allis—I mean, King Balor—say how many souls could be contained in one mirror?"

He tapped his chin, thinking. "You know, I do recall her saying something about that. I—I think, if I remember right, the size of the mirror determines how many souls it can hold. And how much of a person's soul it can hold. A small hand mirror, for example, wouldn't be able to hold an entire soul—"

"—But something of this size would be able to," I finished.

The king closed his eyes and turned his head away.

"What is it, Endri?" Pazho asked me in a low voice.

I frowned. "When I first met Princess Laersa, one of her hands was bandaged. She had cut her hand—I assumed she had dropped a glass or a pitcher, and injured herself while cleaning it up. Later, she told me that she had touched this mirror. But—it didn't take her right away. Why the delay?"

"While part of me is sure King Balor can only speak lies, perhaps in this case he spoke the truth," Queen Jennica said, studying the mirror. "The spell he placed on it beforehand may have needed his guidance to finish it. But when the princess interacted with the mirror, prior to the spell's completion, she may have upset the process. Which could be why it took Princess Laersa physically, instead of just taking part of her essence like it was supposed to."

Pazho tilted his head, thoughtful. "And that may explain why King Balor's Shadow was so intent on bringing her back here. To finish the spell, or correct it. Magic is a tricky thing—if it's not done just so, all sorts of things can go wrong."

King Tahrin said, "Well, if she's in there, let's just break it and set her free. It worked before, at the lake. Why can't we do it again?"

Queen Jennica shook her head. "I think it worked because Endri was caught in the lake's spell with us. If he had tried to break it from the outside—well, I'm not entirely sure, but he might have condemned us and all of Annlyn to death."

King Tahrin deflated. "So we can't break it then?" At Queen Jennica's somber nod, he sighed. "It's too late, then. My daughter is truly lost to me, forever."

"No."

Queen Jennica, Pazho, and King Tahrin all gave me curious looks, surprised at the conviction in my voice. To be honest, even I was surprised at how sure I sounded.

Or maybe it wasn't sureness, but my sheer stubbornness.

Queen Jennica shook her head. "I hate to say it, Endri, but I think King Tahrin is right. It is too late. I don't see what we can do. If we break it ..."

I took a deep breath.

"We're not going to break it. I'm going in the mirror after her."

49

CHAPTER FORTY-NINE

THE BIG QUESTION, THEN, was *how* I was going to jump into the mirror after Princess Laersa.

"I could just try walking into it," I said dubiously.

"Not without some magical protection, first," Queen Jennica said.

"I don't think I'll need to worry about being able to breathe on the other side, like I had to when I was in Lake Vitrum," I pointed out.

"No, but there might be other things in the mirror that could hurt you. Princess Laersa might not be the only living thing on the other side."

A good point. I fell silent as Queen Jennica muttered a spell, waving a hand at the mirror. Her spell hit the center of the glass, and a blueish-purple glow spread from the middle outward.

She stepped back to survey her handiwork, and nodded, satisfied. "That should do it. When you pass through the glass, that ward will cling to you and protect you, for a few hours at least."

I studied the swirling colors. "It—it doesn't cover the glass, entirely."

The queen pursed her lips. "I'm afraid I'm not as skilled as Farrah is at creating wards. Just make sure you go directly through the center, and you should be okay."

"Okay," I echoed.

I started to move closer to the mirror, when a hand on my shoulder stopped me.

"You don't have to do this, you know."

Pazho's hand felt like a lead weight, as if he could physically burden me so I couldn't jump into the mirror. I turned, giving him a hug.

"I know, Father. And I don't even know if this will work. But I have to at least try."

He nodded, tightening his arms around me. "Every day, you make Denaan and me more and more proud. Just ... make sure you come back to us, son."

"I will." *I hoped.*

"I wish there was some way we could still communicate, once you go inside."

"If there is, you know I'll do so."

"Take care, then, Endri."

Pazho released me and stepped back, wringing his hands. I'd never seen him do that before—my father was usually so calm and composed. Denaan was the one who usually showed strong emotion, not Pazho.

With a nod to King Tahrin and Queen Jennica, I stepped into the mirror. I could feel Queen Jennica's shield morph and mold around me, clinging to me as I moved through.

My entire body was nearly through the glass when I slipped. I flung out an arm to steady myself, trying to find something to grab onto.

"Ow!"

My hand came back with a fresh red line down the center of my palm. I squeezed my hand into a fist, willing the blood to stop. But it wasn't the blood loss that bothered me. It was getting cut by the mirror, when I had been warned to avoid that.

I sighed. Well, what was done was done. I couldn't change that, so I would just have to be more careful in the future. For now, I would need a makeshift bandage. Already I was cursing my lack of preparedness. I should have at least brought some supplies with me instead of just running right through the glass.

I opened my hand, ready to rip off part of my shirt to use as a bandage, while resigning myself to the inevitable bloody mess that would result. But when I looked at my palm again, the blood had already clotted. The wound looked like it had happened a day or two ago, and not just mere moments before.

A chill crept down my spine. Whatever magic the mirror possessed, it was now definitely in my body.

I turned, figuring I could step back through the glass and have Pazho and Queen Jennica look at my wound. They would take care of any lingering magic, and I could return here with necessary items like bandages and food. But there was nothing behind me, just a blank silvery-white wall.

In fact, everything around me was blank and silvery-white and misty. The only things of color were me, my clothes, and the blueish-purple ward that clung to me, looking like a richer version of my ice dragon scales. Although I was sure my feet were firmly planted on the ground, the mirror's interior gave me the feeling that I was detached and floating.

Well, at least it should be easy to find Princess Laersa in this, I thought.

A faint shuffling noise caught my attention.

Wary, I looked around, but couldn't see anything except that never-ending, eye-blinding, silver-white landscape. I drew my sword—one of the few things I still had with me—and tensed, ready to fight.

And then a spot of color—blessedly familiar—stepped out of the white.

"Endri!"

"Princess Laersa!" I started to put my sword away, then stopped. "Uh—it is you, isn't it, princess?"

She tilted her head, confused. "Of course, it's me. Who else would it be?"

I still didn't let down my guard. "If it's you, tell me something to prove it. Something only I would know."

She raised an eyebrow, but humored me. "Okay, then. I like to use the secret passages in the palace to spy on Father's council meetings. And we both practiced shifting together. You started turning blue. And as for me ..."

She put a finger up, indicating I should wait. I was about to ask her what I should be waiting for, when her form began to distort in front of me.

No, not distort.

Shapeshift.

Her nose elongated into a purple snout, the same one I had seen hinted at when we practiced days before. Deep purple scales sprouted along her tan skin as her body began to grow bigger and longer. Astonished, I stepped back a few paces to give her room.

Rearing up, she extended two majestic violet wings and roared. A bolt of yellow lightning shot from her mouth. My hair stood on end as the air around me crackled and sparked. The sensation faded quickly, and Princess Laersa settled back on the ground. Lowering her head, she regarded me with mesmerizing golden eyes.

I laughed. Only Princess Laersa could make a dragon look smug.

I clapped my hands in excitement. "You learned how to shift! That's amazing! You're so beautiful!"

Belatedly, my words reached my brain, and I coughed in embarrassment. "I mean—you're already beautiful as a human, but you as a dragon—ah ... um ..."

The purple dragon made a loud wheezing sound. I looked at her sharply, dismayed, until I realized that the princess was laughing at me.

I chuckled. "I'm proud of you. I bet you can't wait to show your father. Once we get out of here."

The lightning dragon nodded as its form began to collapse in on itself. Soon, Princess Laersa the human was standing before me.

I raised an eyebrow. "Wow. And I'm impressed. You make changing back look so easy. Do you know how hard it's been for me to flip back and forth between both of my selves?"

Princess Laersa giggled. If I had any doubts before that the person standing before me was the true Princess Laersa, I didn't anymore. "Well, I've had a lot of time to practice while I've been stuck in here."

She sighed, her mirth fading. "Nothing but endless time. I've wandered everywhere around here, and tried everything I can think of, but I can't figure out how to get out of here. And now that hateful man brought someone else here. It's nice not to be alone, but ..."

"Someone else is here? Who?"

"Oh—the lavender-haired woman from Calia we met on the call. I think her name was—Lady Farrah?"

50

CHAPTER FIFTY

I followed Princess Laersa through the endless white void to where she had left Lady Farrah. I don't think we walked very far, but the lack of landmarks or color, plus the mist that occasionally swirled around us, made it feel like I was traveling forever. I wondered how Princess Laersa was able to find her way around here.

I was right about to ask her when she stopped abruptly. "Here she is."

The silvery-white mist cleared to reveal Lady Farrah lying on the ground, her eyes closed.

I knelt down, trying to ignore the uneasy feeling that we were floating in the air. "Lady Farrah! Are you all right?"

She didn't answer me. And her eyes stayed firmly shut.

"She's been unconscious since she got here," Princess Laersa said. "I've tried to wake her up, but ..."

"You mentioned some man brought her. Did he say what his name was?" Although I think I already knew.

The princess shook her head. "No. He just appeared—yesterday, I think? I lose track of time in here—and said, 'Keep an eye on her, if she dies you'll wish you had, too.' And then he vanished."

"What did he look like?"

"Long blond hair, with two black strands framing his face. Scary long black fingernails. Melodic voice." She tilted her head, considering. "You know, he reminded me a bit of Ambassador Allisandra. Like they could have been related—brother and sister, or maybe cousins."

"That's because he was Allisandra." I filled her in on the events that had happened since she had been captured, up to when I released the people of Annlyn from Lake Vitrum. But when it came to explaining the exact reasons for why she was in the mirror, I hesitated.

"Oh, gods, that's horrible," Princess Laersa said after she heard my tale. "I'm so glad you were able to free our people. They must have been so scared."

"Everyone seemed a bit dazed afterwards. I'm sure by now the magnitude of what they went through is hitting them."

The princess balled her hands into fists. "I have to get out of here. I need to be back in Annlyn, working alongside our people to repair the city and offer them comfort. Father will do what he can, of course, but the people tend to fear him, instead of welcome him. They need me. Father needs me, too, even if doesn't always acknowledge it."

She paused. "But I don't understand something. Why was Father so keen on learning this mirror magic?"

Oh, dear. This was it. The part of the story I had been dreading telling her.

I took a deep breath. "Princess Laersa, you might want to sit down for this."

She gave me a funny look, but sank down beside me. "Endri, what is it?"

I took another deep breath and began talking. "There's an old story ..."

I relayed the tale Pazho had told me about the magician and his daughter. Princess Laersa listened politely, but I could tell the story didn't really interest her. But as I began relaying how King Tahrin's grief caused him to look into ways to make the fabled story come true, she sat up straighter, eyes wide, focused on every word I was saying. By the time I finished my explanation, the princess burst into tears.

"How could Father do this to me? To the kingdom? He was willing to risk my life and our kingdom's future on an old story, which may or may not even be true!" She sniffled, trying to get herself under control. "I can't believe it. No, wait. I *can* believe it."

She turned watery eyes on me. "Ever since Mother died, he hasn't been the same. I should have known he would go crazy in his grief. I should have stopped this. Checked in on him more. I should have ..."

I pulled her to me, putting a comforting arm around her. "There's nothing you 'should' have done. You did everything you could. He should have been watching out for you. He's your father, after all."

She leaned into my embrace. "We're supposed to be watching out for each other. That's what family does."

"Not all family is like that." Thinking of my birth family, the words slipped out of me.

Princess Laersa's breath hitched. Hastily, I continued speaking. "Blood ties don't always mean what we hope they mean. But sometimes you find something better. Something stronger, and more true."

The princess nodded into my shoulder as she relaxed. But then, her eyes widened and she abruptly sat up. "I wonder—maybe that's why ..."

"Why what?"

She swallowed, fear veiling her beautiful dark eyes. "When the Shadow brought me here, I was so weak. But I didn't know why. I only knew that I felt more and more drained. I thought it was from all the excitement—you know, our people turning into animals, and disappearing, and then us running from the black cloud. Once I was in here—this odd mirror world—I could barely open my eyes, let alone fight back. The Shadow hovered over me, and I felt myself get even weaker, but I didn't understand what was happening."

She buried her face in my shoulder. "It took all I had to call you for help. You ... you heard me, even if you didn't know where I truly was."

I tilted her chin slightly so I could look into her eyes. Even with tear streaks down her cheeks and her nose red from crying, she still looked beautiful to me. "Finding you was my biggest priority. I was just glad you gave me a hint."

Princess Laersa sniffled again. "Really?"

"Yes. Also, I know your father regrets what he did. He wants nothing more than for you to come home safely."

She paused. "Thank you."

A lone tear slipped down her left cheek. Tenderly, I wiped it away with my thumb. But before I could withdraw my hand, she caught it with her own.

My skin felt all tingly, like it had earlier when the princess had demonstrated her new ability with lightning. Except I was fairly certain no more lightning lingered in the area. Still, the space between Princess Laersa and me felt just as charged.

Slowly, I leaned towards her.

A mocking, slow clap sounded behind us.

51

CHAPTER FIFTY-ONE

WE BOTH JERKED AWAY, looking up to see who was clapping.

"Oh, don't mind me," a familiar, languid voice said. "I was just reveling in the joys of young love."

Princess Laersa shrank behind me, trying to hide herself from the newcomer. Seated on the ground, I was at a severe disadvantage to look menacing, but I did my best to position myself so I was protecting both the princess and the unconscious Lady Farrah.

King Balor leaned down to get a better look at me. "Interesting. I recognize you. You're the young man who was with Lady Farrah at the lake." He smirked. "I wondered where you went. How lovely to see you again."

"I'm afraid I can't say the same." I tried to sound defiant, but the slight tremor in my voice gave me away.

"Funny, I seem to get that sentiment often. Usually from your friends." He waved a hand at Lady Farrah. "I'm sure if she was awake, she would say the same as you."

"What did you do to her?"

"I? Do anything?" The Fae king played with the cord around his neck.

That creepy eye pendant was, thankfully, hidden under his shirt, but I worried that he would bring it out and use it again. If he did, there was nothing I could do to fight its magic. And unless Princess Laersa had acquired more magical ability during her confinement than I was aware of, she would be just as powerless.

King Balor clicked his tongue in mock sympathy. "It's just a mere side effect of being caught up in my Eye's gaze. Lady Farrah is lucky. When my Eye looks upon most living creatures, they usually end up dead, not unconscious."

He sounded disgruntled, as if what he really wanted to say was, *How dare Lady Farrah not die like she was supposed to?* It was small comfort, but it gave me hope nonetheless.

"But why bring her here?" I waved a hand to indicate the silver-white void surrounding us. "She needs a healer. And if you didn't want her alive, you could easily have killed her back on the shores of Lake Vitrum."

King Balor frowned. "I suppose I could have. It would have made things much easier. But Lady Farrah is much more useful to me alive than dead, at this point."

His gaze sharpened on me. "You don't know much about mirror magic, do you?"

I shook my head.

He smiled, a frightening sight. "It's such a lovely thing. I think everyone should try it at some point. Not only does it amplify your power when you use a mirror, but inside a mirror is a wonderful place to store things until you need them again. Time is suspended here. There's no need for food, but, as at Lake Vitrum—"

"—Lady Farrah's magical power will drain out over time while she's in here." My blood ran cold.

King Balor clapped again. "Aren't you the smart one? Yes, since I lost my magical reserves at Lake Vitrum, I needed a little something to draw from, however small the source. Lady Farrah, with her magic, was so conveniently there for the taking. I must say, it was fascinating to be able to wander above ground during the day, something I would never have been able to do without the amplified magic. And speaking of Lake Vitrum, you must be fairly clever, if you were able to escape my enchanted mirror within it. Perhaps you should join with me. I could use someone like you."

I wondered if Princess Laersa also heard the slight emphasis that King Balor put on the world "use". I shuddered. "No, thank you."

"Pity." King Balor looked beyond me to Princess Laersa, who was doing her best to go unnoticed. "And, as for this fetching creature behind you—I'm afraid I was in a bit of a hurry last time to introduce myself properly. My dear Princess Laersa, don't be shy. I am King Balor, ruler of the Unseelie Fae."

The princess buried her face in my shoulder, as if hiding could make the Fae king go away. He put a long black fingernail under her chin, forcing her to look at him.

"You look a lot like Tahrin, although much more pleasing to the eye. But don't tell him I told you so. After all, royals can be so incredibly vain." He smirked. "And unfortunately, my experiment failed. Once you came here, a copy of your mother was to emerge, with my Shadow controlling her. But we got that simulacrum of you instead. Sad, really. I was looking forward to manipulating Tahrin through his new 'wife.'"

He shook his head in mock sadness. "Well. I'll figure it out for next time."

He straightened, towering over us. In the limitless silvery-white space, with the mist haloing his blond hair, he looked like a giant—or a corrupted angel. Mentally, I kicked myself for not seeing any of the warning signs sooner. But he had been quite convincing as the helpful, sweet Ambassador Allisandra.

"Well, my dear princess, I thank you for keeping my captive alive in my absence." King Balor sketched a bow in our direction. "But now, as lovely as it has been to talk with you, my prisoner and I must be going. Once she's settled to my satisfaction, I'll come back for you both. Hopefully all your magic won't have drained out of you by then."

"What are you going to do with our magic?" I hoped King Balor didn't hear the little squeak of fear that crept into my voice.

He smiled. "Why, my dear boy, there is a gateway to the gods that I want to open. My last try failed—" he threw a pointed glance at the unconscious Lady Farrah "—so I thought perhaps if I bolstered my magic another way, I would be successful. And perhaps the gateway needs power that is more rooted in the Gifted Lands, than the wild magic I tried to harness before."

King Balor sniffed the air, like a bloodhound ready to track another animal. "Mmm. You both have some lovely shapeshifting magic, it just pulses with Gifted Lands energy. Although you—" he pointed at me with one long black fingernail "—have a good deal more power than she does. Hers is still weak. Perhaps it was stealing part of her essence that weakened her. And it's only Lady Farrah's human magic that is so appealing to me."

He lowered his voice to a conspiratorial whisper. "Just between us, human magic is not even that great.

"But your magic, my dear boy, will be absolutely delicious. I will quite enjoy draining you of your power, although it might prove difficult. I hope I don't spend more energy trying to extract your magic than I can get. Oh, well, we shall see what happens. Until then."

He raised a hand, ready to cast the spell that would let him leave.

"Wait."

King Balor lowered his hand, his eyebrow raised. Princess Laersa tugged on my sleeve, trying to warn me against speaking out. Or against doing something foolish. Probably both.

Glancing at the still form of Lady Farrah, I cleared my throat. "I understand that the Fae enjoy making bargains."

The Fae king pursed his lips, but I could have sworn his eyes kindled. Hadn't Lady Farrah said that the Fae loved a good bargain? "Speak on."

I stood up, with my hands out, palms up, to show I meant no harm. "Here's what I propose. Let Lady Farrah and Princess Laersa leave the mirror, unharmed, and return to Annlyn."

King Balor snorted. "That's your bargain? That's hardly worth it to me."

"And in exchange, I'll stay here. I have more—and better—power for you to use. I'll let you drain me, just like you wanted, and I won't fight you on it."

Princess Laersa gasped. "Endri, no!"

I kept my eyes locked on King Balor's face. "Do we have a deal?"

52

CHAPTER FIFTY-TWO

THE FAE KING STEEPLED his hands. His long nails clicked against each other as he wiggled his fingers together, thinking. "Ooh. All that delicious power, and your complete cooperation? That does sound lovely."

I shoved my hands in my pockets. My hand brushed against the ice dragon figurine, which had been my constant companion throughout this whole craziness. I rubbed my thumb against it, taking comfort in its familiar lines.

King Balor tapped his chin thoughtfully. "I can't think of any downsides. My two failed experiments leave, and I get a new minion. And if you ever cross me or I tire of you, I can always kill you."

I tightened my fingers around the carving, feeling it turn cold in my palm.

The Fae king shrugged. "Hmm. Sounds good to me. Perfect, actually. Yes, I agree to your deal."

I nodded in acknowledgment. "Good. What do I need to do?"

He looked me over, noting the faded scratches along my arms, and even across my collarbone. "It looks like you've already been marked by my mirrors."

"Yes—from Lake Vitrum, and then just recently, from walking into this one." I surreptitiously hefted the figurine. It had grown heavy, absorbing the chill from my fingers. A slight bit of frost had begun to form on the little dragon's wings.

"Perfect. Then there is nothing else we need to do. Your blood has already bound you to me."

"All right, then."

A choked sob made me turn and look behind me. Princess Laersa was now kneeling beside Lady Farrah, tears streaming down her face. "Endri, this isn't right. You shouldn't have to stay. I'll stay."

I knelt down to look her in the eye. "No, princess. You have a country to take care of, and a father to help heal. You're needed in Annlyn more than me."

She looked away, distraught. We both knew the truth of my words. Slowly, she nodded.

King Balor snapped his fingers. To his right, the silvery-white mist started to gather, then swirl around a central point. It grew bigger and bigger until it was easily my height.

He waved at the portal. "Enough crying. Princess, are you ready?"

She sniffled, then whispered, "Yes."

She stood, and she flung herself into my embrace. "Endri, I'll miss you. And I'll never forget you. Thank you—for everything."

"I'll never forget *you*, princess. Be well out there."

There was a pointed cough from the Fae king. "Can we *please* get on with it?"

Princess Laersa looked down at Lady Farrah. "But how am I to move her?"

I moved to stand by the unconscious noblewoman's feet. "If you pick her up by her head, I'll lift her from this side. Once you get through the mirror, I'm sure someone will be nearby to help you.

When I left, Pazho and Queen Jennica were standing just in front of it."

"O-okay." Awkwardly, the princess put her arms under Lady Farrah's shoulders and lifted. I picked up the noblewoman's feet, and we sidestepped towards the swirling mist.

With one last tear-stained look at me, Princess Laersa stepped through the portal. Lady Farrah's upper body disappeared along with the princess, and suddenly I felt Lady Farrah's weight removed from my arms.

"Well, that was nice," King Balor said. He snapped his fingers again.

When another swirling white portal appeared, he waved at the new gateway. "And now, onto Faerie. You'll love it there, the Underground is so ... well, I wouldn't say scenic, necessarily, but it is quite interesting at times."

He held his hand out to me. "Shall we?"

The ice dragon figurine weighed down my pocket, and the cold that had infused it now seeped through the fabric. Perhaps my desperation was affecting it. But even though I could feel its chill, my palms were sweating.

I seriously hoped this worked.

"Before we go, I have something for you."

The Fae king eyed me curiously. "Is it your sword? I have no need of mortal weapons."

"No." I withdrew the dragon carving from my pocket. A thin layer of ice coated the tips of the dragon's partially outstretched wings, giving it an ethereal look. "This is for you. A pledge, of sorts."

King Balor took the figurine from me, holding it up so he could look at it closer. "How lovely. And it looks just like you. Well, your other you. How sweet."

While he admired the carving, I reached inside of myself, willing my dragon self to come forward. As fast as I could call it up, faster than I ever had before. My second self rushed to the surface, ready to seep into my skin and reknit my bones, but instead of allowing it to settle into my body, I held myself separate from my dragon self.

And then I pushed it out of me.

My second self was reluctant to leave, but I threw all my mental weight against it. With every bit of my being, I focused on expelling my dragon form from my human one. At any and every point where my ice dragon self was connected to me, I imagined severing those ties, throwing up a barrier so it couldn't come back to me.

I think I screamed.

My tourmaline soulstone grew as chilly as the dragon carving had. Both items had helped me when I was first learning to transform, and now, knowing that they were inextricably linked, I whispered to my second self, *Go to the figurine.*

I gave one final push.

My severed dragon self floated to the carving in King Balor's outstretched hand. I could feel its sadness, how forlorn it felt without me. Apart from me, it loomed over the Fae king, large and imposing.

"What is this? What is going on?" I could hear King Balor asking. He sounded flustered—and furious—but I focused on my connection with my second self.

Thank you for being there for me, even though it took me so long to find you. I'm so sorry it has to end this way.

Even though the ice dragon couldn't talk, I could sense its acceptance.

Goodbye.

And then I jumped through the portal.

53

CHAPTER FIFTY-THREE

As I PASSED THROUGH the portal, the swirling silver-white mist clung to me, making it near impossible for me to see what was around me with any clarity.

I could see some forms moving about, grey silhouettes against the white, and for a heart-stopping moment I thought, *What if I jumped through the wrong portal?* The mist distorted the shapes, and I couldn't tell how far away they were.

And then I hit the ground, hard, and my breath whooshed out of me. I closed my eyes, gritting my teeth against the pain.

From somewhere above me, I heard someone exclaim, "Oh, gods. It's Endri!"

I became aware of smooth, cool stone under my cheek.

Another voice said, "He's alive! He's all right."

I turned onto my back and opened my eyes.

Color had returned to the world—and I was staring into the concerned and relieved faces of Princess Laersa, Queen Jennica, and Pazho. Above me, I could see the criss-crossed wood and stone work of the throne room's high ceiling.

And behind my friends, the mirror I had just jumped through still hung on the wall. Milky white mist swirled in the glass.

The portal was still open.

I struggled to sit up. Princess Laersa, realizing what I was trying to do, said, "No, no, Endri. Stay still."

"N-no," I gasped. "I need to—the mirror."

Pazho scooped an arm underneath me and gently helped me sit up. Princess Laersa and Queen Jennica both stepped back, giving me a clear view of the enchanted mirror.

Was I imagining things? I thought I saw the shadow of a tall man in the glass, with a larger shadow hovering over him.

A chill bloomed at my neck. Touching my soulstone, I realized it felt just as cold as the figurine I had given King Balor.

They're still connected.

I screamed, my already raw throat throbbing harder. Yanking my soulstone from my neck, I threw it with all my might at the swirling mist.

As it flew through the air, I envisioned myself sending an icy blast after it.

And to my surprise—and perhaps the surprise of everyone else in the throne room—my imagined stream of cold air materialized, shooting from my open mouth towards the hurtling soulstone. It hit the necklace just a moment after the soulstone touched the glass, pinning the tourmaline to the mirror. A pale blue-green spread against the glass, and threads of ice began to spread from the center.

King Balor's face appeared in the mirror, perfectly visible despite the swirling mist. His face was snarled in rage. The ice dragon—my former self—harried him with each step, forcing the Fae king to stop and raise his arms in defense. His progress was slow going, but in mere moments, he would be through the portal.

I yelled again, throwing more frost at the mirror.

Additional cracks bloomed on the glass, forming quickly and growing larger.

Within the mirror, King Balor flicked his fingers at the ice dragon. It shrieked, stiffening, and fell to the ground.

"No!" I flung myself forward, intending to stand and run to the mirror, but Pazho held me back.

"Endri, don't!" Pazho said.

King Balor's other hand, balled into a fist, punched through the mirror. Black mist dripped from his long midnight-tinted fingernails as he started to open his clenched hand.

Behind him, the ice dragon rose, roaring as it made one last attempt to knock King Balor away from the portal.

And then the mirror shattered.

Within the glass, the spiraling silver-white mist abruptly stopped. A force within the mirror sucked the colorless fog backward, drawing a screaming King Balor with it. The ice dragon also disappeared.

As shards of glass sprayed in all directions, I fell back to the ground, instinctively rolling over onto my stomach and shielding my head with my hands. A weight dropped on top of me.

"Laersa! To me!" King Tahrin shouted from somewhere nearby.

A boom reverberated through the throne room, swallowing the crashing sound of the breaking mirror. A wave of magic followed the sound, washing over us all. It settled on me, making my skin tingle.

The deep sound faded.

The tingling sensation stopped.

I breathed in shallowly, trying to get my racing heart under control. The weight on me lifted, and I slowly turned around and sat up again.

Next to me, Pazho leaned back on his knees. "Are you all right, Endri?"

I took quick stock of myself. No new cuts, and no bleeding, at least that I could see. "Yes, I'm fine. How are you? How is everyone else?"

"I'm fine as well. Miraculously, I didn't get cut."

I looked around. A few paces away, Queen Jennica was warily sitting up, carefully shaking bits of glass from her long black hair. She was trying to avoid getting any glass shards on Lady Farrah, who was lying on the ground in front of her. The queen must have shielded Lady Farrah with her own body when the mirror broke.

Across the room, King Tahrin and Princess Laersa huddled together. Sensing that the danger had passed, they looked up and around.

And everywhere—on the stone floor, on the twin red velvet thrones, on a wooden side table—shards of glass sparkled, beautiful but deadly.

I gaped. The mirror had been large, but I hadn't thought it contained this much glass.

Pazho turned to Queen Jennica. "My dear Jennica, how about you? And Lady Farrah?"

"I'm good," the queen said. "And so is Lady Farrah, I believe."

"Your Majesty? Your Highness?"

"We're all right," King Tahrin said. Next to him, Princess Laersa nodded mutely.

"Well, then." Pazho surveyed the throne room. "I suppose the next thing we should do is get away from all of this mess."

Carefully, my father stood up, bits of glass falling from his clothes as he did so. He held out a hand to me and helped me up to the tinkling sound of more falling glass.

Pazho turned away to help Queen Jennica to her feet. At the other end of the room, King Tahrin slowly stood, then helped his daughter to her feet.

I looked down at my tunic, holding the bottom part away from my body so I could examine it better. It was no better than Francis the guard's shredded uniform, with a big rip on the bottom from where it had been caught in the trap, wrinkles and dirt from my many falls, and now, prickly little sharp objects covering it. "There's glass embedded in the fabric."

I squinted at Pazho. "In your shirt, too."

Pazho shook his shirt out, to no avail. He sighed. "That will make changing clothes rather tricky. Perhaps it might be best to cut the fabric off instead, to avoid getting sliced by glass."

"I'd be happy to provide you all with new clothing," King Tahrin said. "And probably soon. It can't be safe for us to run around in glass-filled clothes."

We all murmured our thanks. Then Queen Jennica said, "But what are we going to do about Lady Farrah? She's still unconscious. And with all this glass around ..."

An uncertain cough sounded at the throne room's entryway. A timid page ducked his head into the room. His eyes widened as he got a good look at the destruction. "Um. Excuse me. Your Majesty? Is everything all right? I just wanted to see—we heard a loud noise in here—and shouting—"

"Ah, it's good that you're here," King Tahrin said. "If you could escort my guests to some rooms where they could rest, and fetch Healer Arens to attend to them. Find them some new clothes they can change into. Send a few guards back here with a litter to transport Lady Farrah. And have a few others come in here to sweep up."

The page blinked, trying to remember the to-do list King Tahrin had just thrown at him. "Ah ... yes, Your Majesty. Right away. If you would follow me?"

This last part was directed to Pazho, Queen Jennica, and me. I made my way towards the page, wincing at the sound of crunching glass under my feet. I hoped the broken shards wouldn't also lodge themselves in my sandals. Pazho turned to Queen Jennica, holding out a hand to escort her.

She shook her head. "I'll wait here with Lady Farrah until that litter comes."

Pazho nodded. "A commendable idea." He picked his way through the sea of glass, joining me at the entrance.

The page stepped aside to let us pass. "Come with me, please."

Together, the three of us left the throne room.

54

Chapter Fifty-Four

The palace hallways hadn't fared much better than the throne room. In addition to the destruction the transformed citizens had wrought in their animal forms, the mirrored mosaic pieces had shattered as well. Our steps *crunch-crunch-crunched* as we walked over piles of broken glass. The once beautiful walls now had empty stone sockets surrounding the colorful painted tiles, like missing eyes.

Eyes. That reminded me of King Balor and that grotesque necklace of his. I shuddered.

"Are you sure you're well?" Pazho asked me.

I nodded. Two servants passed by, brooms in hand. Our guide stopped them.

"Where are you headed?"

"We were going to start sweeping the hallway outside the royal apartments," one of the servants said.

Our escort shook his head. "I have orders from the king. One of you, head to the throne room and start cleaning up there first. For the other, go to the guardhouse and tell them we have an unconscious woman in the throne room that needs to be carried to a guest room."

The two servants nodded and headed towards the front of the castle. The page continued on, waving at Pazho and me to follow.

"Excuse me," I said to the page's moving back. "But I was just wondering at the hallways and all the glass on the floor. When did this happen? And how?"

Without breaking stride, the page said, "It happened just a few moments ago. Some of us heard screaming coming from the throne room, and I was sent to investigate. On my way there, all the glass suddenly fell out of the walls."

He raised his hands, showing off a criss-cross of fresh cuts. "I did my best to protect myself, but ..."

Pazho frowned. "Oh, my. It looks like you could use a healer, as well."

"I'll be all right."

"Nonsense. Make sure you get that looked at."

The page nodded, only half listening as he turned a corner. It was clear he was thinking of all the things that King Tahrin had requested he do.

He stopped in front of a closed wooden door. Down the glass-littered hallway, I could see other closed doors lining both sides. "This wing houses chambers for our guests. Feel free to pick whichever one suits you. I'll be back with some new clothing for both of you."

"And a knife or a pair of shears, if that's not a bother?" Pazho smiled at the confused look on the young man's face. "It will make destroying our clothes much easier."

"Uh. Of course."

"I have my sword," I said, patting my belt.

"Shears will be better," my father said. "I'd be worried about cutting you with a larger blade."

The page blinked, and then his face smoothed over into a more neutral expression. No doubt he was used to odd requests from his sovereign and various courtiers. With a quick half-bow, he left, his hurried steps crunching glass down the hallway.

I opened the door to find a serviceable, plain-looking bedroom. Compared to my room back home at Pazho and Denaan's, it was quite grand, but it lacked the rich furnishings of King Tahrin's and Princess Laersa's chambers.

Suddenly feeling weary, I started to sink down on the bed.

"Stop! Don't sit down!"

Hearing the panic in Pazho's voice, I popped back up. "What? What is it?"

"I just didn't want you to sit on any glass."

I surveyed the bed, then the rest of the room. There was no glass, broken or otherwise, on the bed. The room didn't even have a mirror, and the walls in this chamber were made of grey, mirrorless stone.

"I don't see any glass," I pointed out.

My father waved at my tunic and pants. "Not on the bed. On your person."

Oh, yes. I had nearly forgotten. I sighed. "Thank you for warning me. I would not enjoy having glass in my behind."

Pazho chuckled. "Just saving the palace healer from having to do extra work."

"I hope that page returns soon."

A knock on the open door made Pazho and me look over. I ducked my head, embarrassed at being overheard. But I was also secretly pleased that my wish had been granted and I didn't have to wait long.

Another page, this time a young woman, entered the room holding a pile of clothing. "I have some items for you both to look over."

"Thank you," Pazho said. "You can put them on the bed."

As she put the clothes on top of the bed's blue-and-white quilt, another knock sounded at the door. A tall woman, about the same height as Pazho, stepped into the room. "I am Healer Arens. I understand my services are needed here?"

"Well met, Healer Arens," my father said. "I am Pazho, and this is my son, Endri."

I murmured a greeting. Healer Arens nodded at me in acknowledgement.

"The one who really needs your help is Lady Farrah, but I do not believe the guards have brought her this way yet," Pazho said.

"Is Lady Farrah the purple-haired woman, the one who is unconscious?" At our nods, Healer Arens said, "She is on her way here. I will wait in the hallway for her. But are you sure there is nothing either of you require?"

What I truly wanted—my second self within me again—was beyond the healer's power to give. Now that it was separated from me, I felt off-balance and empty, bereft and heartsick. It had hurt when my birth family had abandoned me, and I had eventually realized they would not be coming back for me. I had thought no pain would be worse than that.

I was wrong. This was so much harder to bear. I had lost an intimate part of myself, one I had just been getting to know. And even at the end, when I ripped it away and forced it to stay behind, it had fought for me.

In answer to the healer's question, Pazho shook his head, but I rubbed at my lower back and said, "Actually, I've taken a few hard falls recently. If it's possible ..."

The healer smiled. "Say no more. I'll make up a poultice for you, then return to look in on your friend."

"Thank you."

Healer Arens left. The page said, "If there's nothing else you need, I'll get going."

"Wait," Pazho said. "We're going to leave our old clothes out in the hallway. Please advise whoever cleans that area not to touch our things with their bare hands."

"I will."

"And I think it will be true of our companions, Lady Farrah and Queen Jennica, as well. Maybe even King Tahrin and Princess Laersa, too. Like us, they were caught in the explosion of glass earlier in the throne room, which made all of our clothes unusable."

"I see. I will pass on your warning. Is there anything else?"

"Hmm. Did you bring some shears?"

The page withdrew a pair of scissors from her belt. "Here you go, sir. You can return it to me when you're done with it."

"Thank you."

With that, the page left us. I closed the door after her, then picked up the scissors and motioned to Pazho. "Turn around." I eyed his shirt, glittering with glass. "We should have asked for a pair of gloves, too."

"I think we'll be fine. Just be careful."

55

CHAPTER FIFTY-FIVE

I SLICED THROUGH THE back of Pazho's tunic, gingerly ripping the fabric until it fell away from his body. He did the same to my outfit, and from there it was easy to step out of our trousers and avoid cutting ourselves. The light linen clothes that the page had brought were plain, both in color and pattern. After trying on a few items, I found an outfit that fit me.

Pazho, being taller than me by several inches, wasn't as lucky. I chuckled as I saw the outfit that he finally decided on. The sleeves of his new tunic were a little tight and short, giving off the impression that he had just gone through his growth spurt and had to make do with his current wardrobe. Meanwhile, his pants were too big, and my father had to roll the waistband several times to make them fit him—somewhat.

Pazho gave me a sour look. "Don't tell Denaan."

"Of course I'll tell Denaan. He'll be so mad he missed this."

Pazho shook his head, also chuckling. "I take back what I said earlier, about being proud of you. Shame on you for being such a disobedient son."

Still laughing, I opened the door and nudged our discarded clothes out the door with my sandaled foot. A few servants were in the hall, sweeping. And headed towards us were two soldiers, carrying Lady Farrah on a litter. Queen Jennica and Healer Arens followed behind.

I waved at the soldiers. "You can bring her in here."

The guards entered the room. It got a bit crowded, what with Pazho and I already in the chamber, but between us and the guards we were able to gently transfer Lady Farrah from the litter to the bed. Thanks to Queen Jennica's quick thinking in shielding her friend during the mirror's explosion, Lady Farrah's clothes didn't have as much embedded glass as the rest of ours had. Still, I knew Queen Jennica would be eager for us to leave so she could help her unconscious friend change.

Once the guards left, Healer Arens walked in, holding something. "Out, please, all of you. Let's give her some space."

Queen Jennica stood in the doorway, her arms crossed. "I'm not as good at healing as Farrah is, but if you need any magic at all, I am at your disposal."

"That's a generous offer, Your Majesty. But I suggest you rest for now. If I need you, I'll let you know."

For a moment, the queen looked like she wanted to argue. Then she deflated. "All right. But she needs to get out of those clothes, just in case there's any glass in them."

"I will see to it," Healer Arens said.

"I'll escort you to your room, Your Majesty," I said.

"Oh—before you leave." Healer Arens handed me the small cloth she had been carrying. "Put this on your back where it hurts. It might be easier to sleep directly on top of it."

I thanked him, then walked Queen Jennica to one of the empty bedrooms. As I turned to go, the queen said, "I haven't thanked you yet. For saving Farrah from the mirror—and King Balor. She's one of my dearest friends. If she had been trapped in that mirror forever ..."

Tears pricked her lovely dark eyes. I stood there awkwardly, not sure what to do. Pazho probably would have hugged her, but he had known the queen much longer than I had.

I settled for bowing to her. "Your Majesty, I am glad I could offer any assistance. I only wish I could have done more."

She nodded. Two tears slid silently down her cheeks. She turned to go into her room.

I blurted out, "She'll be okay. She's such a strong person. I'm sure she'll wake up soon."

Queen Jennica gave me a sad smile. "Yes, I hope so. Rest well, Endri."

She closed the door.

I headed to another empty room, which looked much the same as the one Lady Farrah now occupied. I drew back the covers, placing the poultice on the bed. I undressed and then settled myself on top of it. I promptly fell asleep, where my dreams were troubled by hazel-colored eyeballs staring at me from mosaic tiled walls.

I woke up feeling stiff and sore. But at least the soreness wasn't as bad as it had been before. The healer's poultice must have worked.

I became aware of a light tapping at my door.

"Who is it?" I called out.

"Princess Laersa," came the response.

"Oh! Give me a moment!"

I hopped out of bed—or tried to, anyway. My head felt groggy, and I moved slowly.

My clothes were lying in a heap at the foot of the bed. Wincing, I bent down to retrieve them. The poultice had helped, but I still had a ways to go before I felt completely better. Speaking of the poultice—I grimaced when I saw the mess of dried herbs and paste in the center of the bed. The poor palace servants were already working so hard to clean up the messes of the last few days, and here I was, just adding to their workload.

Princess Laersa knocked again. "Are you decent?"

"Yes! Come on in."

The princess opened the door, hesitantly peering into the room. When she saw me, she paused. For a moment, we just stared at each other.

The next thing I knew, she hurtled herself into my arms.

"Ow!"

The princess stepped back, embarrassed. "Oh, dear. Did I hurt you?"

I pulled back the sleeve of my shirt to show her the cuts all along my arms. "I remembered them just now. It's all right, a hug from you is worth the pain."

She giggled and embraced me again. With her face buried in my chest, she said, "I really thought I would never see you again. I was trying to convince Father to send some of his men into the mirror—a whole army, if that would have helped—when you tumbled out of it."

She looked up at me. "How were you able to leave?"

I swallowed hard. Although sacrificing my second self had been necessary, I still hadn't come to terms with it. "Remember my dragon carving, the one that we used to contact Queen Jennica?'

The princess nodded.

"I summoned my dragon self, then severed my connection to it and forced it into the carving. I left the carving with King Balor and jumped through the portal."

Her eyes were wide. "That other creature in the mirror—was that your dragon self?"

I nodded. "It was a gamble—I wasn't sure that what I was doing was going to work. But it did, and ... well, you know the rest."

She chuckled. "Yes, I do. It was quite the spectacle, when the mirror broke."

I laughed. "If I never see a mirror again, I'll be quite happy."

"I agree, although they can be useful." At my horrified look, she said hastily, "I don't mean for magic. Just for normal, mundane uses, like seeing how my lady-in-waiting dressed my hair."

I smirked. "Not something I've ever used a mirror for, but I understand."

She playfully swatted at my arm, then looked embarrassed when I winced. "Sorry. I forgot."

"It's all right. But I should probably ask Healer Arens if she has something for all these cuts." I looked around, but the curtains were drawn. My stomach grumbled, and I realized that I was quite hungry. "What time is it?"

"It's evening. You've just missed dinner, but I'm sure the servants can find something for you to eat."

"Evening only? That's not too bad."

She grimaced. "Well, it has been about two days since the mirror incident."

"*Two* days?"

She smiled sympathetically. "You've been through a lot. Healer Arens said your body just needed time to recover. But I was worried about you, during that time."

She stepped back. "You probably should talk to Healer Arens, now that you're awake. But before you do—I'm sure you saw how all the mirrors in the palace are broken, yes?"

I nodded. "I asked the page who escorted Pazho and me about it. From his description, I would guess all the mirrors shattered at the same time. I wonder if the same thing happened to any of the mirrors in the city, too?"

"Hmm. That's a good question. I'll send someone to ask around later. For now—" Princess Laersa withdrew a small object from her dress pocket.

"When I got back to my chamber, there was glass everywhere, just like in the rest of the palace. My vanity mirror had broken. I hope it can be restored. It was my mother's." She sounded regretful.

Sighing, Princess Laersa shook off her sadness. With a smile, she said, "But after my room had been cleaned, one of the servants gave me this. I believe it belongs to you."

She handed me the item. Dumbfounded, I stared at it.

It was my ice dragon figurine.

56

CHAPTER FIFTY-SIX

THE LITTLE BLUE ICE dragon carving stood proudly, firelight from the wall torches glinting off of its outstretched wings. It lacked the icy layer I had last seen it with, and it no longer held the cold weight I had infused it with in the mirror.

Pazho, Queen Jennica, Princess Laersa, and I sat around the long wooden table in the palace's dining hall. Although I still had to talk to Healer Arens, my growling stomach demanded I eat first. Upon hearing that I was awake, the other three had decided to join me for a late-night meal.

And now, with the dinner dishes cleared away, we all stared at the statuette I had placed in the center of the table.

"I can't believe you got it back," Princess Laersa said. "I could barely believe my eyes when my chambermaid gave it to me."

"It may have dropped from King Balor's hand when the mirror shattered," Pazho mused. "Although I don't know why it would have been in your room, Princess, and not the throne room."

She shrugged. "I don't know much about magic. I barely figured out how to transform into my second self. But when the Shadow brought me back to the palace, it first locked me in my bedroom. And then eventually pushed me through the mirror on my vanity."

"And when I entered the mirror world through the throne room mirror, you found me," I said. "The world inside the mirrors must have been connected. Or somehow, King Balor connected them."

"As evidenced by all the mirrors breaking," Queen Jennica said. "Yes, that would make sense. We should ask—ah, I meant to say, I will look into this some more."

She refrained from saying our best authority on mirror magic was still unconscious. Although I had awakened after two days' deep sleep, Lady Farrah had yet to wake after all this time. Whatever was afflicting her was obviously magical in nature, but the healers in Annlyn lacked the arcane knowledge to treat her.

Princess Laersa had instructed that servants attend Lady Farrah around the clock, keeping an eye on the noblewoman and making sure she was fed, bathed, and made comfortable. If there was any change, the servants were to inform the Princess immediately.

And that was another thing that had changed while I slept. King Tahrin, ashamed of how his actions had nearly destroyed his family and his kingdom, had hidden himself away in his chambers. Princess Laersa had taken over running the kingdom in his absence, and in the short time had proven herself a capable leader.

I think it helped that she was already so beloved by the people of Annlyn. Her taking over seemed effortless, natural, and ... right.

"What are you going to do with it, Endri?" Pazho asked me now.

I reached out to take the statue. Now that it had been returned to me, I felt better having it on my person at all times. "I'm not sure. It doesn't seem to have the magic infused in it that it did before. I guess it's just a simple carving now. A sweet reminder of my other self."

I rubbed the top of the dragon's head, as if it was a miniature pet.

Its head turned, the creature's bright eyes fixing on me.

I gasped. Around me, I heard similar sounds of astonishment from my friends.

The little dragon stretched, flexing its wings. The carving began to glow, a cool blue color the same shade as the dragon's hide. It no longer felt like light wood in my hand, but warm and weighted, and steadily growing heavier.

Hastily, I placed the carving back on the table.

The sound of chairs scraping back echoed through the dining hall. The dragon figurine was still changing and growing, and the magical glow quickly covered the edges of the table and threatened to spill over onto anything nearby.

The pulsing glow was now about half the size of the room, easily three times larger than the dining hall table, and nearly reaching to the tall ceiling. With one final shimmer, the magic faded.

In its place sat a large, pale blue ice dragon.

It lowered its head and looked directly at me. And in the depths of its blue-green eyes, I knew.

My second self had returned to me.

The dragon wasn't as large as I had been when I had been able to shift into that form. It might have been because it was separated from me, or perhaps it had instinctively stopped growing due to the size of the room.

A low rumbling came from its throat, sounding like a cross between a growl and a purr. I reached out, placing a tentative hand on its long blue snout.

Its scales felt warm underneath my hand. Tears sprang to my eyes. It was real.

"Endri! Is that—" Pazho began.

I nodded, not caring that I was crying in front of everyone. "Yes. This is what I transformed into, when I finally learned to shapeshift."

"Amazing. And impressive."

"I wonder if it has a name?" Queen Jennica wondered.

—I do not. Perhaps you should name me.—

I blinked, surprised at the unexpected voice that sounded in my mind. The voice was light and airy, making me think of wind blowing across a field of snow.

I stared into the dragon's mesmerizing eyes, realizing that was where the internal voice had come from.

—Did you just speak to me?—

—I did. I was a part of you, and am a part of you still, even if we are not joined together any longer. So I am able to communicate, but only with you.—

—Oh, gods. I don't know what to make of all this.—

—It will take time. But for now, let us be glad we at least have time together again.—

—Yes.—

"Are you all right, Endri?" Princess Laersa's warm hand found its way into mine.

"Yes," I said, sniffling. "I—I'm just a little overwhelmed, I think. I didn't expect to ever see my second self again."

"I don't think any of us did. This is wonderful!"

A cracking sound caused us all to jump. The noise grew louder, and the ice dragon gave a little yelp. As the wooden table split down the middle, the dragon disappeared in a cloud of blue-green mist.

When the air cleared, Pazho, Queen Jennica, Princess Laersa, and I all peered into the middle of the room.

The large dining hall table had snapped in half, buckling under the ice dragon's weight.

Lying in the middle of the splintered wood was the small figurine. Carefully picking my way around the ruined table, I picked up the little dragon and turned to an astonished Princess Laersa.

"Um. Sorry about that. I hope King Tahrin won't be angry when he finds out."

She giggled. "Don't worry about it. It was completely worth it."

57

— • —

CHAPTER FIFTY-SEVEN

THE NEXT MORNING, I stood in the flat lawn area just to the side of the castle, where Princess Laersa and I had talked on the night when all the citizens of Annlyn transformed.

The king hadn't reprimanded me for ruining his dining hall's table—with all the other destruction in the palace, what was one more thing?—but Pazho had privately advised me to try any experiments with my newly restored dragon outside of the building. Outside of any building, really. Preferably in a large, wide-open area with no innocent bystanders nearby who could get hurt.

Princess Laersa had said we could stay in the palace as long as we wanted, but Pazho and I had opted to go home after our dinner. Queen Jennica decided to stay, since Lady Farrah was safely set up in one of the castle's guest rooms. Before Pazho and I had left for the night, the princess told us we could use the castle grounds for any experiments I might need to do.

Which was a smart idea. Not only was the area around the palace large enough for the dragon to grow without destroying anything, but it was secluded enough that most people wouldn't be able to see what was going on. Although Annlyn was a kingdom of shapeshifters, I had a feeling that to see me and my second form standing side by side would be too much for most people to handle.

I took out the dragon figurine, wondering how this worked. Would it transform into the real dragon if I just willed it so, or did I have to say or do something specific?

And most importantly, would I be able to merge with it again?

Like I had last night, I touched the dragon's head. When it started to glow, I quickly put it in a safe place—on the ground, away from any gardens or fountains or furniture. A few stray flowers did get smushed. I hoped it wouldn't be too noticeable.

Soon, my former second self stood before me, majestic as always. Now that we were outside the confines of the dining hall, the dragon appeared in its full height—nearly as tall as the palace, minus some of the upper levels.

—Endri. I am so glad to see you again.—

—As am I.—

—Have you decided on a name for me?—

—I have.—

I had stayed up late into the night thinking of suitable names for the dragon, and had finally settled on one that felt appropriate.

—Mestarendri.—

I eyed the pale blue dragon uncertainly.—That is, if you like it.—

—Mestarendri. Champion.— The dragon sounded out the name, testing it. I could sense its amusement. —And specifically, Champion of Endri.—

—I hope that's all right. I can come up with something else, if you like.—

—No, no. I like it.—

I smiled. —Good. I'm glad we've settled that. Now, onto the other things we need to discuss.—

Mestarendri's laugh washed over me, a pleasant rumble that reverberated in my bones.—That sounds serious.—

—It is. How do we re-merge?—

Mestarendri's mirth faded. —That I do not know.—

Footsteps sounded nearby. Queen Jennica approached, fanning herself. "It's a beautiful day, although I had forgotten how hot it gets in the southern Gifted Lands."

—Ah, the lovely dragon queen.— Mestarendri inclined his long, sinuous neck towards Queen Jennica, his version of a bow.

The queen beamed, although she had no way of knowing what, if anything, Mestarendri had said. Perhaps fellow shapeshifters had an empathetic bond.

I turned to the queen. "Your Majesty, you're a shapeshifter—and a mage. Do you know of a way to bring Mestarendri and I back together again?"

"Mestarendri?" She smiled. "That's a clever name."

"Thanks." I nodded at the ice dragon. "He thought it was clever, too."

—That's one way of putting it.— Mestarendri's laughter vibrated through me once more.

"Anyway." I gave the dragon a mock glare. "We'd love your thoughts—and your help."

Queen Jennica frowned. "I'll be honest, I've never seen—or heard of—anything like this before. I came into my shapeshifting powers later than most, and I didn't grow up in Annlyn, where one would most likely encounter this kind of situation. Did Pazho have any insights?"

I shook my head. "Father and I talked about it on the walk home last night, and he's never heard of anything like this, either."

"Hmm." She tilted her head, considering. "If only we were back in Calia, where I have all my books and supplies. But there might be a few things we can try, even with limited resources."

"I'm willing to try whatever you suggest."

—And I, as well.— Mestarendri inclined his head.

Queen Jennica pushed back her sleeves and smiled. "Let's get started, then."

We spent the better part of the day trying everything the queen could think of. She tried short spells and long incantations. She sliced open my hand and Mestarendri's claw and had us touch, palm to claw, hoping our blood would call to each other. She mixed up a few different potions, pouring them over our heads or having us ingest them.

Nothing worked.

"You could eat me, that's one way of merging back together," I said sourly to Mestarendri during a rest.

Queen Jennica looked thoughtful. "That is an intriguing thought. He'd have to swallow you in one piece, though. As long as he doesn't accidentally bite off an arm, I think we could try it."

Horrified, I said, "I was just joking."

Above me, Mestarendri shook his head so emphatically that several nearby trees suddenly lost quite a bit of their leaves.

Queen Jennica chuckled. "So was I."

I raised an eyebrow. "Were you?"

The queen chuckled again, then sighed. "Perhaps you should come back to Calia with Lady Farrah and me. With more magical scholars and supplies at my disposal, we could continue trying to solve this problem."

"When are you leaving?"

"Soon. I'll be flying back with Lady Farrah. I'm just waiting on the servants to finish the special litter King Tahrin commissioned so I can carry her safely. By the time it's done, her intended, Lord Rhyss, should be here. I told him not to come, but he insisted. Probably riding himself—or at least his poor horses—ragged to get here. If I leave before he arrives, I'm sure I'll see him on the road."

"I should never have let her separate us."

Queen Jennica smiled sadly. "She wouldn't have wanted it otherwise. And she's a strong woman. She'll come out of this. Eventually."

We fell silent for a moment. Then, I asked, "Do—do you think it's possible that King Balor will come back? Or is he trapped in the mirror world?"

"That I do not know." She bit her lip, thinking. "And I think there are bigger questions we must ask. For example, are all mirrors connected? King Balor may not be able to return to Annlyn at this point, but has he left that other world through a mirror in another kingdom? How would anyone even monitor that? And what should King Tahrin—or for that matter, any ruler—do to keep his or her kingdom safe? Should we outlaw all mirrors?"

"And what about bodies of water, if he was able to use Lake Vitrum for his own purposes?" I grimaced. "I see your point. Perhaps it's better to just be vigilant and prepared, in case he does return."

Queen Jennica nodded. "Wise words."

We became quiet again.

"You know, Your Majesty, I think I'll take you up on your offer," I said. "To go to Calia and try to re-merge with Mestarendri. I've never traveled beyond Annlyn. It will be interesting to see other parts of the Gifted Lands."

"Really?" Queen Jennica's face lit up in a smile. "I think you'll enjoy it. And it won't take long, flying by dragon."

"That's true. And Mestarendri and I can bring Lady Farrah's intended back to Calia, as well. Unless he'd prefer to ride with you and Lady Farrah."

—Hey!— Mestarendri yelped. —Since when did I become a giant flying horse?—

I chuckled, remembering my clumsy attempts to fly with passengers. —You'll get used to it. I wouldn't ask it of you if it wasn't important.—

—Fine. I'll do it for you. But you'd better not ask for it too often.—

—I see through your fake grumpiness. You can't fool me. You *are* me, remember?—

I felt Mestarendri's laugh throughout my body. —How can I forget?—

58

Chapter Fifty-Eight

Two days later, I stood at the gates of Annlyn's capital city just after sunrise, joined by Denaan and Pazho. Mestarendri lay nearby, eyes closed, enjoying the early morning heat.

Lady Farrah's betrothed, Lord Rhyss, had arrived yesterday. As Queen Jennica had predicted, his unkempt red hair and the dark circles under his eyes were proof that he had barely slept, instead pushing his mounts to their limits in order to get to Annlyn as fast as possible. I think, if Queen Jennica had been willing, he would have turned right around and rushed back north to Calia. But when he had dismounted—practically falling off his horse, his legs buckling underneath him—Queen Jennica took one look at him and ordered him to bed.

"One more day won't hurt anyone, least of all you," she had told her friend. "And we can't have you falling off a dragon's back on the way home."

So while Lord Rhyss fell asleep in the Red Antler Inn's best bed, Denaan and Pazho helped me pack for my indefinite trip to Calia.

It was the "indefinite" part that was hard for both of my fathers to handle. Truth be told, I wasn't handling it too well myself.

"Who's going to help me with the evening meal?" Denaan said now. "The twins are great, don't get me wrong, but—"

"Now, Denaan," Pazho said, patting his mate on the shoulder. "Don't start giving him a guilt trip, or he'll never go."

Denaan sniffed. "That's the whole point. I don't want him to go."

I gave Denaan a hug. "I don't want to go either, not really. But if I don't go, then Mestarendri and I will stay separated forever."

"Even if you do go to Calia, there's no guarantee that you and your dragon will reunite."

"I know. But I—we—have to at least try."

Denaan nodded, looking unhappy. "You'll write, won't you?"

"Of course. And I believe Queen Jennica said she was going to enchant an item for you, so we could call each other." I frowned as a thought occurred to me. "Although I might need to get a new calling stone as well. Mestarendri's already not too keen on the idea of being a flying horse. He'd probably hate his carving, and thus him, being used as a calling spell conduit as well."

—You know I would.— Mestarendri didn't even open an eye.

I chuckled. Denaan and Pazho looked at me and then at the ice dragon, knowing something had been communicated between us, but of course not knowing exactly what.

"He really is a majestic creature," Pazho said. "And even if you two can't come back together, just knowing that he's there should be a great comfort."

"It is," I said. "And who knows? Maybe it'll be better this way. We'll figure it out."

"Regardless, you and Mestarendri will go down in the history books."

Princess Laersa's voice sounded behind us. "Why wait for a distant future? I'd rather they were hailed as heroes now."

Mestarendri chuckled as the princess joined us. —I like the way she thinks.—

She slipped her hand in mine, smiling up at me. "I'm a bit jealous. You're going to go off and have all these adventures, and I'll be stuck here in Annlyn."

"You could come with me," I suggested, knowing as I said it that it couldn't happen.

Sure enough, she shook her head. "I'm needed here. At least until Father recovers and becomes the ruler he once was. The one I know he can be."

Privately, I doubted that would ever happen. Princess Laersa had proven herself more capable and beloved than King Tahrin had ever been. While I had been sleeping—and then experimenting with Mestarendri—Princess Laersa had gone into the city, helping in the rebuilding efforts, overseeing the cleaning, settling disputes between citizens whose nerves were already frayed from the forced transformations. Even if King Tahrin suddenly changed, stopped hiding, and wanted to rule again, I didn't think the people of Annlyn would let him.

"Hopefully it won't take too long working with Queen Jennica, and I can return to Annlyn soon," I said.

"I hope that's not because my company is that detestable," Queen Jennica teased as she approached us. A tall red-haired man with a smattering of freckles on his face, looking to be in his late twenties, walked next to her. Although he moved slowly, he looked a lot more alert than he had when I had first seen him.

Behind them, four soldiers carried a brand new litter that bore the still form of Lady Farrah. This litter, unlike the previous one, had walls and a ceiling around the noblewoman, enclosing her in a little tent. A fifth soldier walked behind the litter, holding a bunch of fabric in his arms.

"Definitely not, Your Majesty," I said. "I'm looking forward to our time in Calia. But I also hate leaving behind my loved ones here in Annlyn."

"I understand," she said. "And we're all here, I think? Then let's get going. The sooner we go, the sooner we can get you home, Endri."

After a quick introduction to Lord Rhyss—who decided to ride with me atop Mestarendri, since it would be easier to keep an eye on Lady Farrah's litter that way—we prepared to leave. Princess Laersa walked away to talk to the soldiers.

"You'll need this," Denaan said, handing me a heavy bag.

"Wow. What's in this?" I wondered as I shifted its weight.

"Just a little bit of food for the road."

"A little bit?" I opened the bag, closing it quickly to avoid spilling any of the near-overflowing contents. "I think you packed the entire Red Antler in here. Besides, we should be in Calia by the end of the day."

Denaan shrugged, but his cheeks turned a little pink. "Just looking out for you, son."

I gave him a big hug, then turned to Pazho and brought him into the embrace as well. "I'm going to miss you both so much."

My fathers didn't respond, just held me tighter.

Nearby, Queen Jennica transformed, the morning sunlight glinting off her golden scales. The soldiers brought the litter to her. One of the soldiers shook out the bundle of fabric, revealing a large, dragon-sized harness that they carefully fitted around Queen Jennica. Once it was secure, the group of soldiers stepped back and saluted.

The golden dragon flapped her majestic wings a few times, hovering just high enough in the air so that the litter dropped gently beneath her belly. Two soldiers moved forward, making sure the litter was also secure, not tangled or askew. When they were satisfied, they moved away from the dragon queen, saluting her again.

"We'll probably have to land first, to help Jennica," Lord Rhyss said to me. "Once we're safely in the air, I can call ahead to her husband, Beyan, to make sure he has people ready to assist."

"That sounds good to me," I said. Personally, I wouldn't try a spell in mid-air, but I wasn't as practiced as my companions.

Lord Rhyss grinned at me, the first smile I had seen from the obviously worried man since he had stepped foot in Annlyn. "Let's hope I don't drop my calling stone while we're flying."

He walked over to Mestarendri, who, sensing Lord Rhyss's approach, opened a curious eye.

I started towards the ice dragon, meeting Princess Laersa along the way.

"I'll miss you," I said to her.

"And I, you." She touched my cheek. "Come back to Annlyn—and me—soon."

"I will."

I caught her hand up in mine. "If there weren't so many people—and dragons—around, I'd ..."

She grinned mischievously. "You'd what?"

I blushed. "Uh ... I'd ... you know ..."

Princess Laersa laughed, sparing me from further embarrassment. "Maybe next time."

"Definitely next time."

Now it was Princess Laersa's turn to blush.

From atop Mestarendri, Lord Rhyss called out, "Endri! Are you ready to go?"

Nodding, I called back, "Yes! Coming."

I kissed Princess Laersa's hand. Together we walked to where Mestarendri and Lord Rhyss waited. I climbed onto Mestarendri's back, then waved goodbye to the princess.

As Mestarendri began to rise into the air, Princess Laersa said, "Make sure you look back, once you get in the air!"

"All right." I was curious about her statement, but with the ice dragon rapidly ascending, I didn't have time to ask her any questions.

Mestarendri joined Queen Jennica, who was already hovering above the city, waiting for us. The shining golden dragon turned and started flying north, the litter dangling from her harness. Mestarendri soared after her.

Remembering Princess Laersa's words, I looked back.

Rising above the gates of Annlyn's capital, a beautiful, bright purple dragon shot into the sky.

The princess.

She flew in a figure-eight pattern, then stopped and blew an arc of lightning into the air. Brilliant yellow-white bolts crackled in the air, looking like a spiked crown above the city.

She roared a farewell. I waved in return, then turned to face forward.

Towards Calia. And towards my future.

EPILOGUE

VIBRATIONS FROM THE UNDERWATER explosion that had impacted Lake Vitrum sped along the waterways of the Gifted Lands.

They spread north, dying out just before they reached Orchwell. They completely petered out before even reaching the western kingdoms of Bomora and Rothschan.

But the vibrations stayed strong as they headed east, traveling through the rivers that would eventually feed into the land of Graenir, and the sea beyond.

They slammed into a river island just outside of Graenir, causing a small, unexpected earthquake on the islet. Some of the force from the vibrations faded, but the rest of them carried on.

But the earthquake grew larger, and more intense. The ground continued to rumble, and it seemed like it would never stop.

And as the walls began crumbling around her, the river island's guardian knew that nothing would ever be the same, again.

Dear Reader: THANK YOU

It's such a joy and an honor to be able to share my stories with you! Thank you so much for reading *Heir of Illusions and Others*. If you're new to the series, welcome! And if this is your return adventure in the Gifted Lands, thank you for continuing to follow the series! I hope you enjoyed this sixth book in the Kingdom Legacy series as much as I enjoyed writing it.

If you have the time, a short review on Goodreads or wherever you like to buy books and learn about new titles would be awesome!

Want to be the first to know about new adventures? Let's be friends!

□□Sign up for the Newsletter: http://www.rachanee.net/newsletter

□□Instagram: http://www.instagram.com/rachaneelumayno

□□TikTok: https://www.tiktok.com/@rachaneelumayno

□□YouTube: https://www.youtube.com/@rachaneelumayno

□□Twitter: http://www.twitter.com/rachaneelumayno

□□Join the community on Discord: Kingdom Legacy

— • —

READ ON FOR A PREVIEW OF THE FINAL (FOR NOW) JOURNEY IN THE GIFTED LANDS

CHAPTER ONE

"HAS ANYONE TOLD YOU, you're the prettiest girl here?"

I giggled as I turned my face to Tahn, a silent—and hopefully alluring—request for another kiss. "You have to say that, silly. And technically, I am the *only* girl here."

Tahn obliged my unspoken request. "I don't have to say it. And I wouldn't say it if it wasn't true."

I giggled again, snuggling into the crook of his arm. Together, we leaned back against the large oak that also conveniently hid us from prying eyes. In the distance, I could hear the faint voices of laughter and talk from near my house, but I didn't care. The party would keep. It wasn't like I was the guest of honor, anyway. No one would miss me.

Our lips had just met again when a pointed cough sounded somewhere above.

We broke apart to see my brother, Alistair, standing just a few feet away, a pained look on his face. "Forgive my interruption," he said, not sounding sorry at all. "But Mother and Father—among other people—have started noticing your absence, Idessa. I told them I'd go look for you."

I frowned. "Can't you cover for me?"

Alistair's frown matched my own. "I already did. Several times. Come on." He turned to go.

I sighed heavily as I stood up, brushing some dirt and leaves from my dress. Tahn followed suit, and I grabbed his hand. We started after my brother, who paused, looking pointedly at our clasped hands. "Maybe you should return separately."

With that, he walked through the trees, not waiting to see if I'd follow.

I sighed again. "I guess I should go. Count to thirty, then follow me?"

Tahn shrugged. "Or maybe I should just go home. I don't think I can spend several hours being glared at by your brother."

"Oh, just ignore him," I said. "You haven't really met my parents yet. I know they'll think you're wonderful, just as I do." I looked up into his deep brown eyes, batting my eyes for good measure. "Please?"

He shrugged again, but nodded.

Smiling, I stood on my tiptoes for one last stolen kiss. Then I turned and hurried after my brother.

To my surprise, Alistair was waiting for me just on the other side of the trees. "You ready, already?"

"I thought you had already gone back to the house," I said.

He snorted. "Not likely. If I don't bring you back personally, Mother and Father will have both of our heads. Besides, I know you. If I don't keep an eye on you, you'd just stay out here with Tahn. Or worse, wander off with him."

"I don't know why all of you are always so down on him," I complained as we started walking.

"Because, Idessa. You can do so much better than him," Alistair said.

I rolled my eyes. Not this again. Ever since Alistair had returned from his Guardian Year, he'd been insufferable. Gone was my fun-loving older brother, only to be replaced by some stuffy, boring person who was better suited to a straight-laced government job than his original dream of adventurer-for-hire in the Gifted Lands.

Which was why my family was hosting this party. As we got closer, I saw the painted homemade banner: "Congratulations, Alistair!"

A sizable crowd milled around our house. Their chatter and laughter floated on the air. I stopped my brother before we could reach the group—and while we were far enough away that they might not notice us. "Congratulations, Alistair," I said, echoing the banner's cheery sentiment.

He hugged me. "Thank you."

He tried to pull away, but I wouldn't let him go. "I'll miss you."

He laughed, and this time was successful in extracting himself from me. "Silly. I'll still be in Graenir."

"I know. But you'll be busy all the time, and who knows when we'll get to see you? And you just got back. We've hardly had any time together."

Alistair's smile faded somewhat. "And whose fault is that? I've been around for the last year, for the most part. You're the one who's rarely been home."

It was a familiar argument, and one I didn't want to get into. Not on today, of all days. Still, I couldn't stop the whine that crept into my voice. "Well, I'm not the one who changed. You used to be more fun."

Alistair snorted. "I'm still fun. Maybe not in a way you recognize, but ..."

"You know what I mean."

He stepped back, holding me at arm's length as he looked me straight in the eyes. "People change, Idessa. It's the one thing you can count on. And being a Guardian—it definitely changes you. You'll understand, when your time comes."

"If." It was a slim hope, but it was a hope I held onto nonetheless. I certainly didn't want to be a Guardian, even if it was a required duty.

Well. It's required only if you happened to be unlucky enough to be picked, I reminded myself.

Alistair shrugged. "True enough. *If*. And *if* it happens, then I hope it will change you as deeply as it did me."

He walked away, towards the house, leaving me no choice but to hurry after him.

As we approached, various guests greeted us, calling out their congratulations and well wishes to Alistair. With all that noise, there was no way I could slip in undetected. Sure enough, I soon found myself standing in front of Mother, who was chatting with some neighbors I didn't recognize.

"Oh, and here's our youngest, Idessa," Mother said. "Idessa, meet the Kal and Ellya Arnon. They live down by the pond."

I murmured a polite greeting, trying to avoid Mother's pointed stare. The one that said, *I know you skipped out, young lady. And we'll discuss that later.*

"Idessa." Mistress Arnon beamed at me. "You must be so happy about your brother's new position."

"Oh, I am." I plastered a smile on my face. "Serving as the Prime Minister's aide is so exciting."

What a lie. Honestly, it sounded like the most boring job ever.

"It will definitely keep him busy," my mother said, sounding proud and sad at the same time. "He's only just returned to us, and now we have to give him away again in service to Graenir."

"Oh, that's right," Mistress Arnon said. "And now we're coming on the close of another year. They'll be sending out the summons soon." She turned to me. "Have you served as a Guardian yet, Idessa?"

"No," I replied. "But if I am called, then I will gladly serve."

Another lie. But it was the right thing to say—in fact, the expected response. Mistress Arnon beamed again. "Imagine if that were to happen! Two Guardians in the family."

Inwardly, I shuddered. But I just smiled again and nodded. "That would be exciting. If you'll excuse me, Mother, Mistress Arnon."

Mother waved me away, continuing her conversation with the Arnons. I made my way through the crowd, searching for Tahn's tall figure and blond hair. He should have been here by now. But I didn't see him.

I sighed.

"Why the sad face? It's supposed to be a celebration party, not a funeral," a voice teased.

I looked up. And bit back the groan that threatened to escape. Instead, I forced a pleasant smile on my face. "Hello, Oran." I looked behind him. "No Alistair?"

Oran grinned, waving at a group of people that surrounded my brother. "Not right now. He's lost in his throng of admirers."

I chuckled. "It's not often you two aren't joined at the hip. Except, of course, for when Alistair had to do his Guardian duty."

My brother's best friend—and practically a second sibling to me—Oran had been around for as long as I could remember. It always stumped me, how the two of them could be such good friends. Oran was steady and quiet, whereas Alistair was more spirited and carefree, sometimes bordering on reckless.

Or had been. Ever since Alistair had returned from his Guardian year, he had become more quiet and less fun-loving. In short, a lot like Oran.

Bo-ring.

Oran nodded. "If they allowed seconds, I would have gone. But, alas, I had to stay home."

"You sound like you want to be a Guardian." I pursed my lips, hoping I hadn't sounded too accusatory.

But Oran didn't take offense. "A whole year to just sit and be by myself, with only books and my thoughts for company? Sounds like heaven to me."

I smirked, shaking my head. "Sounds like a prison sentence to me."

He laughed. "Tell you what, if you get summoned, I'll take your place, and serve for you."

This time, a genuine smile bloomed across my face. "Deal."

ACKNOWLEDGEMENTS

I CAN'T BELIEVE WE'RE on Book 6 already! Thank you so much to:

Tom, such a wonderful editor and friend. Thanks for reading each book and being so excited about reading the next one! Also, hearing the words, "I have notes, but they're minor ones" really makes a person smile.

All the coffee shops in my area, for keeping me sugared up so I can keep writing.

And of course my cat Riley, the ultimate writing companion. You keep me on task, mostly because you plop on my lap and won't let me move, or meow your head off until I let you in the recording booth.

About the Author

Rachanee Lumayno is an actress, voiceover artist, screenwriter, avid gamer, and amateur dodgeball player. She grew up in Michigan, where she spent way too much of her free time reading fantasy novels. She still spends too much of her free time reading fantasy, although now she writes them as novels, narrates them as audiobooks, and creates them as improv for various roleplaying campaigns as well. *Heir of Illusions and Others* is her sixth novel, and the sixth book in the Kingdom Legacy series. She is also a staff writer for an upcoming video game. You can find her online at her website, www.rachanee.net, or on Instagram, TikTok, or YouTube (@rachaneelumayno).